'An uncommonly good writer, with th
other gifts besides. A bald recital of th
can only be misleading: you must read | ....is Mr.
Parry's talent, compounded of tenderness and irony, that this novel
though consistently deliciously amusing, never degenerates into
whimsy.'

– John Davenport, *Observer*

'There are few novelists more resourceful and original than Dennis
Parry . . . This novel is prodigal of exciting and entertaining incident,
and I should like to read it again.'

– Daniel George, *The Bookman*

'How well Mr. Parry writes!'

– *New Statesman*

'Mr. Parry writes with wit, ingenuity, and even a gift for surrealistic
fantasy.'

– *The Times*

'The story is preposterous, often wonderfully funny, and the impla-
cable exiled gun-runner gives it a weird perspective which is a nice
diversion for the imagination.'

– *Manchester Guardian*

'He is a superb portraitist, and can bring to life a caustic and bibulous
butler as easily as a covey of ogling flappers.'

– *Time and Tide*

'He is out to amuse . . . and very successful he is at it . . . He has the
wit to temper satire with affection, and to perceive the nobility that
so often lies at the heart of the ridiculous . . . A work of considerable
originality . . . fresh, entertaining, and intelligent.'

– *The Listener*

'Witty and civilized . . . a thoroughly entertaining book.'

– *Sphere*

SEA OF GLASS

DENNIS PARRY

With a new introduction by
SIMON STERN

VALANCOURT BOOKS

Sea of Glass by Dennis Parry
First published London: Hamish Hamilton, 1955
First Valancourt Books edition 2015

Published by Valancourt Books, Richmond, Virginia
http://www.valancourtbooks.com

ISBN 978-1-941147-11-5 (trade paperback)
Also available as an electronic book.

All Valancourt Books publications are printed on acid free paper that meets all ANSI standards for archival quality paper.

Set in Dante MT 10.5/12.6
Cover by Henry Petrides

INTRODUCTION

Sea of Glass, Dennis Parry's tenth and last novel, met with wide-spread enthusiasm from the reviewers when it first appeared, sixty years ago, and has been included in several lists of unduly neglected novels (including one by Edward Gorey, for *Antaeus*, in 1975), but is only now being reprinted for the first time. To say that Parry's novel is a comedy of manners might imply that it does not have much to offer by way of a plot—but while the outlines of its plot are quite simple, Parry manages to fit a significant amount of action into the novel's compact space. Featuring an inheritance dispute, a conniving schemer with kleptomaniac tendencies, an exotic rival claimant from Chinese Turkestan (by turns noble savage and femme fatale), a possible murder, and a back-story featuring a swashbuck-ling, gun-running entrepreneur with a fondness for posing as a *Boy's Own Paper* hero, the tale is narrated by David Lindley, a Cambridge law student whose retiring personality makes him an excellent observer of the others' maneuverings, and whose legal knowledge leads nearly all of the major characters to seek his advice at some point (about settlements, powers of appointment, and the like), thus providing a natural means of allowing them to confide in him or to appeal to his expertise while unwittingly revealing their motives. The ensemble also includes a semi-invalid grandmother, her censorious nurse, and a bibulous butler—and while this latter group may sound like a routine and predictable cast, Parry makes each of them origi-nal and intriguing. The result is a well-plotted, inventive, and urbane story, written in a style that keeps surprising the reader all the way down the page and onto the next one.

Set primarily over David's summer holiday in 1928, the novel begins with David's arrival at Mrs. Ellison's house, where her granddaughter, Varvara (or 'Barbara,' as Mrs. Ellison insists), has only recently arrived from Doljuk (located in northwestern

China, near the borders with Russia, Mongolia, and Kazakh-
stan, according to the geography lesson in chapter two). Parry's
invented address for the Ellison household, 8 Aynho Terrace,
is somewhere in 'West London, one of a row built in the last
century,' possibly in the same area as his own house in Earl's
Court, at 8 Collingham Gardens, which was built in the early
1880s. (The street's name also bears some resemblance to that
of David's friend and sometime rival, Andrew Callingham.)
Almost as soon as he arrives, David has a dramatic confronta-
tion with Varvara that makes him fear for his own safety and
her sanity, but he eventually concludes that her 'persecution
mania' is well-founded, at least with respect to her uncle Cedric, Mrs. Ellison's son. Intent on keeping Varvara from inher-
iting under his mother's will, Cedric tries various tactics, and
even resorts to stealing evidence. This rivalry animates much
of the plot, which is punctuated by Varvara's stories about her
birthplace, where death may come in the form of a venomous
bite from a barking spider, and one of the periodic rebellions
resembles 'a circus as much as a military operation,' conducted
with an array of weapons ranging from 'Genoese crossbows to
bronze cannon,' to pebbles wrapped in 'small pieces of paper
… inscribed with highly damaging curses.' Once these discor-
dant characters have been set in motion, much of the plot cen-
ters on how they interact, as David looks on and occasionally
intervenes.

The novel was greeted with very positive reviews. John
Davenport, in the *Observer*, praised it as exhibiting 'the classic
novelist's virtues.' John Betjeman, in the *Daily Telegraph*, wrote
that Parry had a 'clear legal head,' and described him as a writer
'not to miss in future.' The *Manchester Guardian* called *Sea of
Glass* 'preposterous, often wonderfully funny' and singled out
Turpin, the butler, for praise, as a character who is 'magnificent in unexpected speech.' (The *Spectator* also admired him:
'Turpin is as round and fruity a character as his own port.')
The *Illustrated London News* observed that the novel 'might be
described as marginal—or a long anecdote, which means the
same thing. But an amazingly original and brilliant anecdote'

with remarkable 'wit, farce, penetration and exuberance.' The *Times* summarized the author's talents in the same fashion, observing that 'Mr. Parry writes with wit, ingenuity, and even a gift for surrealistic fantasy.' *Punch* likened the novel's 'humour and scenes of high comedy' to the *Mr. Norris* stories of 'the early Isherwood.'

These terms of praise also recall the traits of a slightly earlier writer in the English comic tradition—Saki. The merits of Parry's novel rival those of Saki in many respects: the events, the cast of characters, and the prose that describes them are strongly reminiscent of his fiction. Saki would have envied many of Parry's epigrams. David observes, about his aunt, that 'she had the true Britannic hatred of ill-defined queerness; at a pinch she would rather have been put down in an unequivocal brothel than a place where one could only say that something funny went on upstairs.' On Varvara's difficulty in adapting to the chic modes of 1928, he remarks, 'However carefully Varvara put on her smart garments she always looked as if she had burst her way forcibly into them and was about to attempt an equally violent exit.' Having eloped with a paramour who contracted a mysterious fever, Varvara's mother 'carried faithfulness so far as to catch the same disease.' A cat, deliberate in its choice of method when stalking birds, sounds like any number of Saki's cats (particularly the one in 'The Reticence of Lady Anne'): rather than 'getting down on the belly and relying on stealth, … this cat strolled towards the prey with an air of disengaged benevolence.' Saki would also have relished the plot, with its concoction of outlandish elements, precipitated into a world where most of the characters (including, not infrequently, David himself) are concerned with keeping up appearances. The only feature missing, to complete the analogy, is the surprise ending that was Saki's trademark. Indeed, some reviewers complained that the conclusion does not adequately redeem the plot that effectuates it; the *New Yorker*, for example, commended Parry's 'fine, intelligent, and amusing style' and called the opening chapters 'astonishingly good,' but found the ending 'highly unsatisfactory.' While perhaps this objection is formulated too strongly, some readers will probably agree with its spirit. The air of mystery at the story's end has a certain logic, but one cannot help thinking that a more dramatic reversal, or a revelation that changes the reader's understanding of the events, would have carried the story to a more fitting close.

David's perspective on the events is a familiar one in Parry's novels, but it is used to especially good effect in *Sea of Glass*. Born in London in 1912, Parry was educated at Rugby School and King's College, Cambridge, where he studied classics, graduating with a first-class degree in 1934. He then read Law and qualified as a Chancery Barrister, and spent four years in law practice before joining the civil service. Beginning as secretary to the Vice-Chief of Air Staff, he ultimately became Permanent Under-Secretary to the Minister for Coal Production. He began his career as a novelist with *Attic Meteor* in 1936, and the plots of his first two novels are focused mainly on the kinds of characters who form the back-story to *Sea of Glass*, featuring adventurous figures in exotic settings. Mark Valentine rightly compares *Attic Meteor* to John Buchan's novels; another candidate might be David Footman, whose novel *The Yellow Rock* (1929) is also set in Chinese Turkestan. Parry's later novels, by contrast, usually have a lawyer, or a legally trained character (and often a Cambridge-educated one), as the protagonist. In *Mooncalf* (1947), the goings-on of a highly variegated group of eccentrics are described by a solicitor who provides, as one review noted, the 'entirely normal' foil for these figures, and who shares 'his author's turn of glancing humour' and 'happy economy in words.' Mark Tillott, the protagonist of *Fair House of Joy* (1950), is an ageing solicitor who regrets his choice of occupation ('Some of his friends said that, with his brain, he should have been a specialist, a Chancery barrister perhaps'); his romantic involvement with a much younger woman ultimately leads to the destruction of his career. In *Sea of Glass*, David's efforts to 'practice his legal caution' whenever anyone consults him, and Parry's integration of legal details into the plot, make the lawyer-narrator a particularly effective figure. Indeed, although David explains that 'sea of glass' is the translation of Doljuk's Chinese name, the phrase might at least as readily be taken to refer to the narrator himself. Parry evidently found the title in the Book of Revelations ('I saw as it were a sea of glass mingled with fire'), and it is David's calming, if not glacial, presence, with its cool astringency, that holds the story together.

Tragically, Parry did not live to write another novel. Less than two months after *Sea of Glass* was published, Parry was injured in a car accident, and he died a few days later. He would probably be much better known today if not for his early death. The mid-twentieth century features few comic writers of Parry's caliber, and having already published ten novels at the age of 42, he would doubtless have kept up the same pace over the following decades, and might even have turned to writing as a full-time career. Although it's unlikely that this new edition, sixty years on, will gain Parry a place in the canon of twentieth-century English authors, it will be welcomed by discerning readers who may agree with Edward Gorey that it has been unjustly—and inexplicably—neglected.

SIMON STERN
August 2015

SIMON STERN received his Ph.D. in English literature from Berkeley and his J.D. from Yale and is an associate professor at the University of Toronto, where he is a member of the Faculty of Law and the Department of English.

That afternoon I had called for a few minutes at the house in Aynho Terrace to leave my luggage, and I knew the way up to my bedroom. It was after eleven when I returned from an evening spent with a Cambridge friend. Turpin, the butler, again opened the door, grinning amiably in spite of the late hour.

'Good night,' I said.

'And the same to you, sir,' he replied heartily. 'God wot!'

Young and innocent though I was, it struck me as an unusual response from a butler. I wondered if he had been drinking. (Not to keep anybody in suspense on this point, the answer was yes, of course.) Turpin wore a claret-coloured livery with brass buttons, and under that a waistcoat striped like a wasp. What I liked about him, next to his amiability, was his dirtiness, which was of the boyish, not the insanitary adult kind. His collar was slightly grubby and one cheek of his broad coarse-skinned face carried a smear of soot.

He contrasted oddly with his surroundings. From the little which I had seen of No. 8 Aynho Terrace it appeared to be most scrupulously kept. It was a huge old-fashioned house in West London, one of a row built in the last century at the zenith of England's commercial prosperity. Even at the end of the 1920s (which is the time I am writing about) only very rich persons like Mrs. Ellison could afford to live in them. Now they have been broken up into slummy flats and stand there looking like elephants in a knacker's yard.

I began to go up the stairs which were rather steep and narrow for so splendid a mansion. My feet sank into the deep pile of the carpet and the plaster on the ceiling leant down towards me in a heavy pattern of grapes and cornstalks and curlicues.

On the first landing I noticed the sculptured bust of a fine old man who slightly resembled Field-Marshal von Hindenburg,

except that he had been hewn out in some stone the colour of toffee. Above him spread a potted palm and at his side was a model of a mechanical pump in a glass case.

I paused for a moment, suspecting that the sculpture must represent the late Mr. Ellison and the pump was one of the products of his engineering skill. If I had then known more about this formidable character I might not have dallied; I should have been aware that he intensely disliked any kind of waste—in which he included burning electric light on stairways whilst they were not in use. Accordingly he had installed at his home a device which is more common in lodging-houses and offices. It was a switch like a large button which one depressed in the hall in order to light up the stairs; as one ascended, the button, which was on a slow spring, gradually worked its way back to the original position; when this happened the light went out. The time-interval had been carefully calculated to allow a fit adult to go from the hall to the attic in good light, but no allowance was made for cripples, dotards, or persons who mooned about. It was not the policy of Mr. Ellison's widow to remove any signs of his genius.

Darkness overtook me just as I reached the third floor, where my room was situated. I was a little taken aback but I thought I could find the way to my own door which was in an enclave at the far end of the landing. It was very dark, however, and I had not gone more than a few paces before I bumped into the wall on one side. At the same moment I became aware of someone breathing within a few inches of me. The shock immediately sent up my own rate of respiration; and for an instant my unseen companion and I joined in making a noise like a kettle near the boil.

Turpin, who had been locking up, must have realized that light might still be needed upstairs. At any rate he again manipulated the time-switch, and a lamp hanging just above my head sprang into life.

I found that I was facing a door in the left-hand wall of the corridor. It was open and in the gap stood a large girl with tawny hair and fierce blue eyes which, despite the sudden change of light, were fixed on me with unblinking hostility. In her right hand, raised shoulder-high, she held a long knife with a curved tip. It was pointed towards myself, and it may have been this which prevented me from obtaining full value from another of her circumstances. Never thereafter could I remember how she looked without a stitch of clothing.

Turpin had made rather a mess of his last essay with the switch. Evidently he had given it a glancing thrust which depressed it only a fraction of the way; with the result that the illumination lasted no more than a few seconds. At this second plunge into darkness my nerve failed. I scuttled for my own door and practically beat my way in through the panels. Once inside I promptly turned the key.

In bed I recovered my composure, and even began to think how, with a little reshaping, the incident might provide that element of romantic madness which had so far been lacking in my reminiscences. I knew several undergraduates, quieter and duller than myself, whose eyes would pop at the story—provided of course that they could be induced to believe it. It seems odd, but I did not speculate much about the identity of the girl or the reason why she went armed by night. Once I had rejected a theory that Mrs. Ellison might have a daughter who was a homicidal maniac, I was content with the certainty that next day could be made to reveal the answer.

This wise resignation was helped by the comfort of my surroundings. I lay in an old-fashioned bed which had curtains strung on a couple of movable brass rails. If it was winter or one wished to exclude the world, the rails could be swung out so that their draperies formed two parallel walls joined by a canopy. Now, however, they were bunched together above the pillows and the sleeper looked up into the stiff convolutions of the fabric as into the groyning of a cathedral roof.

Through the open window came a breeze smelling of jasmin. Before going to bed I had discovered that my room looked down onto a flat roof of the storey below, which projected further than the top part of the house. The roof was laid out with flowers in boxes and wicker chairs and potted shrubs. Below, the cliff-like bulk of the house fell away to a garden proper. All the houses in the terrace were so provided, and though the individual strips were narrow they added up, by moonlight, to a seemingly limitless vista of park and coppice.

I was on the verge of sleep when midnight struck. This was not the usual commonplace event. At 8 Aynho Terrace it began with a mellifluous chirring noise as if a flock of doves were about to take wing. Then chimes broke out from all over the house, striking every note on the keyboard and running in and out of each other like linked cascades. There were big clocks with fruity episcopal voices, and little ones that pinged like mosquitoes. The confusion of sound had—for me, at any rate—a curiously concrete effect. I felt that I was riding up and down on a sea of some tenuous but highly buoyant material.

2

Next morning the same chorus, playing its nine o'clock hymn, accompanied me downstairs. The dining-room, which opened off the hall, was a very big room entirely furnished in dark mahogany. It seemed to speak, in a low rumbling voice, of eight-course dinners attended by company directors. On the overmantel there was a bronze statue of a knight in armour who was prodding a dragon beneath his feet. The knight's visor was open, and in the sepulchral light I jumped to the conclusion that this was another portrait of Mr. Ellison in fancy dress. Later when I had the chance to examine this awful piece of *bric-à-brac* I saw how wrong I had been. The knight had an amiable, foolish, Teutonic expression; Mr. Ellison would have had his mailed pants off him in about two minutes.

A young woman in a nurse's uniform was already at the table. As I came in she looked up and choked slightly. The resultant fit of coughing darkened her high-coloured cheeks until they were almost the same shade as the mahogany. I stood shifting about from foot to foot, trying to look both nonchalant and sympathetic.

Finally she recovered. 'Pardon me,' she said. 'Good morning. I'm Nurse Fillis.'

Not unnaturally it took me several days to discover that she had not introduced herself by her Christian name.

'I'm David Lindley,' I said. 'I've come to stay.'

'I hope you enjoy it.'

'Thanks. I'm used to entertaining myself.'

'Oh,' said Nurse Fillis, 'it's not a question of being lonely in this house. Not as things are at present.'

Her voice carried that supercharge of meaning which somehow I associate with outraged landladies.

Before we could pursue this curious conversation Turpin came in with a pot of fresh coffee which he put down at my side. As he did so he belched slightly.

'Box on!' I thought he said, and it turned out that I was quite right.

Nurse Fillis raised her head from her plate and gave him a look of distaste. The movement brought her face into a shaft of light so that I saw its details more clearly. She belonged to that considerable and unfortunate tribe of young women whose features are individually presentable, but refuse to add up. She had a small clear-cut nose and a neat mouth, but both appeared trivial and slightly vulgar against the wide expanse of her cheeks and her massive but well-shaped chin. She was not fat, but something—perhaps the high complexion—gave her a plethoric air, which combined badly with her obvious nervousness.

Turpin had gone to the sideboard and was rummaging about in one of the compartments. Presently he looked round and addressed her.

'You don't 'appen to 've seen Miss Varvara's 'orn?'

The nurse tossed her head.

'I have not. You don't suppose I'd touch the filthy thing.'

Turpin chuckled resignedly, and sloped towards the door.

'She'll just 'ave to drink out of a cup this morning.'

'Or else she could condescend to come down and look for her own nonsense.'

I thought that the sooner I had some idea what was going on, the happier I should feel.

'What was all that about horns?' I asked when the butler had gone.

She replied: 'As well as you, Mrs. Ellison has a granddaughter staying here. She comes from savage parts—which is putting it mildly, if you ask me. Anyway she owns a dirty old goblet carved from some animal's horn—she says it's a rhinoceros's—and every drop she drinks must come out of it.'

'What's the idea?'

'It's supposed to be a guard against poison.'

I had a vague memory of having heard this superstition before and of its being associated with a particular country.

'Isn't that a Chinese notion?'

Nurse Fillis nodded. 'Mind you, the place she comes from is hardly proper China, where I'm told there are some very nice people. It's somewhere right at the back.'

'Why does this girl think she'll be poisoned?'

'It is the way she's been brought up. You should hear her talk to her grandmother—how Governor This strangled Governor That and did I don't know what to his fancy women—dreadful language sometimes. One makes allowances, but it's time she learnt.'

I remained silent, partly because I could not think what to say next, and partly prompted by an elementary sense of social tactics. About the young woman with the rhinoceros-horn I had no ideas, but it seemed to me that I recognized Nurse Fillis. She was the counterpart of several undergraduates whom I knew, the nervous, introspective ones who believed that everyone was watching them; who had elaborate fantasies under exteriors like suet; who for long periods would converse only in monosyllables, and then suddenly burst into plaints or denunciations followed by still more embarrassing apologies.

Sure enough, silence produced reaction. First she bent over her plate and began to eat as if she were digging her way to the Antipodes. But what she needed was reassurance, not distraction, and presently she addressed me in a subdued tone.

'I hope you didn't think I was talking out of turn, Mr. Lindley.'

'If I had, I shouldn't have listened.'

It was a nasty and priggish remark for a boy of twenty. I can only plead that I was not speaking in my own personality. When I was young my dramatic sense (and also a certain lack of self-confidence) often caused me to substitute other people in the situations which I found beyond me, and to speak with their voices. So now I was snubbing Nurse Fillis in the accents of my aunt who was a *mem-sahib* of the old school, and could smell presumption across half a continent.

Indeed, two years before, when we first met Mrs. Ellison in Brittany, she had once or twice unnecessarily slapped down the nice little Irish nurse who was then looking after the old lady.

Until this summer, Mrs. Ellison had gone every year to St. Plou-les-Navets, chiefly because her husband had done so. Though he travelled widely for business, Mr. Ellison had not really approved of places abroad. But St. Plou he exempted from that category: at which I do not greatly wonder, for it had taken to itself many of the beastlier features of a British seaside resort, including the incivility, the crowds, and the noise. It was not, you would have thought, the place for an elderly woman who had lately suffered a minor stroke. Not that Mrs. Ellison was enfeebled. Although she found it convenient to keep a nurse in attendance, the only outward signs of her illness were a tendency to become confused under mental stress and, even without it, occasionally to forget the context and the company in which she was speaking.

Very likely her excellent recovery was due to self-discipline. So far as possible, she refused to abandon any of her former habits. One of these was doing the crossword in a well-known English paper. This exertion did not turn out so well as some others, for it tended to put too much pressure on her memory. It was sad and comic to see the old lady sitting in the lounge and gnashing her teeth over some elusive clue, whilst Nurse Riordan, who had the brains of a hen, further exasperated her by making imbecile suggestions.

One day when my aunt and I happened to be at the next table she seemed more disturbed than usual.

'I know it, I know it,' she kept on repeating. 'Town in Central Asia. . . . Town in Central Asia. . . .'

'Now me,' said Nurse Riordan, 'I never knew they had any towns in Central Asia. I thought it was all sand and godlessness.'

'My son wrote from there . . . my son. K— and five more letters.'

'Karnak,' volunteered Nurse Riordan. 'Kanton.'

'Please remember, Nurse,' said Mrs. Ellison crisply, 'that it is my mind which is failing.'

My aunt leant across to them. She knew all about Mrs. Ellison and this was an opening which she did not despise.

'Could I help? I think Khotan may be the word you want.'

The old lady was grateful, but she slightly disappointed my aunt by showing no surprise at her geographical knowledge. Some delicate angling was therefore necessary before the conversation could be moved onto the plane of personal reminiscence. But finally the transition was made.

'I just happen to know a little about that part of the world because my husband was sent on a mission there, about five years ago.'

'Ah,' said Mrs. Ellison vaguely.

'Rather outside the normal run of jobs in the Indian Political Service. As a matter of fact it was supposed to be very hush-hush and I wasn't allowed to mention it for at least a year after he came back.'

'But I am sure you did,' said Mrs. Ellison.

Never doubting that she had misunderstood, my aunt continued: 'So naturally I was interested when I happened to overhear that your son had been there.'

'Yes,' said Mrs. Ellison flatly.

'So few people get a chance to penetrate into those regions . . . unless they're archaeologists or missionaries. My husband said that both were doing magnificent work.'

'They were all pests—particularly the missionaries,' said Mrs. Ellison without hesitation.

'Oh! Well ... it depends on one's point of view, doesn't it? I expect your son was tied up in a lot of administrative problems ...'

Mrs. Ellison let the heavy white lids come down for a moment over her eyes.

'Bores like a beaver,' she said in a low sing-song voice. 'And fat.' I noticed Nurse Riordan frown and touch her unobtrusively on the sleeve: at which she seemed immediately to recover her sense of the distinction between speech and thought. 'My son,' she said, 'sold guns to the natives so that they could fight each other.'

'God forgive him his ways!' added Nurse Riordan in a discreet undertone.

You might think that this was a discouraging start to an acquaintance. But once my aunt had decided that somebody was worthwhile it took a great deal to choke her off. Moreover, to her honour, her mind was as large in some directions as it was small in others. She seldom wasted time resenting the fact that people did not like her; she either moved on or set about improving their opinion.

Nevertheless contact remained at the level of formal greetings and remarks about the weather until my uncle arrived in St. Plou. He was an instant success with the old lady, and we used regularly to sit with her in the lounge. Not that my uncle made any conscious effort to charm: it simply happened to be second nature to him. Aunt Edna was the one who had our fellow-guests graded from the first day. Mrs. Ellison came very high on her list, if not actually at the top. I soon learnt that she was a reputed millionairess—or at least the widow of a man who had been an indubitable millionaire.

I still remember another of the few occasions when she mentioned the mysterious son in Turkestan.

'They killed my boy, you know,' she said, her voice wavering not from sentiment but one of her sudden attacks of fatigue. 'But not till he'd led them a fine old dance. He used to write and tell me things ... some of them very unsuitable.'

Later, when our family group was alone, my aunt said:

'I cannot think why Mrs. Ellison persists in pretending that her son was some kind of—well—hobo in Sinkiang. Affectation of that kind is so unlike her.'

'And what,' said my uncle in his gentle lazy tones, 'makes you think that it is affectation?'

'My dear Henry, I wasn't born yesterday. It's perfectly obvious why the son was there.'

'You tell us.'

'He was arranging for his father's firm to get mineral rights. Everyone knows there's a fortune under the ground in those extraordinary places. Or perhaps I should say there *was*: most of it's probably in the Ellison bank account by now.'

'That was not exactly the impression I gathered when I met Fulk Ellison,' said my uncle.

'You met him? You never told me!'

'I meet a lot of people without telling you, my love.'

'Well, what was he like?'

My uncle thought for several seconds.

'He was an amiable and romantic bandit,' he said at length. 'A character . . .' he chortled gently . . . 'and he damn well knew it.'

Unfortunately at this point a little dog belonging to one French family bit a little boy belonging to another and in the electrifying row which followed my curiosity about Mrs. Ellison's son was forgotten. That lapse of memory lasted nearly three years.

For several minutes Nurse Fillis continued to radiate faint jarring waves from some source of interior confusion. Whether she talked or remained silent she was an uncomfortable young woman, and I was glad when she finished her breakfast and excused herself.

'I must go and get my patient up.'

I was reading the morning paper and drinking a final cup of coffee when Turpin made a second appearance. He went over to the sideboard and opened one of the compartments.

'Excuse me, sir,' he said in a tone of unwonted formality, 'but

I thought I'd show you the requirements.'

I joined him and saw that he had pulled out a couple of deep drawers. The top one was stocked with a variety of decanters and bottles; the lower, lined with zinc and fitted with cedar trays, contained hundreds of cigars of various sizes. I was only moderately interested in drink, but I loved cigars, and now with a princely gesture Turpin made me free of that enormous collection.

'But won't Mrs. Ellison mind? I mean, oughtn't I—?'

I think it was my complete ignorance of how to behave with butlers which laid the foundation of Turpin's amiability towards me.

' 'Elp yourself,' he said. 'Make the old lady 'appy. There's a nice nature there, though it is my own employer. Besides, she's seen enough of scrooging and gouging.'

'Well . . . thanks.'

'Mind you,' said Turpin gloomily. 'The drink's no good. Mr. E. didn't 'old with it. That brandy there—strictly for 'ospitality. Anything decent I look after downstairs.'

'Of course.'

'Mrs. Ellison won't 'ave nothing locked. Asking for it!' Turpin winked rapidly, then recited so fast that I could scarcely follow him:

> ' 'Ousemaids sip,
> Grooms soak,
> Nurses nip . . .
> Butlers—occasionally—take—a
> drop—more—than—would—be—
> good—for—other—folk.

Learnt that in me first place, but there's not the same spirit now.'

Not to choke him off, but because I was afraid that if the conversation continued I should let myself down, I said, 'I expect you'd like to clear away now.'

'That's right,' said Turpin. 'You go and 'ave a look round

the 'ouse. 'Ighly artistic. Give you a laugh.' He sucked his front teeth thoughtfully. 'Not but what you should 'ave come ten years ago.'

'Why, was it different then?'

'*You* was. What I've always said about this place, it's made for kids, like the pantomime.'

He escorted me to the dining-room door and opened it, wrapping, as it were, his robes of office about him and from the midst of them producing an unbelievably plummy and flunkeyish voice.

'The drawing-room, sir, is situated on the other side of the vestibule.'

After a few seconds I saw what Turpin meant about pantomimes. Indeed the comparison was surprisingly acute. The drawing-room looked strangely like one of those spectacular sets which appear about halfway through the second part of the programme at Drury Lane or the Lyceum, depicting Princess Baldroubadour's Boudoir or the Hall of Dreams in the Fairy Queen's Palace. They rely on chandeliers and a generous use of gilt and mirror-panels: in the middle there is often a giant confection—ostensibly a bed or a throne—which is decorated partly with spangles and metalled brocades and partly with human figures arranged in plastic poses.

The resemblance persisted despite the fact that Mrs. Ellison's drawing-room was overcrowded with furniture, whereas stage-sets are necessarily rather empty. The accumulation of *bric-à-brac* in the one seemed to counterbalance—indeed spiritually to replace—the swarms of coryphées and courtiers in the other.

It was a very big apartment running through the whole length of the house. One set of french windows formed part of the façade of the house, the other looked onto the garden at the back. A grand piano stood in the front embrasure, a splendid Bechstein, but round it, as though for a kindergarten lesson or tea-party, were grouped six or seven little chairs of a truly frightful winsomeness. One—evidently of Swiss manufacture—had a carved Berne bear on each arm: in the worst and biggest the back panel was adorned by an inset plaque of two pre-Raphaelite maidens looking into each other's eyes with an expression which would cause comment nowadays. The feature which they all had in common was a distinct thickening or downward protuberance of the seat. I even toyed with the idea that they might be a collection of high-minded commodes.

In fact, as I discovered later, they were musical chairs. If they were wound up and one sat on them, the boxes inside played a variety of tunes including *Abide with Me* and *The Minstrel Boy*.

The same contrasts between tawdriness and magnificence persisted throughout the room. Hanging on the walls or standing on cabinets and on the marble overmantel was a part of the grand chorus of chiming clocks. (Other smaller squads were distributed elsewhere about the house.) A few of these were pieces of considerable beauty, but they were outnumbered by the product of Bavarian woodcarvers and imitators of celebrated buildings. A cuckoo popped out from the eaves of a chalet next door to a model of the Leaning Tower executed, apparently, in the substance of moth-balls.

At the further end, near the garden-window, the centre of the floor was held by a tall octagonal cabinet. I opened two or three of its glass-fronted partitions and took out objects at random. I noticed how many of them had a Far Eastern origin. There were at least a dozen Chinese snuff-bottles, several small jade screens, and a model of a junk in ivory. At the time I supposed that Mrs. Ellison's son must have sent them as gifts to his mother. This was not correct. They had, in fact, been collected from various sources for Mrs. Ellison's sister who was a congenital cripple. With that strange mixture of good sense and incomprehension so typical of the Victorians it was decided at an early stage that she must be given an interest in life. So a museum was started in order to make her forget her wasted spine. Everything went into it, as into a hot-pot—postage-stamps, sea-shells, coins, an uncut ruby worth a thousand pounds, and hundreds of *objets d'art*. The collection, begun in her own family home, was transferred to that of the Ellisons when she went to live with them. It had originally been housed in a single room at the top of the house which still held the core of it; but after her death Mr. Ellison, who combined a keen sense of economy with the aesthetic taste of a Yahoo, had seen no reason why all these rarities should not be used for the general embellishment of the house. So they were duly parcelled out, the drawing-room receiving the articles which were thought to have the highest monetary and decorative value. I believe the cases of sea-shells were put round the servants' bedrooms.

I had heard no sound of footsteps, but when I looked up from replacing an object in the cabinet, there, standing a few inches behind me, was the girl whom I had seen on the upstairs landing. This time she had no knife and she was dressed in a long frock of printed cotton. Her fierce blue eyes eclipsed the feeble colours of the design and her tawny hair and skin glared leonine against the white background.

'Good morning,' I said.

'Good morning,' replied the girl in a voice which was foreign in texture rather than accent.

'I'm David Lindley.'

'I am Varvara Ellison.'

'I think we met for a moment last night.' I tried to smile engagingly. 'You rather scared me.'

From the outset the girl had worn an expression of intense watchfulness. It did not respond to my attempt at levity.

'I am on guard in the nights,' she said briefly.

'But . . . why?'

'Lest someone should kill me.'

'Why?' I repeated in a flabbergasted voice.

'For gain,' said Miss Ellison, as though it were the most natural thing in the world.

From utter bewilderment I leapt again to the theory which I had entertained on the previous night. Mrs. Ellison's granddaughter had been sent home from the wilds suffering from mental trouble which took the form of persecution mania. I thought I might have been warned that my invitation involved

sharing the house with a deranged person and one who did not
appear to be subject to any close control.

'Oh come,' I said. 'I'm sure it's not as bad as all that.'

Varvara looked at me with contempt.

'My grandmother wishes to see us,' she said.

She led the way upstairs to the first landing where she tapped
on a door. Nurse Fillis opened it and motioned us to enter.
Inside, Mrs. Ellison was sitting up in a bed resembling my
own, except that the draperies were even more elaborate. She
had aged perceptibly since our last meeting. Her eyes seemed
paler and vaguer, and the artificial plaits which she wore like
a coronet round her head looked top-heavy against the thin
foundation of her own hair. Nevertheless she still diffused an
air of aristocratic benevolence which inspired confidence in her
control of her surroundings—sometimes rather misleadingly,
as I was to find out.

'My dear boy,' she said, holding out her hand. The diamonds
between the clay-coloured wrinkles looked as if they were finding their way back to their original matrix.

I started to thank her for her hospitality, but she cut me
short: 'You are doubly welcome,' she said. 'For your own sake
and because it will be so good for Barbara'—she pronounced
the name that way—'to have a companion. Everything in England is strange to her.'

'That I do not find,' said the girl.

'Ah,' replied Mrs. Ellison, 'we must learn to know the wood
before we can recognize the trees.'

The sudden tautening of phrase was unaccompanied by
any change of manner. And this somehow made the mild snub
more effective.

Varvara disengaged herself with a shrug and wandered over
to the dressing-table where she began to play with a galaxy of
toilet articles cut in the solidest and most ornate silver which I
have ever seen. She stole (unobserved, I hope) more than half
the attention which I should have been giving to the old lady.

'. . . very sad,' said Mrs. Ellison, 'and, of course, a terrible pre-
dicament for a young girl. Not much better than being locked

up in a cage with a lot of wild beasts after they had eaten their trainer. However she was most sensible. She set out for England a few weeks after the funeral.'

Varvara looked round, and for a moment I could see the line of her body under that shapeless djibbah. She was solid yet sinuous, like a young puma just come to its full growth.

Suddenly the significance of Mrs. Ellison's words dawned upon me. I was shocked to think what an impression of lacka-daisical callousness I might have conveyed.

'I'm sorry,' I stammered, 'terribly sorry about your son. I'd forgotten that he was—'

'Quite right,' said Mrs. Ellison. 'The young should not fill their minds with thoughts of death.'

Nevertheless when I was sixteen my aunt had very sensibly taught me the skeleton of a letter of formal condolence. All I could think of was one of its marmoreal phrases.

'You must have suffered an irreparable loss.'

'That is not how I regard it,' said Mrs. Ellison quite kindly. 'At my age it may be repaired any day.'

Varvara dropped a nest of scent bottles with a loud clatter. As she came over to the bed with arms outstretched, her face seemed to be lit by an internal fire which rarefied the blunt handsomeness of her features.

'Those are words of God,' she said, taking Mrs. Ellison's hands. 'We shall meet him again in the bosom of the blessed and immortal Christ who will have forgiven his errors and his blindness. . . .' She appeared to consider for a moment. 'At any rate by the time I come to die,' she added thoughtfully.

Mrs. Ellison did not attempt to withdraw from the embrace. But her eyelids batted in deprecation of this excessive and un-Anglican display.

'We are given every grounds for hope,' she said quietly.

Up to this point the old lady had controlled the interview with tact and firmness. Possibly the introduction of an emo-tional note upset her. But more likely, I think, she was simply tired by coping simultaneously with two diverse creatures from whom she was widely separated in age and outlook. At any rate her grip began to waver. No longer did the ends of sentences entirely match their beginning; and an increasing number of her utterances took the form of commands—not always directed to any clear object. She made Varvara pull back the heavy tasselled curtains to the end of their runners although they were already admitting a blaze of sunshine. Even so she was not satisfied. She seemed to be looking for something beyond the window, but she could not explain what it was.

In the middle of this impasse Nurse Fillis entered and summed up the situation at a glance.

'Time for a nice rest now, Mrs. Ellison.'

'I . . . want . . . to . . . see . . . my . . . flowers.'

'Now you know we had the window-boxes taken away because Dr. Conway thought they stuffy-ied up the room.'

'My . . . flowers,' repeated Mrs. Ellison sadly.

Nurse Fillis put a finger roguishly to her lips.

'Now, I'll tell you something. We've just had our order in from Harrods. Two dozen lovely roses, like a lot of princesses in satin petticoats. I'll bring them in the moment Gibbons has arranged them.'

'Drip, drip, drip,' said Mrs. Ellison distinctly, in her 'accidental' voice.

Unhappy Nurse Fillis! Amongst other comparisons still less flattering, she resembled a pair of those linked buckets; of which, when one rises, the second sinks into the depths. As she pulled her credit up with one hand, she let it down with the other. No sooner did I start to respect her professional competence, than she shocked me by showing an unexpected addiction to sickroom whimsy—though perhaps I am being unduly harsh about a defensive habit forced on her by a succession of melancholic and querulous invalids.

'Now,' she said, plumping the pillows on the bed, 'we'll just lie back and rest for a bit. Otherwise we shan't be fit for our visitor this afternoon.'

Varvara said: 'Who is coming this afternoon, Grandmother?'

Nurse Fillis made a shooing motion behind her back, clearly indicating that we should get out. It seemed to me that she was entirely justified: it was not a time to ask idle questions—still less to ask them in the steely, rather menacing tone which the girl had employed.

Sacrificing manners to example, I went first through the door.

I knew that Varvara was following by a peculiar noise which I could not at first identify. Then I realized that she was grinding her teeth.

'What's the matter?' I said.

'They are making a tool-pigeon of my grandmother,' she replied.

The atmosphere, super-saturated with eccentricity, was telling on my nerves.

'Tool,' I said. 'Or stool-pigeon. Take your choice. They both seem equally unlikely.'

'That is because you know nothing.' She stopped and put her hand on my shoulder, slewing me round so that she looked into my face. She was very strong. 'Are you my friend, David?'

'Yes, of course.'

She sighed.

'I think that you are a person who will see both sides before he chooses where to give his friendship. Well, that must happen, and I am not afraid because your heart is pure, though ignorant.'

I spent the rest of the morning sitting in the roof-garden which I had observed from my bedroom, and smoking one of Mr. Ellison's cigars. The garden was in effect an unroofed extension of the sitting-room on the second floor. This was the room which Mrs. Ellison chiefly used when she was out of bed. The décor was less flamboyant than downstairs, though a case containing a large stuffed fish with razor teeth looked odd on top of the bookcase. But there was also a high-fidelity gramophone and a magnificent collection of white-label records, to which I later spent many hours listening.

The discovery of the gramophone cheered me at a point when I needed cheering. For some while I had been asking myself whether I was going to enjoy this visit; and the answers which came back were increasingly dubious. When every allowance was made for the narrowness of my horizon, No. 8 Aynho Terrace remained a very peculiar place. If my aunt had gauged the oddity of its inmates, I was convinced that she would never have let me come. She had the true Britannic hatred of ill-defined queerness; at a pinch she would rather have been put down in an unequivocal brothel than a place where one could only say that something funny went on upstairs.

But of course Aunt Edna had never had any great opportunity of judging Mrs. Ellison's domestic background. After the return from Brittany she and my uncle had several times been asked to Aynho Terrace for tea or dinner. Seen thus fleetingly, and without the presence of Varvara, I could imagine that the household had appeared quite conventional. When my uncle's leave expired and they went back to India the friendship continued by letter—Mrs. Ellison was a surprisingly active correspondent—and it was in the course of these exchanges that she had so kindly offered to help with the perpetual problem of what to do with me during the vacations.

After I had been sitting out for a while a thought struck me and I returned under cover. I went to the bookcase with the fish on top and looked along the lower shelves. As I had expected in a house of that type I found one devoted to books of reference: as well as copies of Whitaker and Burke and Kelly's *Landed Gentry* it contained a large leather-bound atlas. I took this out into the sunlight and opened it on one of the tables at the page which showed Western China and Eastern Turkestan. The map was coloured for contour, so that the dark masses of the mountains to the south and north-west looked like thunder-clouds encroaching on the Gobi and the Takla-Makan, the great deserts whose pale lemon floor shaded off to a dull white where the land dropped below sea-level.

A shadow fell across the book. Varvara who had left me after our talk with Mrs. Ellison was standing behind my chair. She moved very silently for a girl of her size. I was embarrassed by being caught in an occupation which was so obviously inspired by her.

'I hope you don't think it impertinent,' I said, 'but I was wondering exactly where you lived.'

She studied the map for some seconds, as if she was not very familiar with such things. Then she put her forefinger on a spot under the Northern Tien Shan mountains in that section of the range which is called Bogdo-Ola. Where she pointed there was quite a cluster of small towns, but the scale was large enough to show which one she meant.

'Hai-po-li' I read slowly, and no doubt with an utterly false pronunciation.

'Doljuk,' said Varvara like an oath or a battle-cry.

She picked up my fountain-pen which happened to be lying on the table and scored through the printed name, cutting the strong paper in her vehemence. Then above the erasure she scrawled in the name which she preferred.

I missed the point because I knew nothing about the politics of Sinkiang. Whilst I was still wondering how to respond, the tubular gong in the hall began to warble, its notes mixing with the quarter-chimes of the innumerable clocks which simultaneously announced the hour of lunch.

The meal was not a very happy one, in spite of the excellence of the food. Considering the small degree of supervision which its mistress could exert, the household at Aynho Terrace ran with surprising smoothness. This was partly due to the unexhausted strength of tradition, and partly to the fact that, for all appearances to the contrary, Mrs. Ellison had collected round her an exceptionally honest and conscientious nucleus of upper servants.

The trouble was, quite simply, the presence at the same table of Varvara and Nurse Fillis. They obviously hated each other.

This intense hostility struck me as something actuated from beyond visible causes. Each had her social disabilities, but in neither did they seem to take a form which should be particularly liable to rile the other.

As at breakfast, Nurse Fillis got up and left the table whilst we were still eating. If I had had to guess about a move which interested me so little, I should have said that she did so either from an inflated idea of her duties, or else in recognition of the fact that the family and their guests might like a chance to talk in private. Varvara, however, had a more original theory. As soon as the door closed behind her enemy she gave a loud, gruff giggle.

'Now she goes upstairs to wash her armpits.'

'Why on earth do you imagine she's doing that?' I said when I had recovered a little.

'From desire,' replied Varvara in a sombre tone. *'Elle fait la cour au roi des hyènes.'*

I had not noticed that the butler was in the room during these exchanges. Otherwise—prig that I was—I should certainly not have abetted them. Now, however, it was too late. Turpin who was doing something mysterious in a corner with the remains of a bottle of white wine gave a loud liquid chortle followed by the almost anguished cry of 'Box on!' As he went out of the room, still choking with mirth, Varvara observed:

'Turpin is a man of God.'

It had been made clear by Mrs. Ellison that I was expected to devote the afternoon to entertaining her granddaughter. Nor had I any intention of welshing. I merely hoped that Varvara, like myself, would prefer some sort of active amusement. Nevertheless for fear of seeming stingy, I felt bound to begin by suggesting a matinée or a visit to the cinema. To my delight she rejected both without hesitation.

'I wish to walk in the town,' she said.

I took her by a circuitous route to Kensington Gardens. At the bottom of Queen's Road we saw a disaster. A middle-aged man lay, either dead or insensible, on the outer edge of the pavement. One constable was bending over him whilst another kept back the usual ring of spectators. Since no vehicle seemed to be near, there was more than the usual scope for speculation.

'Poor chap,' I said, 'I wonder what's happened to him!'

This presented no problem to Varvara.

'He was robbing in the street,' she said confidently, 'when the guards of the magistrate came by and shot him.'

After a pause I said:

'How long have you been in England?'

'Now, three weeks and three days,' she replied.

'Well, if I were you I shouldn't be in a hurry to jump to conclusions.'

If I had been brave enough and cruel enough I might have added: 'On the other hand, if you like to learn up a few of the simpler conventions, you can't be too quick for me.' Like most very young men I was gravely embarrassed by any eccentricities of behaviour or appearance. I certainly did not dress well myself, I was not even neat, yet I was capable of suffering acutely in the company of someone who wore brown shoes with pinstriped trousers. Any breach of the rules by a woman was even more excruciating. Nineteen twenty-eight is not very long ago, but it is an effort to recall how much more conventional people were in those days. For instance, if a girl had walked about the London streets without stockings, the dirty thoughts would have been swarming up her legs like centipedes. Varvara did wear stockings, though without much attention to their grip or alignment. On the other hand she had no hat; her tawny mane seemed to have a peculiarly elastic quality which caused it to bounce and flare out round her head as though a galvanic current were running through it. The garment which I incorrectly thought of as a djibbah was not intrinsically daring, but a piquant effect could be obtained by leaving the buttons which ran down the front open as far as the waist.

It is a curious thing, which I have confirmed more than once, that a woman who comes from a country where there are strict rules of female modesty from which she is exempt will not unconsciously approximate to those standards; much more probably she will go round in a way which would cause comment in a licensed quarter.

But at least I had a companion who never allowed any one embarrassment to chafe monotonously. Brisk as raindrops came half a dozen more, making their impact in as many different quarters.

'We should be friends,' announced Varvara, as though she were triumphantly refuting some furious argument to the contrary. 'We have the same misfortune.'

Oh no, we haven't, I thought. My shirt is done up in front.

'You also are an orphan—yes?'

'Yes.'

'We fight alone.'

'I didn't know your mother was dead too,' I said, for something to say.

Varvara rolled up her magnificent eyes until practically only the whites were visible.

'God rest her, my beloved Serafina Filipovna. She had a terrible death. I shall tell you about it and see if you weep.'

'Let's take a chair,' I said, feeling that it might be easier to force a few tears from a sitting position.

We arranged ourselves to look over the Round Pond, above which a faint water-vapour was shimmering in the brilliant heat.

Varvara began: 'In the summer at Doljuk it is so hot that nobody can sleep in the houses. At night they go into the cellars which are dug deep beneath the yards. But before you lie down you must be very careful. You must search the *Kang* and search the ceiling and you must burn along the cracks of the wall. Otherwise the pests will come out and empoison you in your sleep.'

'Bugs?' I queried.

'Pests,' said Varvara firmly. 'Scorpions, many bad flies, and also *nobbol*.'

'What's *nobbol*?'

It was more easily asked than answered. There was a gap in Varvara's English about *nobbol* and not one which could be easily filled by circumlocution or gesture. After several feverish minutes I had accumulated a number of disconnected items about them; for instance that they were about half the size of her palm, they had hair, appeared to be generally unloved and—to make it more difficult—they uttered a noise which she rendered as a sort of bark. But none of this added up to any coherent picture. And since *nobbol* were clearly essential to the story, it looked as if I might miss the horrible end of Serafina Filipovna.

Presently, however, a little dejected by her failure to explain, Varvara allowed her eyes to wander. Of a sudden she stiffened and pointed with a cry at the ground beside her chair. I looked down and saw a tiny spider clambering round a piece of stick.

'*Nobbol*,' she said triumphantly.

'But they don't bark.'

'In Doljuk,' she insisted.

'Well, it's your story!'

Here I will admit that subsequent research shows that Varvara was speaking the literal truth. In parts of Sinkiang is found a species of very large spider covered with reddish fur. It is capable of making a noise which natural history books usually compare to the snapping together of two boards. It bites fiercely and injects some sort of venom whose effects are highly unpredictable. Some people suffer very little, but in others the stuff produces intense lassitude followed by swelling and coagulation of the blood round the wound.

Apparently Varvara's mother was sleeping alone in the cellar, because her husband and daughter were away on one of the former's business expeditions. I suspect that Serafina Filipovna may have prepared herself for a lonely night with several hearty drinks. At any rate she fell asleep without making the usual precautionary search. By bad luck not merely one but two *nobbol* dropped on her and bit her simultaneously on the breast and the side of the neck. She had never been attacked before and neither she nor anybody else knew that she was violently allergic to the poison. Before she could seek aid she fell into a stupor, during which great buboes of stagnant blood came up at the points of injury. Presently fragments broke away from the main clots and were washed round in her circulation till they reached her heart and brain. So I suppose she died from a kind of multiple thrombosis.

The tale was my first introduction to life in Doljuk, and it indicated the general flavour not badly—the savagery, the inconsequence, and an element of absurdity which prevented the most frightful blows from acquiring any spiritual significance. It is an awful thing to be bitten to death by barking spiders, but it is not tragedy.

I should have liked to ask Varvara how her father had perished. But I thought it might seem a morbid insistence on the details of her orphanship. Besides I was conscious how very little I had to offer in return: merely one pneumonia and one motor accident.

After a while we strolled on, going down to the Serpentine and then along its banks as far as Lancaster Gate. From there we cut up into Hyde Park. We were not very far on the way to Marble Arch, and the heat was already making me think of a return by bus, when a few yards ahead of us I recognized a familiar figure.

Andrew Callingham had rooms on the same College staircase as myself. He was a year older than I by birth, and at least a decade by experience. His father was a financier, who received a good deal of mention in the newspapers. I suppose he was what they call cosmopolitan and had brought up his son likewise. At any rate by the age of twenty-one Andrew was at home in London or New York or Paris. Brighton suited him equally well—though this did not dawn on people till later.

I don't know why he bothered with me, except perhaps that I was useful whenever he wanted to get rid of a surplus of worldly wisdom. His visits to my rooms were usually paid late at night after his return from some gambling party in Trinity, or, more often, a gallant visit to Town.

'Don't get caught up in it, David,' he would say. 'I dropped eighty tonight,' or, 'I thought I should never get rid of the little bitch'—depending on the way he had spent the evening.

'Don't let yourself be drawn into it,' he would repeat.

Simple though I was, I realized at an early stage that if by some chance I disregarded his advice and began to rush round gambling and fornicating, Andrew would be very, very angry. I should have destroyed a delicate but essential constituent in our relationship.

If I had been in control of our progress, I would have daw-
dled so that we never caught him up. Unfortunately Varvara set
the pace, and it was a brisk one. There was nothing for it but to
swallow my mean fear of being laughed at for going about with
a wild woman. Andrew did a good deal of quiet sniggering at
the comic lack of sophistication around him.

'Hallo,' I said, as we came level.

He stopped and raised his pearl-coloured trilby.

'David, my dear chap! And accompanied!' He smiled at
Varvara. 'David always pretends to be such a woman-hater.'

'This is Miss Ellison,' I said. 'From Chinese Turkestan.'

'No!' said Andrew. 'Or is that an example of your famous
poker-faced humour?'

'He speaks the truth,' said Varvara. 'Why should you doubt
him?'

'I don't really,' said Andrew. 'It is just that I've never met
anyone from those parts before. In fact I can't miss the chance
of making good the gap in my education. Why don't we all go
and have tea at Tytlers.'

Tytlers lay just behind Park Lane. It was one of the most
fashionable teashops in London. There, sitting on small gold
chairs with bars like harp-strings across the backs, one could eat
the nicest ice-creams and cakes which I have ever tasted. Two
things only I hoped: first that Andrew would pay, for I had very
little money on me; and secondly that Varvara's dress would
not attract stares—though on this point I was somewhat reassured by Andrew's calm acceptance.

Accidentally or by design they put us at a secluded table.
As usual the place was pretty full and it was not numbers that
Andrew was thinking of when he said:

'I don't know what's happening to this place. You practically
never see anyone here nowadays.'

'To me there seem many,' said Varvara.

'He means people of importance,' I said.

I don't know why, but I thought this explanation might make
her annoyed or contemptuous. Those seemed to be the proper
reactions of a Noble Savage. But on the contrary a look of inter-

est animated her face and her fierce blue gaze swept round the room like an arc-lamp.

'They are peasants?' she said.

Andrew began to laugh.

'Oh dear!' he said. 'That's very nice. Yes, I see several who could be described as honorary peasants.'

'At first I must say strange and foolish things,' said Varvara with dignity and also with an unsuspected humility. 'But in the end I shall come to speak as a true-born residing native.'

'God forbid!' said Andrew. 'It would be a descent from champagne to soda-water.'

Here I will anticipate a little. From her father she inherited great linguistic gifts which were developed by the hotch-potch of races amidst which she had lived. As well as English, she spoke fluent Russian, French, Chinese, and Turki—the last being a language of quite fantastic difficulty. But like most polyglots she was prevented by the range of her accomplishments from becoming absolutely at home in any of them. Nobody who talked to her for five minutes would have believed that she was English. And yet her actual solecisms were few and her mispronunciations still rarer. It was the odd turn of phrase—the dignified word when one expected a colloquialism—which gave her conversation its foreign ring.

Her mother knew little English and Russian was usually spoken in their home. Apart from this, there was another reason why, despite the possession of an English father, she grew up without the slipshodness and the slang which mark the indigenous speaker. Fulk Ellison probably went out of his way to avoid teaching her his own habits of speech. He was considered very foul-mouthed in a genial way and no doubt he realized that it would add to his daughter's handicaps if she returned to civilization cursing like a navvy.

Presently Varvara got up and went to the Ladies. Andrew looked at me with quizzically raised eyebrows.

'Well, well,' he said. 'You tempt one to coin a phrase about dark horses. What a striking, not to say staggering, young piece!'

'She's very simple,' I said deprecatingly.

'So's a tidal wave. But it doesn't make any the less impression.'

I now began to see that I had acquired prestige instead of losing it. So far from being ashamed of my previous cowardice, I was puffed up with smug complacency.

'She still has a lot to learn. For instance about dressing,' I said.

'But nothing, nothing. If you take away that sack and those delicious boats she has on her feet, you'll destroy half the effect.'

'Oh well,' I said rather gruffly, 'if you merely regard her as a sort of comic turn!'

'Me!' said Andrew in an outraged voice. 'I think she's one of the most magnificent creatures I've ever seen. I can tell you, David, some pretty crude thoughts have been passing through your Uncle Beastly's brain.'

'I doubt if there'd be much doing in that way.'

'Why?'

I did not really know, but I managed to improvise an answer.

'I rather think that at present she's preoccupied with other things.'

'For instance?'

'Well ... she seems to imagine that someone is trying to murder her.'

'Oh, lovely!' said Andrew, closing his eyes in ecstasy. 'How right! A dash of persecution mania is just what's needed to bring out the values in that face. . . . By the way, have you discovered who's supposed to be after her?'

'Not yet.'

'Well, it doesn't matter. I prefer to supply my own assassins. I think that before she fled from Sinkiang she pinched the gigantic ruby which formed the eye of an idol worshipped by a particularly foul and esoteric cult. Their yellow slant-eyed priests have followed her to England . . .'

Andrew did not do this kind of foolery badly. He practised it a good deal—largely, as he once told me, for the benefit of that wide range of young women who were in love with Dornford Yates's Berry characters. It often got results which would never have been countenanced at White Ladies.

On this occasion he was interrupted by the return of Varvara. He called for the bill and waved aside my offer of a contribution. He was a generous chap in a way which is too often and too lightly despised: there is still virtue in giving what one can well afford.

On the baking pavement our ways parted. Andrew was going back to his father's flat in St. James's and I intended that Varvara and I should catch a bus at Marble Arch. Before he said goodbye, Andrew took the telephone number of the house in Aynho Terrace.

'One day soon,' he said, addressing Varvara, 'I'm going to offer my services as a guide. I'm sure David does his best but I believe I could drag you down at least two circles lower in the pit of iniquity.'

Varvara did not reply; but when we had progressed about twenty yards on our way home, she suddenly said:

'He is one of the children of this world. What is the name of that smelling stuff which he puts on his hair?'

As was her custom, Mrs. Ellison came down to dinner. I was a little surprised that she had been allowed to do so this evening, for she looked old and tired and worried. The last expression was new to me and it conflicted with my conception of her unshakable aristocratic calm. Whilst she was taking some medicine at the beginning of the meal, I whispered to Varvara who was sitting next to me that her grandmother looked rather ill.

'Is it strange?' she replied. 'All afternoon the fiend is with her and she wears herself out against his snarlings and persuasions.'

'What do you mean—the fiend?'

'My uncle,' said Varvara.

She spoke rather louder than she intended. Mrs. Ellison looked up at us over a glass of frothy pinkish liquid. In her regard there seemed to be a curious and subtly disquieting mixture of emotions: sympathy, disapproval, and the cold quiet amusement of the ancient who know that very soon now somebody else will have to hold the baby. All she said was:

'Did you have a nice walk, my dear?'

'Yes, Grandmother,' replied Varvara in a subdued voice.

Mrs. Ellison turned to me.

'I am sure you saw that she did not over-excite herself. It is all so novel and stimulating for her.'

The cool, faintly astringent tone was certainly intentional. The old lady knew a good deal more about the cross-currents in her household than one would have expected.

After dessert it appeared that I, as the solitary male in the company, was expected to sit on for an indefinite time in front of a decanter of port. Very wearisome my solitude would have been if Turpin had not appeared after about five minutes. He had poured some interesting-looking sauce which I could not remember figuring on our recent menu over his wasp-striped waistcoat.

'Mrs. E. pops off right after,' he said.

'You mean, goes to bed?'

He nodded.

'There's not much doing in the evenings round 'ere—unless you'd like to warm up the Fillet.'

I must not let down Aunt Edna, I thought, by exchanging lewdities with the servants.

'Turpin—' I began severely.

But like the rabbits and birds which I had occasionally hunted he would not remain still whilst I took my shot.

'What about the Gorgeous East, though? All right, eh? Lot of character and body like this Château Ickham.'

He held up a bottle of the rich aromatic Yquem which we had been drinking at dinner.

'About four years ago,' he continued, 'we had another young chap come 'ere. Mr. Sampson, the Honourable Elwood Sampson. Sounds a bit starchy, eh? That's why I 'ave to laugh. Because you'd never guess. This young Honourable, every night 'e was down in my pantry 'aving a cag with me.'

Having dropped his tactful and unassuming invitation, Turpin swept up an armful of tableware and loped through the

door, trailing one decanter at the full stretch of his arm, like a
Neanderthal man with his club.

At first it seemed that convention was going to win the day.
Against my inclination I went upstairs. But I found it was quite
true that the social life of the house broke up immediately after
dinner. The big sitting-room stood empty and so did the roof-
garden beyond. There was no indication of Varvara's where-
abouts. Perhaps she was upstairs sharpening her knife. Anyway,
Turpin's comparison between her and Château Yquem made
contact at another point: both had a very strong flavour and the
palate could temporarily become surfeited with it.

What finally decided me was the risk that Nurse Fillis,
freed from her evening duties, would come into the sitting-
room. Turpin did not impress me as a man who often spoke
at random, and I wondered whether he had meant to implant
some warning in his jest about warming up the Fillet. She
was obviously an emotional young woman. At that age I had
a marked fear of becoming involved for life with some female
who was totally unattractive to me. This was, I think, largely
the work of Aunt Edna; when I was eighteen, she had delivered
a long lecture about various men of her acquaintance who had
been trapped and compromised into marriage with designing
hussies. Neither I nor even she realized that these stories dated
back fully thirty years, to an utterly different social climate: and
that all the victims were covered in strawberry leaves and drip-
ping with money. 'Poor Jack Froggett,' she would say, 'he was
only the second son, but he had ten thousand a year and the
place in Gloucestershire. Still, it didn't go far with that woman
and her relatives on his back!'

I could have saved myself a lot of trouble if I had realized
that anybody who trapped me would be doing so for the sake
of a Cambridge scholarship tenable for four years and a capital
sum producing £286 a year at 3½ per cent which I would inherit
on my twenty-first birthday.

I made for the pantry. Above-stairs and below-stairs probably differed far more in an eighteenth- or nineteenth-century
mansion than the hall and the dungeons in a medieval castle.

The basement at Aynho Terrace was not intrinsically sordid: it was the seemingly deliberate imposition of certain disadvantages which rather shocked me. For instance, need it have been dug so deep that only the last quarter of the barred windows peeped up above ground-level? And why line all the passages with grey stone, when a facing of coloured plaster would have cost hardly more?

Whatever the case had once been the hardships were now more aesthetic than practical. I looked in at the kitchen where the enormous leaded range still occupied most of one wall, but the work was done on an electric cooker of the most modern design. A little further on a door was ajar and inside another large room—the servants' hall, I suppose—a whole covey of females were seated round a table sipping cups of tea, as earlier in the day, I had seen some of them sipping away the dust with brush and pan from the *bric-à-brac* upstairs.

Turpin's pantry was at the end of the central corridor. It was lighter than most of the other basement rooms because it looked on to an area. The wall on the house-side was fitted with cupboards and where one or two of them were open I could see the massed silver standing on a lining of green baize cloth. Turpin himself sat at the table with a bottle before him, polishing a multiple candlestick which I never at any time saw used during my stay with Mrs. Ellison. This made not the slightest difference to Turpin who had been trained to an hieratic tradition, in which one of the rites was polishing silver.

Along the wall by the window where they would obtain whatever sun seeped into the area were several birds in cages —a jackdaw, two budgerigars, and a linnet. No doubt the R.S.P.C.A. would have condemned their situation, but I am confident that their lives, though perhaps shorter than the average, were happier than most. Turpin loved his pets, and he was their sun. At intervals they were taken out and allowed to flutter round the table where he fed them on currants and sips of sweet white wine.

Turpin always insisted that all his birds were fluent talkers. Personally I never heard one of them utter a word. On several occasions, however, I did see Turpin, much mellowed, address them very movingly and then reply to himself in a variety of small piping voices which he thought suitable to their personalities. He appeared to be quite unconscious of his share in this performance.

At my entry Turpin rose and said in his episcopal voice:

'This is indeed a pleasure, sir.'

'And to me,' I replied.

'Will you take a glass of wine?'

He poured out some port which, even to my uncultivated palate, was much superior to the stuff that appeared upstairs.

After these preliminaries I was seized by shyness. I could think of nothing to say. The evening stretched before me in a vista of agonized speechlessness. To hide my embarrassment I wandered round the pantry, pausing at random before a reproduction of Landseer's *Monarch of the Glen* which hung over the door.

Turpin's eyes followed me.

> 'The stag at eve 'ad drunk 'is fill—
> No wonder 'e felt bloody ill,'

he recited in his ordinary tones.

The ice was appreciably thawed.

'Did you make that up?' I asked.

Turpin shook his head.

'It was one of Mr. Fulk's rhymes. 'E 'ad some 'ot ones.'

'Who was Mr. Fulk?'

' 'Er father,' said Turpin, jerking his eyes at the ceiling in a way which made his meaning clear in defiance of all logic. 'And one or two others, I shouldn't wonder!'

'So you knew him?'

'I came as footman about four years before the bust.' Seeing the incomprehension on my face, he explained: 'Bust with 'is father, of course. Mr. Fulk was away a lot of the time, seeing to the business abroad. But didn't we know when 'e came back! Not ten minutes 'e'd be in the 'ouse before you'd 'ear 'im and the old man damning and blasting each other all round the place. "Confounded young puppy!"' trumpeted Turpin in a voice which went well with port, ' "— — old — !"' he replied to himself in a voice like a young bull. 'Nothing churchey about Mr. Fulk's language.'

'What did they quarrel about?' I asked, fascinated.

'Business.'

'Wasn't Mr. Fulk very good at it?'

'The way I 'eard 'e was a top-notcher with the machines and the men—all round, in fact, till it come to putting on the bite. Then maybe 'e'd let someone get away with tuppence-'alfpenny. Well that wouldn't do for old Mr. Ellison. People said 'e chewed 'is tanners till 'e'd flattened 'em into bobs.' Turpin paused, took a refreshing draught of port and refilled both our glasses. 'Mind you,' he went on, 'I don't reckon that was at the bottom of it. The real trouble was the same as 'aving two cocks in one pen. Each 'as to show the other. . . . Still, I never believed it would come to anything serious. I thought they could go on shouting the odds at each other like you get in some families and underneath the blood's as thick as glue. But then one day, bango, Mr. Fulk's shaken off the dust and that's the last time 'e came near England, let alone this 'ouse.'

'Do you know what happened?'

'Ask me, Mr. bloody Cedric 'ad 'is 'and in it,' said Turpin. 'Christ, 'e didn't 'alf 'ate 'is brother! See, where the trouble was, Mr. Fulk could never leave alone; when 'e saw a bastard 'e 'ad to kick 'im. And anyone who can look at Mr. Cedric without putting a name to 'im wants 'is eyes examined!'

I noted the present tense with surprise. I had not fully realized that Mrs. Ellison had another son who was alive.

'As live as any other snake,' said Turpin in answer to my question. 'It wasn't no ghost that came round this afternoon and told me at me own door that I'd better smarten up. The dirty sod! And the way 'e goes on at 'is mother. Wheedle, wheedle, wheedle—bully, bully, bully. I never take in the tea to them but I expect to see the poor old girl stretched on the 'earth-rug while Mr. Cedric tries to make 'er sign something with 'er last twitch!'

A peculiar suspicion for which it would have been difficult to give any logical grounds had begun to form in my mind.

'Do you think his niece is scared of him?'

Turpin did not seem in the least surprised.

'I shouldn't wonder. And I dare say if the truth was known, she got cause.'

'Why?'

'Money,' said Turpin succinctly.

Something seemed to be slightly off-centre in his reasoning. 'I suppose this Cedric does something?'

'Manages the firm now.'

'Well, then, he must be pretty rich . . .'

'Look,' said Turpin, laying his hand paternally on my arm, 'it's like as if a man's tit-struck. 'E 'as a girl, but 'e can 'ardly wait to finish the job for fear 'e might be missing the chance to 'ave another. Well, it's the same with money, if you got it bad. Give the old man or Mr. Cedric an 'undred million and they'd ask you in the same breath for the stamp they lent you yesterday.'

The volatility of Turpin's talk stopped me from following up the interesting sidetracks which it disclosed. Undistracted, I should certainly have asked him how money came to be a source of rivalry between Varvara and her uncle. And since he was extremely shrewd I should probably have got the correct answer: that the conflict was concerned with Mrs. Ellison's will. Beyond that I am sure he could not have gone; even the most trusted servant could scarcely have learnt the facts, and if he had he would not have understood their legal implication.

At the present stage of our acquaintance the conversation had reached one of its natural boundaries. (Considering I was a guest and in the second day of my visit, I could hardly complain that it had lacked range and latitude.) We turned to less dramatic topics. They were also less exacting and this began to suit Turpin at a time of the evening when the decanter was running low. For the rest of the time we talked mostly about his pets. Just before I went to bed he did his strange, and somehow pathetic, act of ventriloquism.

3

The fortunes of the Ellisons were based on mining-machinery, particularly pumps. I believe Joseph Ellison liked in later life to pretend that he had set out as a bare-foot boy; in fact he was the son of a prosperous doctor who gave him a good education. But his ascent was still remarkable. In his twenties he went to Mexico where he obtained a position in the silver-mines and persuaded the management that it would pay them to expand with the help of certain machinery from England—on the sale of which he drew a large commission. When he returned to London he went to see the manufacturers who were so impressed by his astuteness that they made the mistake of inviting him to join them. Three years later he was at the head of a completely new Board.

For a long while he continued to travel widely, undeterred by the most frightful hardship. He was nearly frozen to death in the Bolivian Andes; a poisonous snake bit him on the West Coast of Africa. But all the time his empire grew and money, always responsive to personal attention, came pouring in.

Just after the last war I was in a small South Coast hotel. Its battered library of a dozen volumes included the reminiscences of an aristocratic old *flâneur* who had been About Town in the late Victorian and Edwardian eras. I read with increasing boredom until I chanced on the name of Joseph Ellison, who seemed to have stung the author into his only gleam of wit.

'Whenever I met this Napoleon of commerce,' he said, 'I was filled with a sense of guilt. Presently I found out why: it was because I had never bought anything from him.'

For me this rings true. Only a missionary sense of the sacredness of gain could reconcile the two sides of the picture; on this the grim old eagle with his fierce independence, on that the super-salesman who would sell a 1,000 horse-power pump to a sheik in the middle of the Sahara.

If Ellison had stuck strictly to his own business I suppose he would have ended merely as a very rich engineer. But he graduated into the realms of high finance by the usual means of moving more and more of his interests on to paper. He started, almost accidentally, to accept shares in and mortgages on mines in payment for the equipment which he supplied; and this led, in some instances, to his taking over and running his security. Soon he was going in for such arrangements as a matter of policy.

I have no idea how much he was worth at his peak, which probably occurred in the first decade of the twentieth century. Five or six millions perhaps. But already at that date a flaw in his empire was beginning to show itself. The bulk of his estate— that is, the investments other than his own business—was situated abroad, in the form of immovable property. From the time when Queen Victoria died foreigners were becoming, if not more dishonest, at least braver. They were no longer terrified by a couple of gunboats in the harbour and a few white shell-puffs over the Presidential palace. They pinched the property of the British pioneers, they legalized their thefts in rigged courts, and finally offered a derisory sum of compensation. What with war in Europe and rising costs and the multiplicity of offenders, it became impossible to bring them to heel. Before his death Joseph Ellison had been robbed of a good part of his profits in South America and China; he died just in time to avoid seeing many more thousands vanish in the Russian revolution.

Still, it was only by the standards of Rockefeller and Morgan that his family had anything to complain of.

He had married at a date which now seems incredibly remote—1873. An advantageous marriage was needed to lift his social position onto a level with his bank account. Mrs. Ellison was, I believe, the daughter of a baronet. My aunt, who always knew these things, said that she was selected only after Joseph had been turned down by several Honourables.

'And she wouldn't have had him either, except that her father was gravely embarrassed. In those days girls were sold like sacks of coal.'

She pulled down the corners of her mouth in an equivocal

way which indicated disapproval of such treatment, coupled with regret for the filial spirit which led young women to submit to it.

Whatever the truth about her marital situation, I am sure that Mrs. Ellison met it with good manners and fortitude.

After the evening in Turpin's company, I did not feel well. I woke up with a headache which I put down to vintage port. But as the morning wore on and the headache was reinforced by fits of shivering, I suspected that I had caught a germ. That summer there was a good deal of mild 'flu about. I should not have been sorry to go to bed, but I did not like to play the invalid in a strange house. So I lay about in chairs for most of the morning, pretending to read, but with my eyes closed.

Fortunately my services as chaperon did not seem to be needed that morning. I saw nothing of Varvara until just before lunch, when I woke up from a doze to find her standing in the doorway watching me with an air which could not be mistaken for affection. When she noticed that I was awake, she said:

'They tell me you are a lawyer.'

'A student only. I'm reading Law at Cambridge.'

'But still, no doubt, you have training to cheat inheritances.'

'Nobody would be fool enough to allow me near an inheritance,' I said.

'You are humorous,' said Varvara. 'But I think now I see why you have made your appearance on this scene.'

'Please go away, or talk sense. I don't feel very well.'

She appeared to choose the first alternative, but after a moment she put her head back through the door.

'In Doljuk,' she said, 'when the Tungans revolted, they put all the lawyers on sharp stakes. Up their bottoms,' she said, lest I should miss anything.

I was feeling too muzzy to speculate on the reason for this outburst. It merely struck me as mildly surprising that she should have troubled to ask her grandmother about my future calling. Yet within the same day I had another and stranger example of interest directed to the same quarter.

*

Soon after lunch Mrs. Ellison came into the morning-room, walking slowly with the aid of a stick. She seemed disconcerted to find me there, and said something about the lovely weather outside. I was too embarrassed to tell her that I did not feel well, but I think she saw that I was in some kind of difficulty, for she immediately took my side, as it were, against herself.

'When my sister Fanny became so ill that she could no longer move about I remember saying—no doubt in a very silly and sentimental way: "My poor dear, how I pity you for not being able to go out into the sunshine and the fresh air." But Fanny said: "If you only knew how tired I've become in these last twenty years of people forcing me to leave warm fires for wet fields and cool conservatories for scorching lawns, you would not have such an exaggerated idea of the horrors of being crippled." Myself I always thought it was a very sensible remark.'

'I think so too,' I said.

Mrs. Ellison was looking at the mantelshelf, on which stood a faded cabinet photograph of a woman in Victorian dress. She lay propped up on a sofa. She might have been rather pretty but for the emaciation of her face which tightened the skin and gave her eyes an unnatural prominence like those of a Belgian hare.

'Poor Fanny,' said Mrs. Ellison, 'later on it was harder for her.' She fumbled the next words, then said quite distinctly: 'We tried to take her mind off, to distract her. We made her a museum and she was very patient about it . . . but it's not the same thing having a museum as the use of your backbone.'

In Mrs. Ellison's company I often felt that I was being sprinkled with an incredibly bland and refined irony. It fell as lightly as droplets flicked off the fingers. But to this day I cannot tell whether it was a real attribute or one with which I invested my hostess out of my own mind.

'Still,' she said, 'you might find some of the curiosities amusing. They're kept in the room above yours.'

In spite of her courtesy I suspected that she was anxious to have the sitting-room to herself. I went upstairs and lay down on my bed. After an hour I felt distinctly better and boredom began to seep in. Since I had neglected to provide myself with a book, I thought I would accept the invitation to look over the museum.

It was rather a pathetic place; the threadbare intention of comfort which was behind it peeped through the assorted muddle. Who really believes that sea-shells can exorcise the loneliness of the bath-chair or snuff-boxes the fear of death? Trays for the smaller objects ran along the walls; whilst in the centre of the room there was a huge cage of glass, with sliding partitions, which contained stuffed humming birds and a stuffed monkey and an armadillo which had undergone some kind of embalmery. On a rack hanging from the roof rested a couple of long Tibetan devil-trumpets.

These were the hard core, the intractables, among the curios. As I have already explained, the specimens judged capable of domestication, including the clocks, had long ago been dispersed for the general beautification of the house. I should have liked to see the museum when it was full: the density of the whole mass must have been roughly that of plum-pudding.

Some of the articles were genuinely interesting. Placed across a corner near the windows stood an enormous screen made out of mother-of-pearl and the feathers of kingfishers. I examined it for several minutes and then was filled with a desire to see how the constructor had dealt with the reverse side. Presumably he could not have left it as a mass of rough matrix and quills.

I slipped behind the panels, where I was concealed but not blinded, since the fabric of shell and feathers, though ostensibly solid, was in fact pierced with numerous tiny peepholes. I had scarcely gone into this accidental retreat when the door opened and there entered a big man with wavy iron-grey hair. He walked slowly down the left-hand row of cases, pausing at intervals to inspect them. Finally he appeared to find the one he wanted, for he opened its lid and took out an object which I could not see.

It suddenly struck me that my situation, originally excusable on grounds of surprise, was quickly becoming that of a spy.

I stepped out from shelter, coughing modestly. At the same time my head again began to ache abominably.

When he saw me the man's face assumed an expression which is seldom seen except in diluted form. It was concentrated suspicion. And yet in spite of its idiosyncrasy the look was strangely familiar.

'I was up here glancing at the things,' I said.

'You're that boy,' he said, as if to himself.

Unless today's young man of twenty has changed it is no way to his heart to refer to him as 'that boy'.

'I'm staying with Mrs. Ellison,' I said stiffly.

All over his face, he switched on an entirely different sort of stage-lighting. The violence of the change and its blatant artifice made the comparison inevitable. I remember thinking that this trick should be played in the drawing-room to complete the atmosphere of pantomime.

'My dear chap,' he said, 'I'm Cedric Ellison. I've heard so much about you. I know we shall see much more of each other.'

Here he made one of the absurd little miscalculations which were typical of him and which, in my later judgment, sprang from some very deep-seated lack of co-ordination. He was always pulling so many strings that he could never remember which of them might have crossed.

On this occasion he held out his right hand, forgetting that it still contained the object which he had removed from the case. Suddenly he realized that he was holding a foreign body. He withdrew his fingers and carelessly transferred a small yellow coin to his pocket. Immediately I remembered and identified it from my previous inspection, which was not hard, seeing that a gold Macedonian *stater* stood out from the general junk in the coin-tray like a diamond among ashes.

Cedric Ellison said: 'Excuse me, David. When I drop round here I often pick up some little curio to amuse my girl. It's such an awful magpie's nest, but one can still find a few things that will stimulate a child's imagination.'

'I expect so.'

He looked at me closely. He had eyes of a peculiar light-grey which should have suggested vacillation, yet, in some mysterious fashion, indicated an extraordinary hardness.

'I feel,' he said, taking off his gold pince-nez, 'that you're a person who has ideas about education. So I don't mind saying that I believe one of the finest things you can do for a young person is to give him or her a sense of the romance of past ages.'

I felt the gratuitous falsity of his sentiments like a physical slap. And yet, even as an older man, I have been taken in by characters far less intrinsically skilled in deceit than Cedric Ellison. But he had a kind of self-defeating mechanism inside him. Later I began to see how it operated: he was so utterly absorbed in himself and the part he was playing that he forgot he was being observed by an independent human intelligence. All the springs and weights and counterweights in his mind lay bare like the works of a gramophone. You could practically hear him saying (as it might be): 'Now I am being subtle,' or 'Now I will put him off his guard,' or 'It's about time I applied the whip-hand.'

Such signals reduced the amount of damage which he could do; but it would be wrong to suppose that they rendered him harmless. He was not a clever man, but he had cunning and endless pertinacity. Failing to get in by the door or the window, he would turn up weeks later through the chimney, when you thought he had forgotten his objective. I do not think that he could ever have acquired great wealth or power for himself; on the other hand he knew how to keep and use them.

'Of course,' he said with a sincerity so highly charged that it would not have deceived an infant, 'of course, anything that I borrow for Deirdre is returned after a few days. It would never do to let the child get the notion that even odds-and-ends are there to be walked off with.'

I knew then that Cedric was stealing the *stater*. And I was quite right. Later I learnt from Turpin that for years, whenever the acquisitive fit was on him, he would pop round to Aynho Terrace and pinch something out of the museum. It was a kind of intermittent outlet, such as is necessary in many types of mania. Over the years it had, so Turpin told me, visibly diminished the contents of the collection. He also said that Mrs. Ellison was aware of it. Certainly the servants knew. Some time before there had been a head-housemaid who particularly loathed Cedric. She invested several shillings of her wages at Woolworth's in sixpenny rings out of which she prised the stones. These she placed in an inconspicuous corner of the museum—and had the amusement of observing their steady disappearance during the following months.

His vice was not so much that of the plain thief as the magpie or the miser, for by all accounts his personal income was in the region of £20,000 a year.

'I hear,' he said—and the machinery of flattery started up with an audible purr, 'that you're a young man of quite remarkable talents. A future Haldane or Stephen.'

I muttered something about 'having a long way to go'.

Then he said: 'You're modest. I expect if the truth were known a good many people have already benefited by your advice.' Feeling that the second show of interest in my embryonic profession could not be pure coincidence, I gave him much the same rejoinder as I had given to Varvara.

'Nobody in his senses would consult an inexperienced undergraduate.'

'Oh,' said Cedric with great smoothness, 'not about the kind of detail which one only picks up with practice. But advice on matters of principle ... I often think that comes as well from a young, as an old, head.'

I suddenly made up my mind to string along with him, if only to see where he was going.

'What sort of matters had you in mind?'

'Well ... for instance ... respect for the Law ... making people understand they can't play fast and loose with it or with documents made under its authority.'

'Such as?'

'I don't know. Deeds, perhaps, or wills. There are a lot of simple unbusinesslike people who imagine that if you don't like what's written in them you can ignore it.'

'It should be easy to squash that notion,' I said.

'It just needs a word or two of disinterested advice.'

I continued to wear a bright, astute expression, but he suddenly shut up. I suppose I had played my part too vigorously and he felt that I was trying to push him into some concrete proposition before he was ready.

We left the museum and went downstairs together. In doing so we had to pass the door of Varvara's room. It was open and I could see her inside seated in front of a mirror, like the Lady of Shalott.

'Good evening, my dear,' called her uncle.

She must have been able to see our reflections, but she did not reply nor did her face flicker. Perhaps, I thought, it is one of those conventions which play such a part in Chinese life that people observing others through a mirror are themselves notionally invisible.

Cedric sighed. 'A poor, wild, uncouth creature!' he said in a lowered voice. 'I suppose it's a miracle she survived at all in that terrible wilderness. What my brother can have been thinking of, all those years . . .'

'I've wondered why he went to a place like that,' I said.

Cedric nodded gravely.

'Yes,' he said, removing his spectacles and fixing me in a light-grey stare. 'Yes, you must have wondered. Well . . . there's no sense in being squeamish about old scandals.' He paused so that his words should gain emphasis. 'My wretched brother betrayed our father's trust.' For a moment I was not quite sure whether the victim's name should be spelt with a capital F or not: then he went on. 'Fulk obtained money as an agent and failed to account for it.' (This seemed to rule out the Deity.) 'In those days society had no place for swindlers.'

It is a significant fact that the possibility of believing him never for an instant crossed my mind.

'It must have been very disturbing,' I said cautiously.

'It was,' Cedric agreed, 'to persons with standards of honour.'

His awful naïve cunning sometimes achieved results by a kind of double bluff. It filled persons of sensibility with so much

vicarious shame that they could not bear the insult to humanity involved in showing him up; consequently they sometimes
pretended to have noticed nothing and allowed him to achieve
his object. This, of course, led to a vicious circle, since each triumph was put down by its author to a Borgian subtlety.

By this time we had reached the hall and Cedric was collecting his hat and his gold-topped malacca cane. I looked round,
hearing a noise from the staircase, and saw Nurse Fillis coming
down the treads two at a time.

'Oh, Mr. Ellison,' she said, 'I'm so glad to have caught you!
You left your spectacle-case upstairs.'

'Thank you, Sister,' said Cedric. 'Most kind! It's so seldom
you youngsters realize how much we old fogeys depend on our
props and crutches.'

He squared up his body, which for a man in his fifties was
a pretty good one. I caught an enlightening glimpse of sickly
adoration on Nurse Fillis's face.

'What nonsense!' she said in slightly breathless accents.
'Everybody says how young you look.'

Cedric coughed sharply, a displeased bark, and you could
see her shrinking back to the station to which St. Thomas's or
Bart's had called her. Then—feeling, I suppose, that the scene
must otherwise end a little bleakly—he inquired:

'Is my mother resting now?'

'I've just given her a sedative,' said Nurse Fillis, 'to stop
her—'

But though it passed me by she obviously received another
warning of displeasure, for she broke off abruptly.

'You stimulate her so much, Mr. Ellison,' she finished syco-
phantically.

I next saw Varvara whilst we both waited in the morning-
room for dinner to be announced.

'Now,' she said with biting scorn, 'you have found a new
friend and master. You shall be his lice!'

I was feeling distinctly ill again, and my patience was short.

'Please don't talk drivel,' I said. 'If you want to know, I

think your uncle is one of the most god-awful skunks I've ever
seen.' I squinted at her maliciously, for migraine was setting
in. 'And that,' I added, 'is in face of a good deal of local competition.'

At this stage in her career Varvara never used the emotional
staircase: she dived straight down (or up) the lift-shaft. The disgust in my tone must have carried instant conviction.

'My dear ally,' she said, coming forward with her gesture of
the outstretched hands, 'I knew you must hate him. . . . You do
hate him?'

'I don't know him well enough. But he makes a very nasty
impression on me.'

This apparently satisfied her.

'We shall plot together,' she announced.

'Not me.'

Varvara and Cedric Ellison cannot have met very often
before my arrival on the scene. She had not been in England
long enough. And yet her hatred of him was already full-
fledged and she seemed to have a singularly complete apprecia-
tion of his character. This, I think, can only have been due to
a course of preparation beginning in childhood. Fulk had had
good reason to distrust his brother and he was not one to mini-
mize his wrongs.

Presently the gong sounded and we went downstairs. For
the next forty minutes I had to make a show of eating rich food
and simultaneously carrying on polite conversation without
being sick. It was Turpin who keyed up my resistance. He must
have noticed my greenish appearance, for when he bent over
me with a dish he said in a commiserating mutter:

'These bloody little afternoon boozers—clubs in mewses—
they're no good for a young chap!'

With that interpretation hanging over me, there was no
longer any possibility of quitting the table. But by the time I
was left alone with the port (which did not appeal to me even as
an emetic) my head was spinning.

I was sitting with my back to the door, and when I heard it
open I assumed that Turpin had come in.

'I don't think I'll join you downstairs tonight,' I said without looking round.

To my surprise I was answered by Varvara.

'You must go to your bed. I have watched you and you have a fever.'

She put her hand on my forehead. It was slightly rough, but cool, and her touch seemed in itself to have a special quality. I am not producing the usual mystic gibber about healing hands and electric 'fluences. Varvara had 'touch' in much the same way as we use the phrase of a professional billiards player; and, I suspect, for much the same reason, namely abounding self-confidence. A fraction of this was transferred by the contact and from it I derived a definite, though momentary, alleviation of my symptoms.

'You must be cured,' she said.

'I don't want to trouble them to send for a doctor.'

'I shall cure you myself,' she said with a certain condescension.

'Do you know how?'

'My nurse taught me. She was a witch. She could poison and she could heal.'

It was not really a very auspicious testimonial. I must have been feeling damned ill; otherwise I should never have surrendered myself to second-hand Asiatic sorceries. But had I not, I should certainly have missed something.

We went upstairs, my skull opening and shutting at every step. Varvara stopped at the door of her own room. I hesitated, but, seeing that I was obviously meant to enter, I did so.

'Lie down on the bed,' she ordered. 'Take off your shoes first.'

'I should have done that in any case,' I said coldly.

Through a haze of fever I watched her preparations. In a corner of the room, looking wildly out of place against the rich smug Victorian furniture and hangings, was a large and hideous tin trunk stamped with the initials F.J.E. She opened it and took out a box with the same black japanned surface, which contained a number of little jars and bottles made of coarse china. From one of the former she measured out on to

her thumbnail some small slivers like fragments of dried hari-
cot, and tipped them into the famous rhinoceros-horn goblet,
a dingy vessel which a quiet word from Mrs. Ellison had lately
caused to be banished from the dining-room. Then she added a
few drops of reddish liquid and began to pound the strips with
the handle of a hairbrush. There was nothing antiseptic about
Varvara's medicine.

Lying still on my back made me feel better, and consequently rather more observant. I noticed Varvara's clothes, to
which I had become hardened of late. In those days there was
no question in a house like Mrs. Ellison's but that one dressed
for dinner. Her evening frock was about the right length for current fashion, but its fabric reminded me of nothing so much
as those curtains of string and beads which are still found in
old-fashioned pubs.

She must have seen the direction of my gaze in the mirror.

'Why are you staring at me, David?'

I was not up to social evasion.

'I was looking at your dress,' I said, 'and wondering where
you got it.'

'Passing through Shanghai on my way to England. At a shop
for the modes.'

'Ah,' I said, 'the modes.'

She gave me the look of sorrowful nobility, which, on occasions when she had been insulted or injured, alternated quite
unpredictably with tigerish rage.

'I know I am dressed laughably,' she said. 'At home I wore my
trousers and coat, like the other women of the country, and I
am not used to your clothes.'

'I didn't mean to be rude,' I pleaded unhappily.

Varvara continued: 'My father had an English proverb: First
things first. Thus, first I shall defeat my enemies. Second I shall
become fashionable so that I fill everyone with desire.'

'Oh, I don't think you do badly as it is,' I mumbled.

Varvara blushed and went back to triturating the contents
of the horn. Though she said nothing, I knew that I had made
amends for my remark about the dress.

Soon she came over with the medicine. I sat up and drank it. It was curiously bland and rather sickening, and it made me shake my head involuntarily as though trying to expel the after-taste. I put my feet on the floor, meaning to thank her and return to my own room, but she pushed me back on to the bed. (Her push would have been more use in a rugger scrum than mine ever was.)

'No,' she said. 'You must remain quiet. Otherwise it will do you harm.'

I began to feel alarmed. 'What in God's name have you given me?'

Varvara pronounced some long word which was probably Turki. She could not translate it at the time, but later when her English vocabulary improved, I learnt that it meant 'mushroom' or 'fungus'. These are not very reassuring words in the mouth of an amateur doctor, and my ignorance was perhaps fortunate.

But after two or three minutes I should not have cared. All fears or speculations about the future were extinguished by a new intensity of present vision. Despite a tendency to lose the sharpness of their outlines, inanimate objects assumed a vastly increased significance: and also a kind of suppressed activity. Perhaps I can best describe this by saying that now, for the first time, I seemed to perceive that being a chair or a wash-basin or bed was a continual struggle by matter to retain its orderly and useful form, and one in which my sympathies ought to be actively engaged. If it had not been too much effort I should have applauded the furniture.

I do not know what she gave me, except that it must have been some kind of hypnotic. Toadstools with this property are known to be used in parts of Central Asia for inducing trances. But none of the doctors of whom I have made inquiries can explain why a drug of this type should have allayed fever. Apparently its result ought to have been the opposite. Yet the fact remains that as soon as I swallowed the stuff my body began to feel deliciously cool and my headache ceased.

Presently I felt a drowsiness which did not seem to threaten

my heightened interior vision. The latter, I felt, would be continued and perhaps enhanced in sleep. But Varvara had other
ideas.

'No,' she said. 'You must not sleep yet.'

'Why?'

'It is bad.'

'I doubt if I can keep awake.'

'To help you,' she said, 'I shall talk.'

'What about?'

'This will be a long talk and there is only one subject of
which I know enough.'

She meant her own life, which could be practically equated
with the city of Hai-po-li or Doljuk. She spoke with unerr-
ing fluency, never hesitating for a word, as she sometimes
did in ordinary conversation, and her gruff voice took on the
cadences of a rhapsode. Early in her discourse I felt an extension of the drug's power. Whereas before it had merely given
life to inanimate objects, it now began to convert words into
pictures as active and vivid as any on a stereoscopic screen. I
could see what she described to me. It is a curious thing that my
mind supplied many details which were necessarily left out of
verbal description, and supplied them correctly, though I had
no means of knowing this till much later. Unfortunately it is
not possible to make printed words convey a third-dimensional
effect: so that the reader will have to be content with a hotch-
potch of topography, ethnology, and anecdote.

Picture a high mountain in the middle-distance. It is summer
and the snow-cap extends only about a fifth of the way down its
slopes. Beneath there are forests of pine and cedar, though from
forty miles away they appear only as a band of blackish-green.
Below again, the foothills begin. There the soil is intensely
barren; chiefly because it contains a very high proportion of
mica splintered into billions of tiny crystals whose prisms catch
the sun and reflect it with an intolerable brightness. There are
four months of days in the year during which nobody in the
city can bear to look northward for more than a few seconds at

a time. Perpetual dazzle as well as filth plays its part in the eye diseases which are seen everywhere in the streets.

These long burning slopes are the origin of the place's Chinese name, which means Sea of Glass. They end about half a mile from the walls, where the oasis begins. The transition from sterility to luxuriance is astoundingly sudden. Over a brief ellipse, stretching east and west for eight miles at its furthest extent, the desert soil is made intensely fertile by a multiple outcrop of springs. Between the pools and the conduits there are orchards which grow peaches and apricots, and small amber grapes that dry out into currants of unrivalled quality. The fruit on the trees and vines is so thick that a sort of warm glow comes off its massed profusion. There are also fields where cotton is cultivated, but not many because the trade in dried fruits is more paying.

On the other side of Doljuk the ground continues to slope away. Down and down it goes, still fertile for several miles, but gradually drying up. The salt content of the soil increases rapidly. Suddenly the traveller is stopped by a ragged precipice which turns the steady downward grade into a sheer plunge. At the bottom is a salt-crusted wilderness which contends with a spot near the Dead Sea for being the deepest land depression on the earth's surface. For bestial desolation it probably has no rival. Between the white bone-like pans there are rocks, lead-coloured, but dyed here and there by mineral veins of a curious fungoid yellow. Then gradually the face of nature lightens to a mere scowl and the Takla Makan desert rolls out in sand and gravel to the borders of Tibet.

The wall of the cliff contains numerous caves, mostly natural in origin, but extended by human artifice. Between eight and fourteen hundred years ago they formed the homes of a colony of hermits. Or rather two colonies, for though the first inhabitants were Buddhists from China, they were presently joined by a few Nestorian Christians out of the West. Both faiths seem to have coexisted amicably: but this is almost the only example of mutual forbearance, let alone charity, in the history of Doljuk. Where the entrance of a cave has fallen in, anybody who will brave the surroundings may often find not only human remains sealed up in the interior, but also images and paintings on the rock and manuscripts written on leather in the strange Uighur script. At one time, before the First World War, there was a spate of visits from German archaeologists whom the inhabitants complacently robbed and occasionally murdered, not realizing that these imbecile strangers were quietly removing stuff which had ten times the market value of anything taken from them.

Between the Sea of Glass and the nether pit stands the walled city. Its fortifications and all its houses are of mud, except for the residency of the Chinese Governor and a palace which once housed an hereditary puppet-prince. The buildings are very thick and almost windowless to withstand the appalling heat of the summer and the no less frightful cold of winter. Narrow streets, like mole-runs, twist between the high, blank façades. Sometimes they are further constricted by booths and stalls which line them on either side. Where there is a market a sort of roof is often erected from mats and green branches. Struggling up and down, like strange fish swimming in soup, go the people.

There are Tungans wearing long Chinese robes. They also speak among themselves the language of their masters, but there are no other bonds. The Tungans are Mohammedans of a fierce and bigoted persuasion. Nobody knows their true racial background. The Chinese who reciprocate their hatred say that their ancestors appeared on the borders of China many generations ago, proclaiming that they sought only temporary hospitality, after which they would return to their own place. As they never did, the Chinese ironically named them 'Returners'.

And now comes a leather-faced old man with long moustaches driving in an ox-cart which splashes sewage over the cooked meats and fruit in the stalls. He has a high-crowned hat like an Ottoman fez and he is supported by two youths carrying long whips who are his sons. All three wear expressions of mingled good nature and suspicion; the first reflecting natural temperament, the second the experience of a slow-witted race living among five or six who are quicker and more dishonest. They are Turkis and they have the best claim to be considered the basic population of the area. Though they too are follow-ers of Mohammed, not much love is lost between them and the Tungans who have managed by superior astuteness to rele-gate them, as a whole, to the class which provides employees rather than employers of labour. Many of them are carters, and they may make journeys ranging from fifty to a thousand miles across the Gobi: east over the firm gravel to Mongolia and China proper, or west to Dzungaria, or, hardest of all, south-wards through the soft shifting sands and the haunted desert of Lob.

At intervals of twenty years or so the races of Sinkiang forget their mutual distrust sufficiently to make common cause in rebellion against their overlords. The land—not only Doljuk but the cities for hundreds of miles around—flares up like a volcanic pit. Chinese officials are dispatched with unspeakable torture, incomprehensible speeches are made, and small bands of warriors, some wearing old bowler hats, some medieval Per-sian helmets, are to be found riding furiously about the desert to keep strategic *rendezvous* which are always bungled. For a while all the towns are in the hands of the insurgents. Then gradually, like boxers fighting beyond their weight, they feel the exhausting effect of being leant on, and occasionally buf-feted, by a much larger body. Chinese armies arrive. They go to the wrong place, but eventually reach the right one. They are grossly defeated in the field, but somehow remain in possession of it. Finally their adversaries start quarrelling among them-selves. After a well-judged distribution of cash, it is found that most of the revolted towns have been unobtrusively retaken. It is then time for the second series of hideous executions. It has all happened some dozen times since the reign of Kien-Lung and the result is always the same.

From about 1907 onwards Fulk Ellison and his wife (if so she was), Serafina Filipovna, lived in a large house near the centre of the town. Fulk's dealings in arms made him rich by local stan-dards. Moreover the gold deposits which had first attracted him to the place, though disappointing, were not entirely mythical. He derived an income from them which cushioned him against any temporary slackening of violence.

Fulk obtained his stock-in-trade from a variety of sources. The greater part came through China, but in the years immediately following the Russian Revolution there was a brisk flow of Tsarist rifles and machine-guns from over the northern border. The bread-and-butter of his business was sales to individuals, which nevertheless frequently reached quite large proportions, since the rich men of the town had learnt the wisdom of arming their retainers. On a bigger scale he was purveyor to a tribe of Oirat Mongols who made Doljuk the western terminus of their wanderings. These people, and particularly their prince, were his devoted friends and through them he performed a feat which blazed his name throughout Sinkiang.

It was impossible to live in a land so torn by conflicting loyalties without taking sides. There was no doubt where Fulk stood. He was a supporter of the native dissidents against the Chinese. It was curious that for twenty years the latter should have put up with the unconcealed treasonable activities of a foreign devil who was enjoying their hospitality. But the Chinese are curious to our way of thought. Besides I imagine they found that over long periods there was a balance of usefulness in his favour. He was a good engineer and improved the city's water-supply. And though he was hostile to the established government his influence was opposed to mere casual disorders. Possibly, too, they feared that if they drove him out, he would be only too welcome elsewhere. The Russians would no doubt have paid well for his knowledge of a highly strategic area.

Nevertheless, whenever a new broom took over the governorship, an attempt was usually made to assassinate him. This fact was recognized in the Ellison family and laughed over. Later, they knew, relations with authority would settle down into the old groove of amicable mutual vigilance. No one—least of all himself—believed that anything could really happen to him.

*

For a moment of disintoxication her voice came to me as a source of mere words, no longer of vivified impressions. Then, as if a prop had been knocked away from under my eyelids, I fell into a blank sleep.

When I woke the light was still on. Even so it took me several seconds to realize that I was not in my own room. What restored my memory and orientation was a sound of someone stirring at my side. The simple Child of Nature had not seen why she should waste the unoccupied half of a bed. Admittedly she had taken off nothing except her shoes and stockings, but even so the situation invited misunderstanding.

Sliding my feet cautiously to the ground, I prepared to creep out. But sentiment and curiosity impelled me to stop for an instant and look back at the recumbent girl. Purged by sleep of its overcharge of will-power, her face was truly beautiful. Now, too, it had for me the romantic appeal of its associations.

As often happens, intense scrutiny seemed to penetrate to the sleeping brain. Varvara woke up suddenly.

'Are you well now?' she asked, abrupt and unabashed.

'I think so.'

The best proof of my recovery was that I had almost forgotten the original reason for my presence in that room.

'It is good,' said Varvara. 'Sometimes, if the dose is wrong, they die.'

'Ssh!' I entreated her. 'Someone might hear us.'

She looked baffled for a moment, then she said:

'They would think it is fornication?'

'Well . . . necking, anyhow.'

My genteel effort to spare her feelings involved me in explaining to her the difference between the two pursuits. She listened, nodding moodily.

'I am pure,' she said at length, 'but I have a strong instinct for love. I inherit from my mother. When she was young she would lie in the bed yelling with pleasure.'

'Good God, who told you a thing like that?'

'She did,' replied Varvara surprised. She rolled off the bed, landing on her knees. 'There remains one thing more,' she said.

'To ask for you the blessing of God.' Therewith she recited a string of sentences in sonorous Russian. I continued to stand, feeling foolish and at the same time curious. Public piety usually embarrasses me, but I had no more shame in asking Varvara the meaning of the words than if she had been a young actress giving a foreign recitation. When she had finished I asked her what the words meant.

'O evergreen, immortal Christ,' she translated, 'forgive this man for seeking to put off the sickness which Thou hadst sent him for the improvement of his miserable nature: and me for helping him to do so.'

It was a new theological outlook to me and not one that I found particularly sympathetic.

I reached my own room without mishap. But in the short transit I was suddenly attacked by an enormous physical weariness, as if my legs, like my mind, had travelled ten thousand miles.

4

'All I can say,' observed Nurse Fillis, 'is that when my own father died, my mother and I relied on my uncle for everything. When I think of the trouble he took for us—'

'I do not suppose you had anything else worth taking,' said Varvara very rudely.

Nurse Fillis jumped up from the table and flounced out of the room, muttering audibly about 'foreign chits'. She had yet to learn that you do not change the constitution of a tiger by calling it a jackal. On the other side of the door she uttered a further remark which I thought I must have misheard. It sounded like 'the wrong side of the blanket'.

Whether because of this final insult or the general nervous tension, Varvara also felt the need to relieve her feelings. In her case it took the form of seizing a bunch of bananas, biting each of them in half and throwing the ends on the carpet. Then she too went out.

Because Mrs. Ellison was never present to keep the peace, lunch had become an agonizing meal. The two women baited each other incessantly. Nurse Fillis, mouthing her words primly, would talk into the blue about the strange customs of people from savage lands and the idiotic mistakes and breaches of good taste which they were always committing. Varvara, however, had somehow discovered a very deadly form of retaliation. She speculated aloud on the beastly habits and vanity of certain types of middle-aged men and on the frequency with which uncles turned out to be wicked. She had somehow grasped that Nurse Fillis cherished a deep admiration, if no more, for Cedric Ellison, and could not bear to hear him run down.

Turpin entered, breathing heavily, and looked at the mess on the floor with resignation.

'She done it?'

'I'm afraid so,' I said, helping to pick them up.

' "The bud blasteth",' he quoted. 'Three cheers for the Blasting Bud!'

He repeated the phrase meditatively. It evidently pleased him, for thereafter he often referred to Varvara as the Blasting Bud. What point the name had I am unable to say, but it seemed to be vaguely, surrealistically appropriate.

As we finished clearing up the bananas, the telephone rang. Turpin went to answer it.

'Mrs. Ellison's residence,' I heard him intone. He was still speaking mandarin butlerese when he came back to fetch me. 'Mr. Callingham desires to speak to you, sir.'

I had forgotten about Andrew since our tea at Tytlers. His amicable, slightly patronizing voice came crawling over the wire. 'Look, old boy, can I have your reactions?'

'What to?'

'Do you know Pam Kerrison? No, I don't suppose you would. Jeffrey Kerrison's daughter—the sparking-plug man. Well, Pam's going to set up a dress-shop. I should think it might be quite good because she's always had a flair for fashion. But of course one needs to get a start . . . eh?'

'I doubt if one would get very far without it,' I said, practising my legal caution.

'There are lots of ways. But one of the cheapest—and most effective—is to collect a school of really striking young creatures, dress them and then turn them loose for people to stare at and ask where they got their clothes.'

He paused before continuing: 'Of course, in those circumstances there's no question of a girl *paying*.'

'The other way round, I should have thought.'

'How do you mean?'

'Presumably mannequins don't work for nothing.'

Andrew sighed patiently. 'I'm not talking about mannequins. The girls I mean simply receive smart clothes in return for showing them off in the right places. It's a very common arrangement. Anne Butterworth does it; so does Laura de Toffarini.'

(These were names of two of the chic-est and most sexually active débutantes of the season.)

'Why are you telling me this?' I asked mildly.

'The one type that Pam's short on is what you might call the Amazonian and the other day I happened to mention that I'd seen just what she wanted. I mean, most of these big girls are so fat: you can hear everything clapping together. Anyway, it struck me that your Miss Ellison might be ready to enter into the sort of arrangement I've described. What do you think?'

'I think your friend would be wasting her money. Surely the point about that sort of tie-up is that the girl practically lives at race-meetings and dances and night clubs. Varvara's not got the opportunity or the inclination for social life.'

'I wouldn't be too sure about the second,' he said with the laugh which I liked least of his attributes—a fruity sniggering noise. 'It's easy to mix up a country cousin and an ascetic, particularly for a retiring type like you. It wouldn't surprise me if in, say, a year's time Varvara was getting around quite a lot.'

'Well,' I said rather helplessly, 'if you believe it would work, you'd better ask her.'

'Good idea,' said Andrew. 'I knew you'd put me on the right track. I wonder if you'd mind getting her for me?'

I found Varvara on the roof-garden, reading in the sunshine. She received the summons with composed alacrity. My God, I thought, she's been expecting to hear from him!

The more I thought about Andrew's appeal to me for advice, the phonier it seemed. All he wanted was to be able to tell Varvara that he had put his odd proposition to me and to make it appear by implication that it had my approval. I did not believe that Pam Kerrison would be fool enough to spend money equipping a striking but barbarous girl from the wilds of Asia, merely in the hope that she would one day turn into a socialite beauty. If so, Andrew himself must be intending to pay. This showed that since his meeting with her he had revised his opinion as to the perfect suitability of her present weird garments. In other words he had decided to take her seriously.

As well as jealousy, I felt a genuine concern. By no means all Andrew's conquests were invention. He was quite capable of eliciting those hereditary yells of pleasure.

After about ten minutes she returned.

'Well,' I said, too impatient to pretend ignorance, 'do you mean to take the things?'

'Would there be harm in it?'

'In England girls usually fight shy of an arrangement which puts them under an obligation to a man.'

'Why?'

'He might think that it gave him certain rights,' I said with high-principled malice.

A tremendous struggle was visibly enacted in Varvara's face; it was like a virgin martyr deciding to go to the lions, or a wrestler performing under arc-lights.

'Alas,' she said at length, 'I must do it. It is my duty to my grandmother to appear worthy of her station.'

I played my final card.

'If you're thinking of your grandmother, couldn't she meet you halfway by providing some pocket-money, so that you could buy your own clothes?'

Though it was none of my business, I was surprised that some such arrangement had not been in force since Varvara's first arrival. One reason, no doubt, was that Mrs. Ellison tended to be forgetful about the mundane details of existence. The other Varvara gave me herself.

'No,' she said, and the refusal clearly came from her heart. 'I am her son's daughter and either she shall enrich me fittingly, or I will take nothing.'

That evening we went to the cinema together. It was pleasant because she was in a good mood, but the film happened to be extraordinarily fatuous. In it there was a hard-used wife. She had a faithful platonic boy-friend who would turn up at intervals with little gifts designed to redeem the husband's neglect. Once when this happened Varvara caused some scandal by leaning towards me, reading out the caption which displayed the little woman's pure gratitude, and adding in a voice which carried for several rows:

'You see, David? She has had the gift, but she is not dishonoured.'

After the film I tried, as I had done several times of late, to persuade her to speak about Doljuk. But again she refused with a brusque shake of her head. I was not altogether resentful; her performance on the night when she drugged me had been that of a pythoness and too frequent repetition would have depreciated it to the level of a parlour trick.

The first appointment with the dressmaker took place three or four days later. Varvara went off about eleven to an address in Mayfair. Just before one she rang up and told Turpin that she would be lunching out.

My thoughts about Andrew now became very low. I wondered whether he was actuated by anything as healthy and straightforward as physical lust: it struck me that he might have been making a few inquiries about the Ellison family's situation, if indeed he had not known it from the first. He was extraordinarily shameless about such things and I had several times seen him cross-question his host about the income and connections of a fellow-guest, the moment the latter was out of earshot.

Even at twenty, I did not delude myself that as the son of

a well-known financier Andrew would have no interest in out-side sources of wealth. That is not the way most rich people are made. In any case the Callinghams and the Ellisons held their money on quite different terms. Metaphorically speaking, the former had yachts, mistresses, and caviar on a yearly tenancy—which might in fact continue for a decade: but sooner or later, in the nature of their occupation, would come a black period when the markets went wrong and the yachts were sold and the mistresses turned loose to forage. Eventually there would be a grand recovery . . . but who favours a career of ups and downs if he has any chance of sticking exclusively to the former? It was natural that Andrew should envy the Ellisons whose fortunes varied no more between one summer and another than the African sun.

There was one consolation for Varvara's absence: it spared me her daily lunch-time bicker with Nurse Fillis.

'Mr. Ellison's coming this afternoon,' she volunteered.

'He turns up almost every day, doesn't he?' I said.

She had evidently become so used to Varvara's baiting that she saw a sneer in every remark.

'Why shouldn't he, Mr. Lindley? It's surely nothing to be ashamed of, if a son takes the trouble to visit his old mother —particularly when she relies on him so much for help with her affairs.'

As usual when she was upset, she went an alarming puce colour. Whilst I made some soothing reply, I thought of the prevalence of blood-letting in earlier ages. Millions of gallons must have been drawn off—usually, so medical science now declares, with no useful effect. It seemed ironical that Nurse Fillis should have been born after the practice lost its popularity.

In the afternoon I went down to see Turpin. A bottle of Cha-blis was open amidst the knife-powder and the cleaning-rags, and we drank several glasses. Presently one of the maids came in on some trivial errand. This was a rare occurrence; perhaps because Turpin liked to keep his pantry free from feminine influence; although I think that the housekeeper may have had something to do with it.

As the girl passed him on her way out Turpin slapped her saucily on the bottom, at the same time observing:

> ' 'E nothing common did or mean
> Upon that memorable scene.

I don't bloody think!' he continued in the same breath.

'Language, Mr. Turpin!' said the girl, but she did not seem offended.

'You want to watch them little tarts,' said Turpin as the door closed behind her. A sudden fit of class-consciousness swept over him, bringing back for a moment his official voice. 'Not, sir, that I suggest you would lower yourself to misbe'ave with a mere *corpus vile*. I meant it general. I once lost the best place of me life that way.'

'I shouldn't have thought you could do much better than this.'

'Ah,' said Turpin, 'no damned disloyalty—no, sir. But this 'ere, it might 'ave made something of me. And near did! See, I was first footman to Sir Travers Wilkin—'

The name was vaguely familiar. As he talked on I picked up clues which combined with my scattered memories. Sir Travers had been one of the great figures of Victorian archae-ology. Most of the gloomy Assyrian bulls and nervous Persian lions in British museums which had not been acquired earlier by Sir Henry Layard were the fruit of his foraging. He was, in the better sense, a gifted amateur. And this gave him a breadth of taste rare in the present age of subsidies and specialization. For instance, I now learnt that he had been a great lover of Eng-lish literature and vintage port. From him, in differing degrees, Turpin had caught both tastes.

'Drink!' he said. 'The old boy made a bloody camel of anyone else I've seen! Lock 'imself up in 'is study with a dozen Cockburns, and then after two, three hours, you'd 'ear it begin-ning—rumble, rumble, rumble, like a big drum.'

'Do you mean he got D.T.'s?' I asked rather stupidly.

'Not 'im! 'E was reading 'imself poetry—Shakespeare, Tennyson, ones 'ose names I can't remember. Well, after maybe another couple of bottles, 'e'd start thinking 'ow beautiful 'e read and what a pity there wasn't nobody to listen to 'im. That's where I came in. I was only first footman, but the butler was deaf. So when 'e rang I 'ad to go up to the study and act audience for 'im. Many's the night we did a play, a couple of long Brownings, and a handful of tiddlers. I got to like it; though, mind you at first it was a job keeping awake: because 'e made you drink level with 'im. But I knew it was as much as my job was worth to doze.'

I said: 'He sounds a marvellous old pirate. Were the rest of his habits to match?'

Turpin shook his head regretfully.

'Strait-laced as a Baptist over women. That was my trouble. I reckon the ones that are always taking it out on Cleopatra or Queen Guinevere don't see what us others want with the real thing. Caught me in the cellar, doing the under-'ousemaid a bit of good. "Filthy malpractice"—I can still 'ear 'im—"and in the middle of my wine." Still 'e never put a word against me in my character.'

A bell rang, and in a box above our heads a light came under the sign which said 'Morning Room'.

'Now what's that for?' grumbled Turpin. 'It's an hour and a 'alf to tea-time. Besides the old lady's got Mr. flaming Cedric up there, giving 'er the usual pasting.'

He struggled into his coat and went reluctantly upstairs. I sat and waited. On return his first words gave me a sharp surprise.

'It's you that's wanted.'

'Me? Who by?'

'That Cedric. Know what 'e 'ad the bleeding face to say when I told 'im you was down 'ere? 'E 'oped I wasn't teaching you to fuddle yourself in the afternoons! Bastard!'

I was almost as annoyed as Turpin—particularly as I was still near enough to my public school to have a sense of guilt about indulging in sluggardry after lunch.

'I suppose, in courtesy, I must go.'

'You watch out,' said Turpin prophetically. ''E's up to something.'

I found Cedric Ellison pacing up and down the morning-room. As soon as he saw me he leapt forward and gripped my hand, at the same time subjecting me to one of his compelling, man-to-man stares.

'I knew I could rely on you,' he said, allowing his voice to vibrate slightly.

'I didn't,' was what I nearly replied; but prudence won and I merely made a non-committal noise.

'Frankly,' he continued, 'it's a god-send that we have you in the house. It's so often the same story; the man that's needed is the expert who can speak with authority. As an ordinary business-man with no professional qualifications I'm always coming up against that hard fact.'

He gave a rueful laugh that was so rueful it would have got any ham actor turned off the boards.

'What did you want me to do?' I said cautiously.

'Just a little matter of explaining a legal term to my mother. . . . You know about Powers of Appointment?'

'Something,' I admitted.

'Then what are we waiting for?' cried Cedric with ogreish gaiety.

I followed him out on to the landing which he crossed to a door I had never previously seen opened. It gave on to a small room which had been equipped as a sort of feminine study. It contained a beautiful Louis Quinze writing-desk at which Mrs. Ellison was seated.

My first reaction was that the old lady ought not to be bothered with any business matter at all. She looked too ill. She was wearing an old-fashioned black dress sewn with jet ornaments and her face against the dark fabric was chalky white.

'Now, Mother,' said Cedric in a very jolly tone, 'I've brought along our referee.'

'He can't know whether they were married,' she said, mumbling.

Cedric's face hardened, but he maintained a surface of bluff patient good-humour.

'Now, now,' he said. 'We must keep to the point. One thing

at a time. We want to straighten out the legal aspect first—don't we, Mother? Don't we?'

'Very well,' said Mrs. Ellison wearily.

Cedric said: 'Shall I pose our problem or will you?' Without waiting he answered the question in his own favour, and began to address me. 'Supposing a man were to leave a part of his estate to X for life and after her death as X should appoint between the children of Y and Z—that would be quite a usual form of gift, wouldn't it?'

'It's an ordinary Special Power,' I said, relieved to be asked anything so easy.

'Correct me if I'm wrong,' said Cedric, 'but isn't it called a Special Power, as contrasted with a General one, because X cannot give the money to anybody except that one limited class of persons, the children of Y and Z.'

'That's right.'

I saw that he already knew as much as, and possibly more than I did, about the subject. It was crazy to suppose that if he had really wanted information he would not have gone to an accredited lawyer.

'And it would be rather a serious thing if X tried to dispose of the property outside that class—eh?'

'Well,' I said, 'the disposition would be void. Presumably there would be a gift over in default of appointment and that would take effect.'

It was evident that in some way I had run contrary to his puppeteering and had given the wrong answer. I had the impression that he wanted me to help in making his mother believe that there was something near-criminal in exercising a Power of Appointment invalidly. But he abandoned this tack for the time being.

'Now, here's where we really want your assistance, David. In the context of a case, such as the one I've imagined, how would the law interpret children?'

I was baffled by the seeming pointlessness of the question.

'The usual way,' I said.

He gave a cough of pretended embarrassment. Then assuming a sort of roguishness, he said:

'I'm sure we can be frank here. It can't be any secret to you at your age or to mother at hers that children are born outside marriage as well as within it.'

I could have kicked myself for appearing so naïve. But I retrieved a little self-respect by giving the text-book answer.

' "Children" in a will or other legal instrument means *prima facie* "legitimate children". Unless there was something unusual in the will which created the Power of Appointment X couldn't give any share to an illegitimate child of Y or Z.'

'There, Mother,' said Cedric. 'That's just what we wanted to know.'

The old lady sat fumbling with a gold fountain-pen. I had a moment of insight in which I felt the air of the little room grow heavy with the distillations of enormous wealth. She seemed weighed down, logged by the vapour of gold, and its concomitants of greed and jealousy and hatred.

'Cedric,' she said with an effort, 'you can't prove a person a thief—you can't prove a person—you can't—'

'For God's sake, Mother,' he interrupted harshly, 'who's talking about thieves?'

I was disgusted, but I had not the self-assurance, nor even the knowledge, of how older people treated each other to dare to interfere. But Mrs. Ellison could manage without my support. Unsticking her tired mind from its groove, she tried again successfully.

'You can't prove a person a thief simply by reading out the law on theft.'

I suppose she made her point in this oblique form because she did not like referring to bastardy. At any rate she made it. At the same time I belatedly realized what was afoot and at whom all these manœuvres were aimed. Even then it was a shock to me, for I had never shaken off my first impression that Varvara was a melodramatic creature who saw a conspiracy behind every accident.

Cedric was saying: 'Very well, Mother, I won't tire you by

chopping logic. In any case, if you take that line, we can hardly discuss the factual evidence in front of the boy.' (I had gone down a bit from my status as legal adviser.) 'I'll come to see you again tomorrow.'

'Not tomorrow, Cedric,' said Mrs. Ellison faintly.

'Tomorrow,' he repeated firmly. 'Alone.'

He went out, not saying goodbye. I was terribly at a loss, but Mrs. Ellison braced herself in a final effort to rescue me.

'Thank you, David, for your good advice. You'll help a lot more silly old women in your time.'

Her courtesy moved me. I knew that I wanted really and effectively to help her.

'Don't do it,' I said, the words coming out almost of themselves.

'Don't do what?' asked Mrs. Ellison, surprised through her fatigue.

'Whatever he wants you to do.'

She did not reply for so long that I feared she must think me daft or impertinent. But at length, with a jump in thought as wide as my own, she said:

'If you have sons, David, never insist on making business men out of them. Either it doesn't succeed . . . or it succeeds too well.' She bent her head forward which at first I took as a sign of dismissal. In the next second, however, I realized that she could no longer hold it upright; she was on the verge of collapse. I rushed to the door and shouted, 'Nurse! Nurse!'

Fillis appeared with a creditable promptness. She took one look at Mrs. Ellison, then said:

'Stay here and watch that she doesn't fall out of that chair.'

I was terrified that the poor old lady would die during her absence. But she was gone for less than a minute. The hypodermic which she carried must have been kept perpetually charged against emergencies. This was clearly one, for Nurse Fillis ripped up the buttons on the long sleeve of her patient's dress, sending them flying to all quarters.

The injection took effect quickly. Mrs. Ellison sat up looking almost normal. Nurse Fillis said soothingly:

'Now in just a moment we're going to get you to bed.'

That she refrained from saying 'beddy-byes' emphasized the gravity of the crisis. When she took Mrs. Ellison's arm on one side and draped it over her shoulder, I naturally suggested that I should give support on the other. Probably she knew exactly how to manage such operations and I should only have hindered her. At any rate she waved me aside.

I was left with a great deal of new-won knowledge to digest. Automatically I sat down at the little desk, in the place which Mrs. Ellison had vacated. Twenty minutes later I was still there, pondering uneasily, when Nurse Fillis came back.

'What are you doing?' she said sharply.

'Nothing particular.'

'You've no right to be in here.'

'Why on earth not?'

'Mrs. Ellison keeps a lot of extremely valuable and private papers in this room.'

It was too much. I thought again of my aunt. She might have allowed me to be bamboozled and patronized within reason by Cedric Ellison, for she had strong ideas about the subjection of the young to their elders, but she would not easily have forgiven me for submitting to Nurse Fillis's cold-blooded insult.

For once my own sentiments agreed. Unlike most people, I have always been more exasperated by blank rudeness than covert sneers. Rage gave me an instinct for the place to strike.

'Nurse,' I said, 'I'd like to ask you something. Have you had so many friends in your life that you can afford to make enemies quite gratuitously?'

Her eyes dropped miserably. 'I'm sorry,' she said. 'I only spoke like that because I'm on edge.'

Then it was my turn, of course, to feel that I must make amends.

'That's not surprising. It shook me up. I hope Mrs. Ellison's better now?'

'Yes. She'll be all right.'

'Was she actually in danger?'

'There's always danger in her condition . . . if she gets over-excited.'

I said: 'She was worried, and a bit frightened too, I think.'

'Medically we call it over-excitement,' she said stubbornly.

'That damned fellow was shouting at her like a bargee. I suppose that's exciting in the same sense as being shot at, but it's not the way I'd describe it.'

I had quite a lot more to say, but I never said it because Nurse Fillis had gone out of the room with tears on her cheeks.

After a few wet days the weather had again become fine and hot. At the beginning of my stay I had generally sat out on the roof-garden but lately I had taken to going down to the real one. I found it curiously attractive with its mingled smell of soot and flowers, and the noise of the London traffic coming through like the beat of an enormous waterfall. The proportions of the garden mingled impressively with those of the house; it was long and narrow, a strip of, say, a hundred and twenty yards by thirty, and this exaggerated the height and sheerness of those plastered cliffs. Lying in a deck-chair with half-closed eyes, one felt that one was looking up at a mountain with windows. The roof-garden seemed to hang halfway up to the sky. And indeed the impression was not entirely illusory, for there must have been a drop of over thirty feet between the second floor and the railings of the area.

Varvara did not come back for tea. But about half-past five her shadow fell silently across my chair.

'How did it go?' I asked.

'I suffered,' she replied sombrely. 'Lord Jesus, how I suffered!'

'Why?'

'The women mocked me. They came out like slaves, but underneath I could hear them laughing.'

'Damned rude!' I said. 'But perhaps you imagined it.'

Varvara continued morbidly: 'My top clothes are not right. That I know. But they laughed also at my drawers. Only Andrew did not laugh.'

'Surely he wasn't there at the fitting?'

She chose not to answer.

'At least,' she said, brightening, 'I shall soon be dressed so that I do not shame my friends. People will think that I am an English girl of breeding.'

I said: 'I hope that doesn't mean you'll give up being yourself.'

'That is what Andrew tells me. He says I must keep my personality because it is distinguished. Manners are being worn rather *farouches* this season,' she said, obviously quoting.

'Andrew has always had a line in flattery,' I said.

'And you, David, in spitefulness,' replied Varvara calmly. 'It angers you to see people doing what you cannot do, and being what you will not be. And yet you are too proud of yourself to change.'

I cannot remember any home-truth which, for the moment, hurt me more. Part of the impact was pure surprise. Hitherto I had always regarded Varvara as a kind of Valkyrie, a creature full, no doubt, of great thoughts and violent, headstrong, consuming hatreds, but not one to whom you would look for psychological insight. She probably saw that I was shaken, for in her next remark she relented a little.

'I like you better than Andrew,' she said. 'But I do not admire you so much. I pray for you, David.'

'Not for Andrew?' I asked, trying to sound cynically indulgent.

'It would be no good,' said Varvara. She paused before reverting to an earlier line of thought. 'With Andrew I shall make social advances.'

It was taking time and accumulation of evidence to make me realize that she cared about such things. The difficulty lay in overcoming the sentimental belief that noble savages do not envy the trappings of civilization.

Going into the house to dress for dinner, I found a cable for me in the hall. It was signed by my uncle, and it said:

'Called home confer India Office week mid-July. Will notify arrival. Love self and Edna.'

This was most unexpected. Never before, so far as I could remember, had my uncle returned to England in between his spells of leave. Much as I liked him, my first reaction was fear lest my stay at Aynho Terrace should be cut short. Presently, however, I realized that if he had only a single week, and that mortgaged to official duties, it was most unlikely that he would want to disturb the existing arrangements. On that basis his presence would be pure gain.

About half-past nine when twilight was falling, we were sitting alone on the roof-garden looking over the parapet. On the lawn a fat cat was stalking birds. It did not adopt the usual feline method of getting down on the belly and relying on stealth to conceal hostility. This cat strolled towards the prey with an air of disengaged benevolence; when it was near enough, without any tensing or winding-up, it would give a curious stiff-legged bound straight at the victim. In this way it soon killed an unwary sparrow.

Varvara had been watching. Was it some symbolic association of ideas which suddenly caused her to say: 'I suppose my uncle was here this afternoon?'

'Yes, I saw him. I've something to tell you about that.'

'He has tried to suborn you against me?'

'More or less. . . . The point is, I'm afraid you were right, and he has some scheme for preventing you getting any of the family cash. It was damned clever of you to size the situation up so quick. Has your grandmother ever talked to you about her intentions?'

'Intentions?'

'What she means to do in her will.'

'My grandmother,' said Varvara, 'would think that vulgar.' It was true, of course. Only members of the lower middle classes went around dropping hints about legacies given and revoked in a pathetic desire to obtain respect for their latter years.

'It's rather a tricky position,' I said, wondering without relish how I was going to explain the part about bastardy.

'I am an heir,' said Varvara in a stubborn tone. 'Therefore my uncle tries to undo me.'

No doubt in Doljuk there was a simple standardized procedure for undoing heirs; say, with an axe or a horse-pistol.

I was not sure how far she would understand that in the West
there were other techniques of spoliation.

'Heir isn't a word which means as much as it used to in English Law,' I said tentatively. 'Property in general isn't bound in
a line of descent. It's disposed of at the will of its owner. And
anybody who can control or influence that will . . .'

I need not have bothered about her comprehension. Once
a few questions had cleared her mind of the patriarchal conception of society, she caught on surprisingly quickly to such
complicated conceptions as settlements and Powers of Appointment. She may have thought them sissified, but she saw that in
England they governed the physical possession of wealth, just
as surely as did the sword elsewhere.

Presently, as was inevitable, we came to the crux of the
matter, the contention on which Cedric relied to exclude her
from Mr. Ellison's will. I was relieved that she took the point so
calmly.

'Sometimes with men my mother was not married,' she
said. 'Christ, how she repented! But with my father—yes.'

'You could prove it?'

'I know it in my heart.'

'I suppose,' I said hesitantly, 'that facilities existed in Doljuk
—for getting married, I mean?'

'There was Harold,' she replied after a pause.

'Was he the English Chaplain?' I asked, as if Doljuk had been
Montreux or Rapallo.

'Harold was an American missionary of the Church of the
Unleavened Baptists. For ten years he went up and down the
Gobi, preaching. But he preached always in the Chinese which
he had learnt at the Missionary College.'

'Ah,' I said, pleased to be able to show my memory. 'I suppose that annoyed the other chaps you were telling me about
—the Turkis?'

But Varvara shook her head. 'Nobody knew what language
he was speaking.'

'Didn't he get discouraged?'

'He had great faith. Besides it was once fortunate. Some of the Tungans came to kill him because they thought he was a spy for the government. Harold remained on his knees in prayer and saying, as he thought, "Peace be unto you". But the thing he said was, "Enjoyable fish", over and over again. The men consulted and decided that it was an oracle. So they went away.'

I would gladly have let her continue her reminiscences of Harold who seemed to have been an evangelist well suited to his field. But a sense of practical urgency dragged me back to our original topic.

'You do grasp what your uncle is up to? If he succeeds in convincing Mrs. Ellison that she must leave you out of her exercise of this Power and then she dies ... well, you won't have any remedy.'

'Then what must I do?'

It was the first time that she had appealed to me directly for any aid or advice, and it was a gratifying sensation. After all, what did the latest fashions count against an inheritance which might run into myriads of pounds?

I produced the answer which I had been meditating during dinner.

'We can't tell where we stand without seeing your grandfather's will.'

'If my grandmother has it I will make her show it to me.'

She had never shocked me before. But now, catching the steely note in her voice, I was forced to see that hereditary characteristics are seldom entirely absent in any member of a family.

'There is no need for that,' I said rather coldly. 'In England all wills are public. There's a registry at Somerset House where we can look it up.'

Varvara was silent for several seconds, then she began to mutter too low for me to catch the words or even distinguish the language. At length she stopped, and seeing the look of inquiry on my face, she explained: 'I was praying to God to damn the soul of my uncle ... for the sake of my dear mother!'

In the failing light the tears glistened on her cheeks. I could understand how the sense of her own isolation must from time to time sweep over her, smothering the joy of battle, and how the very meanness of the tactics being used against her would produce fits of enervated disgust.

When she recovered, I said: 'If it comes to some sort of legal showdown, you may be asked a lot of questions about your mother and father, so you might start putting your memories in order.'

The very unprofessional thought behind this suggestion was that she had better weed out anything which did not support her legitimacy: after all, we were dealing with a completely unscrupulous opponent. But Varvara understood my remark differently, as an invitation to rehearse what she knew of her parents' story.

First she ran up to her room and brought down an old photograph set in a box of hard wood. It showed a woman with black hair reclining at full length on a couch. Against the dark wood and the yellowed musty background, her face stood out clear in its mixture of energy and sloth, its sensuality tinged with asceticism, and its melodramatic expression which seemed to be half-mocking itself. She looked a silly, intelligent woman. Her prettiness was the only quality which she had without contradiction. She was not as strictly handsome as Varvara, but I think that most men would have preferred her owing to the softer quality of her looks and her more manageable size.

'She was a holy saint of God,' said Varvara, kissing the photograph; and went on to prove in detail that it needed either another saint or a strong partisan to hold so charitable a view.

I have forgotten the maiden name of Serafina Filipovna; also the one which she took from her first (and perhaps her only) husband. She was the daughter of a government official who seems to have been rather like Dostoievski's Marmeladoff, drunken, verbose, tearful, and shameless.

When she was sixteen and a half she raised the family fortunes by marrying the proprietor of a successful restaurant in

St. Petersburg. He was an upright man but cold and excessively
absorbed in his business. He could cope with Serafina Filipovna
when she was virtually a child, but by the time she had matured
she was too much for him.

'It was like throwing shrimps to a seal,' said Varvara with her
usual frankness, quoting, I think, from the person who should
have known best.

The customers, who included some of the best society in
Tsarist Russia, soon began to notice her. Though she did not
work about the restaurant, she was expected to make the gra-
cious appearances of a patronne. She had an ascending scale
of lovers, ending with a millionaire and two princes. Nevertheless she cannot have been a mercenary woman. When she
ran away it was with a simple army colonel and not even one
who carried much military glamour. Igor Igorovitch Prespykin
was the head of a branch of the Military Survey. Although he
was married, the elopement did not finish his career; it merely
caused him to be sent to Vyernyi near the borders of Siberia
and Sinkiang. There in the heart of Asia he and his mistress led
a life of comfortable idleness unbroken by any serious survey-
ing . . . until the Russian War Department decided to lend his
services so that the Khan of Doljuk might have a map of his
domains.

At that time Russia was showing one of those fits of interest in Sinkiang which recurred whenever she herself was free
from embarrassment and the Chinese hold on the province
appeared to be more than usually weak. Colonel Prespykin no
doubt had orders which went far beyond map-making. But he
never carried them out, for when he had been in Doljuk about a
fortnight he caught one of the mysterious fevers which infested
the place, and he died.

Serafina Filipovna had accompanied him on his mission.
She even carried faithfulness so far as to catch the same disease.
She did not die, but she was very ill. For three weeks she lay
semi-conscious. When she recovered she found that Prespykin's second-in-command, a dour Puritan who loathed her,
had marched off with the rest of the survey party. It was a truly

awful situation to be penniless, homeless, speechless in a city where infidel women were on the same level as stray dogs. She did the only possible thing in seeking out the single other European who was at that time in the city. This happened to be Fulk Ellison.

That strange union, whether sanctified or not, was a roaring success. Roaring is the word. Neither was a person backward in expressing his or her feelings. The high windowless room, lit by mutton fat burning in a silver bowl, would echo simultaneously with Fulk's curses and Serafina's analyses of her own spiritual condition—two occupations to which they were respectively much given. As soon as she was old enough, the little Varvara would make her voice heard. Nobody specifically listened to anyone else, but out of the tumult and the confusion and the violence were forged bonds whose strength put to shame many relationships between husband and wife, parent and child that had grown up in an easier climate.

The one thing about which Serafina and Fulk seriously disagreed was religion. The latter was an aggressive atheist; whereas she cherished an excitable, slightly erotic devotion to the two First Persons of the Trinity. At a later stage I shall have more to say about her daughter's inheritance in this respect. There was a time when I thought that Varvara's religion was a pure emotional luxury. This view did not prove altogether tenable, but I am still sufficient of an unspiritual pragmatist to distrust a faith which seldom has the slightest effect on conduct. Indeed, it would have needed very little to persuade her to adopt that distinctively Russian heresy which taught that the more the sins, the merrier, on account of the increased opportunities for repentance.

Presently, alas, it was evident that the story must bring us again to that horrible death by the venom of spiders. In her overstrung state, it would do Varvara no good to dwell on her mother's end. I therefore interrupted her at the first opportunity.

'I'm going to bed.'

We climbed the stairs together.

Outside her room I was seized by a curious mixture of desires: to have pleasure, to assert myself, not to miss my opportunities.

I put my arms suddenly round her and kissed her on the lips. At first her mouth was hard, but rather, I felt, from inexperience than insensitivity. Probably she had never before received a passionate kiss. At least she did not seem to resent it.

'You don't mind?' I murmured—the standard cry of the undergraduate.

'My father said that I should stay chaste until it seemed worse than death.'

She stood back at arm's length examining me amiably, but also with a certain detachment; as if she were trying to calculate whether I should ever be able to make her feel so badly about continence. I would have said from her expression that she did not rate the chances very high, but suddenly she pulled me against her and renewed our embrace. In the interval some subterranean process had been going on—as it were, the conversion of a glacier pool into a geyser. Her body was heavy and soft against me and her lips were wide open.

It was some while before we parted; when we did so it was once more at her abrupt dictation. She simply pushed me aside without warning and ran into her room, shutting the door.

From that close encounter I took away two impressions, one pleasant, the other less so, but both mildly embarrassing. First, though she used no scent, Varvara smelt nicer than any woman I had known; second, she was probably physically stronger than I.

5

'Straight!' said Turpin. 'As true as I'm here! Back into the bottle it went, every drop.'

He was telling me an anecdote about old Mr. Ellison, the money-spinner. In his later years he had some sort of minor eye trouble for which the doctor prescribed a lotion. Three times

a day he bathed his eyes. Other people who earned hundreds
where he earned scores of thousands would unhesitatingly have
thrown away the contents of the used eye-bath. Mr. Ellison did
not see why the same liquid, costing all of half-a-crown a bottle,
should not serve him over and over again. So he poured it back
into the bottle. The pleasing end to this story was that the stuff
finally became polluted and set up inflammation, which made
necessary a long and expensive course of treatment.

Cedric had inherited the same fantastic meanness.

'I reckon his poor bloody wife stopped the worst of it,' said
Turpin. 'Once when they was staying here she said to me: "I'd
stay in Hell to get away from those 'ouse'old accounts!" . . . I
don't reckon they 'ad to carry 'er kicking and screaming to 'er
eternal rest!'

'I didn't know Cedric was a widower.'

' 'Bout six years. Miss Deirdre 'as to stand the racket now,
God 'elp 'er!'

'Is that the daughter—the one he borrows things for from
the museum?'

Turpin permitted himself a queer smile.

'If there's any others, they don't come round 'ere,' he said
enigmatically.

'How old is this Deirdre?'

'Seventeen or so.'

'What's she like?'

Turpin reflected. 'Might be worse . . . considering. Not a
patch on our Blasting Bud, though.'

Cedric continued to make fairly regular appearances in
the afternoon. But I was not again called into conclave. From
external evidence it seemed that he had relaxed the pressure on
his mother: for Mrs. Ellison went through a phase of improved
health during which she not only came down to dinner but also
sat up in the morning-room for a couple of hours after it. On
these evenings I got to know her much better; like most old
people, she was very lonely and she liked to have somebody
by her to whom she could talk about the past. Listening was

no charity on my part; I have always genuinely enjoyed the re-creation of a dead era.

Varvara was not much help. She was always ready with fervid love or hatred, but she could not understand the cool, reserved affection—in her eyes so little distinguishable from an equal degree of dislike—which was Mrs. Ellison's norm of civilized behaviour. At times she grew impatient and almost rude; and then trying to make amends she would come up against those impregnable emotional defences, which were like a moat of China tea. Varvara admired her grandmother, she longed to love her, but she never found out how.

The feeling in the opposite direction was, I think, even more complex. Mrs. Ellison wanted to cherish the child of her son and to make amends for the injustice done to him by his family. But when it came to the point she quailed before Varvara's size and violence and harsh, flamboyant beauty. Besides, by one of those processes which her generation would never have admitted, she may subconsciously have resented the girl as a usurper of her father's place. If there had not been some buried feeling of this kind, I doubt whether Cedric's machinations would have had any effect.

My next sight of that villain was accidental. I was sitting out on the roof-garden and I had moved two or three of the potted shrubs to form a barrier between my neck and the sun. They also incidentally concealed me from the french windows. Presently I heard voices which I recognized as belonging to Cedric and Nurse Fillis. I had no wish to eavesdrop—at any rate at first —but I also wanted to spare myself five minutes of insincere and laboured small-talk. I therefore sat still.

He was saying: 'Now, we're not going to be silly, are we? We're not going to start having imaginary attacks of conscience? Because it doesn't suit us. We stop being rather a specially nice person . . . and our friends don't feel the same at all.'

It was a pretty odd speech, but for a moment I could not understand why it jarred me so sharply. Then I realized that the speaker had usurped the idiom of the person he was address-ing; that jollying tone, those facetious plurals, teetering on the verge of baby-language, were Nurse Fillis's own coin. On her lips they might be irritating; from those of Cedric Ellison they came with an oily, sinister roll.

Without shame I turned quietly in my chair so that I was looking through the branches.

The other two were standing just inside the window, by a big writing-desk. Their bodies had assumed an attitude which was in keeping with the subtle perversity of the whole atmosphere. She was leaning back against the desk, her hands resting behind her on its edge, so that her shoulders were pulled back and the lower part of her trunk was pushed forward. Cedric loomed over her bending in an opposite and complementary curve which made it appear that he was about to fit his body to hers. But in fact, by a considerable feat of muscular discipline, he kept a clear six inches between them at every point.

Nurse Fillis said in a quick breathy voice: 'I don't like it, Mr. Cedric. It wouldn't be ethics. Where'd I be if I was found out?'

'In another job, perhaps,' said Cedric in a teasing voice.

'I'd be struck off the register.'

'Then,' he said, 'I suppose the people who'd got you into this wicked mess would have to look after you. Would you mind being looked after?'

Cedric suddenly lowered his face towards hers. An intervening branch stopped me from seeing whether he had completed a kiss, or was merely tantalizing her. The second I think; he was a prudent man and he cared no more for Fillis than for a bag of hay.

They moved further back into the room, still arguing. I could no longer distinguish the words, but soon one side or the other appeared to have prevailed, for the door opened and the voices faded away into the interior of the house.

I did not mention this scene to anyone, chiefly because it revolted me too much. I felt that my spying had brought me into contact with the nadir of human servitude.

A day or two afterwards we made our expedition to Somerset House. I had previously found out from Turpin the year

and month of Joseph Ellison's death—June 1916—and as I knew
that he had been residing in Aynho Terrace at the time, I did not
expect much difficulty in picking up the trail. We were shown
into the main index-room where the probates are listed by the
dates of grant. When I had looked up the file number of Ellison's will, a clerk went to fetch a copy, for the Registry does not
allow the public loose among its shelves.

Varvara was rather subdued by the atmosphere of venerable
dustiness.

'Afterwards,' I said graciously, 'we'll go out and have lunch.'

I had spent little money of late and I meant to stand her a
first-class meal at Simpson's. It was the sort of place which
should suit her appetite.

'I am sorry,' she replied, 'but I am already lunching. And then
I have a fitting.'

'With Chief Couturier Callingham in attendance, I suppose,'
I said viciously.

Varvara looked at me with reproach. She obviously felt that
I was taking an unfair advantage of the temporary increase in
her dependence on me.

The clerk came back. I received the copy of Joseph Ellison's
will with some misgivings. If you have studied law academi-
cally you will know why. The student performs a sort of minuet
with hard realities like mortgages and executor's accounts,
but contact is seldom established. He can, if he is sufficiently
industrious, write reams about them—and particularly about
various interesting decisions delivered between 1250 and 1780.
But the whole performance takes place *in vacuo*. He has never
mortgaged anything, except unconsciously to the pawnbroker,
his practical knowledge of the marshalling of assets is confined
to a bland confidence that, if his aunt leaves him money, he will
get it. In other words Law only achieves a real meaning in relation to one's own affairs. The university catches young lawyers
too early. I always notice how many people who become successful barristers and solicitors embarked on their careers only
after they had a grasp of the raw material of their profession.

Fortunately Joseph Ellison's will happened to be simple. He

had made a few smallish legacies to servants etc., and a single large one whereby all his shares in Ellison, Dyer Ltd. were to go to his son Cedric Walter Ellison absolutely. As to the residue, he gave one-quarter to the said Cedric Walter Ellison absolutely and the other three-quarters to his dear wife, Eleanor Louise Ellison for the duration of her life.

The crux was in the gift-over after Mrs. Ellison's death. That was where the famous Power of Appointment raised its head.

Cedric had been perfectly correct. In non-legal language, the will gave Mrs. Ellison absolute authority to dispose of the capital in which she had a life-interest in such shares as she thought fit among the children of her own marriage or their children by any *wife*. Even to my inexperienced eye it was clear that no illegitimate child would have the shadow of a claim.

It was a curious will for a man of Joseph Ellison's acumen to have made. For one thing it ran the risk of attracting unnecessarily heavy death duties; for another it left the burden of distributing the bulk of his vast estate to an elderly woman with only a limited knowledge of affairs.

I think that the explanation may lie in the testator's ambivalent attitude towards his exiled son. Perhaps he was never happy about his treatment of Fulk. On the other hand it was foreign to his nature to admit himself in the wrong; and in his eyes the good old Victorian disinheriting act was an essential part of any family row. So Fulk could not be given a halfpenny directly. But if his mother, who made no secret of her affection for him, was given the last word, it was unlikely that he would go empty-handed.

Though she stated it too frequently and with too little tact, there was a lot of moral justification for Varvara's claim that she was entitled to a fair slice of her grandfather's estate.

The clause ended with a gift in default of appointment. If Mrs. Ellison did not exercise her Power, the money would go to the children of the marriage in equal shares, the offspring of a deceased child taking the parent's share. This was awkward for Cedric. *Prima facie* Varvara would share in the distribution. If he wanted to exclude her he would have to adopt the not-very-savoury procedure of instigating an action to bastardize his own niece. No, from Cedric's viewpoint there was everything to be said for keeping up the pressure on his mother.

As we went out into the Strand, Varvara said: 'I have thought. Why should you not come to lunch as well?'

'I don't want to disturb your tender *tête-à-tête.*'

'Do not be bestial,' said Varvara. 'Otherwise I shall be compelled to withdraw my favours.'

I could not help laughing.

'You filthy little blackmailer! All right, where are you meeting Andrew?'

'Near here. At a place called Simpson's.'

I ground my teeth quietly.

Andrew was waiting in the cocktail-lounge on the first floor. When I was in crowded hotels or restaurants I always had to signal wildly for five minutes in order to attract a waiter, but he simply lifted one finger in a fatigued way and instantly a man was at our table.

'I hope you don't mind me tacking myself on,' I said.

'I'm always delighted to see you, David.'

To my inflamed ears there was a tinge of sarcasm in his voice. But obviously it was lost on Varvara; I could see her mentally contrasting my churlishness with Andrew's sunny charity.

'And what have you two been doing with yourselves?'

If it had been left to me I should have made some evasive answer; assuming that Varvara would not want to publicize her family feuds. But she jumped in ahead of me without a trace of inhibition.

'We have been looking at my grandfather's will. Under it there is a great fortune owing to me, but my uncle wishes to cheat me out of it.'

'Nothing is owing to you,' I said, not from pedantry, but because I thought it was important to get the fact straight in her mind.

After that, of course, we had to tell Andrew the whole story. On reflection I was not sorry, for I had begun to feel my responsibility as Varvara's only adviser. Besides, Andrew was extremely shrewd for his years.

In another mistaken effort to spare her feelings, I tried to skate lightly over the issue of legitimacy. But I need not have been so delicate.

'Have I the air of a bastard?' she demanded, glaring at the waiter who was bringing our soup.

As I expected, Andrew's comments were to the point.

'I don't see that there's much to be done, except pray that Mrs. Ellison holds out.'

'Do you think it would be wise for Varvara to try to force some kind of a showdown?'

He shook his head.

'If you once enter a shouting-match you have to accept that the prize will be given for the loudest shouting and not for any of your other merits. She should avoid putting herself on a par with her uncle.'

I agreed; but at the same time I foresaw that it was going to be very difficult to restrain Varvara if Cedric's campaign continued much longer.

'This Cedric chap has a pretty queer name,' said Andrew unexpectedly.

'I didn't realize you knew anything about him.'

'Of course he does,' said Varvara. 'Andrew will know about your family too, and whether any of them has some money and good lineage.'

It was one of the few occasions when I saw Andrew blush. He went back hastily to the main topic.

'My father's had a few dealings with him. Not more than he can help.'

'I suppose he's pretty crooked in business.'

'The old man can look after himself,' said Andrew. 'What he complained of was that Ellison made him feel so damned uncomfortable. Besides he's a terrific nagger and worrier. He'll ring up twenty times a day about some footling detail.'

'Is that all?' I asked, disappointed.

'Not quite,' said Andrew. I saw him glance at Varvara and

hesitate. 'Well ... I suppose we may as well broaden the little snowdrop's mind. It's the only thing about her that needs it.' (This was obviously revenge for the remark about his habits of social inquiry.) 'Seven or eight years ago Ellison nearly landed himself in bad trouble. A girl died after an illegal operation, and the evidence pointed pretty clearly at him as the person who'd procured and paid for it. At the inquest the coroner threatened him with a prosecution for perjury.'

'Did anything happen to him?' asked Varvara.

'No. They couldn't pin the charge. But something will happen one day. I don't go in for gipsy-gipsy stuff, but there's one way I'm psychic: I know a natural-born happenee.'

'Andrew,' said Varvara, 'you please me very much.'

Without any rudeness it was made quite clear that my invitation did not extend beyond the door of Simpson's. I went back to Aynho Terrace by bus, teasing myself the whole way with images of Varvara, statuesque and desirable, being fitted and suavely leered at by Andrew.

Before I had even rung the bell I knew that something was wrong inside. The sound of angry voices percolated through the closed door. It was opened, too, with unusual promptitude, the reason being that Turpin was just inside and was probably glad of anything which might divert the storm of abuse which had broken about his head. Cedric marched up and down snarling out the threats.

'You're going to have quite a lot to explain, my man. I shall be surprised if you can get the police to believe that solid objects dissolve into thin air.'

'Now, look here, Mr. Cedric,' replied Turpin calmly (though it struck me that he was looking rather worried), 'twenty-two years I've been in this 'ouse. If I wanted to steal, 'ow many times d'you think I could 'ave found something better than a dirty old writing-case? Of course, if you tell me it was stuffed with jewels, that's different...'

Apparently Cedric did not feel competent to tell him anything of the sort. His attitude became perceptibly more reasonable.

'But where the hell can it have gone? I wasn't in the cloak-room more than three minutes. . . . You say that you went through to the study?'

'To close the window in case it rains,' said Turpin so speciously that I knew he was lying.

Fortunately the same crassness which made his own conduct so transparent often blinded Cedric to the obvious in other people.

'Well,' he said, 'it's most mysterious, most disquieting. If the thing turns up, you're to let me know immediately. . . . Oh, and one other point, Turpin, I don't on any account want Mrs. Ellison worried by the business. There's nothing that would upset her more than the thought that things were inexplicably disappearing. You understand?'

'Very good, sir,' said Turpin, giving me a surreptitious wink.

Cedric seemed to become aware of my presence for the first time.

'Lost something,' he said brusquely and superfluously. 'Bit on edge today. It's this damned thunder in the air.'

He went out of the door, almost at a run.

'Ah,' said Turpin, bringing out his old favourite. ' " 'E nothing common did nor mean, Upon that memorable scene—" I don't bloody think!'

'Has he gone bats?'

With a mixture of relish and apprehension, Turpin described the events which had preceded my arrival. Cedric had touched them off by his own malice. He had the idea that butlers should be made to jump around for their money. Often when he had been paying a visit to Aynho Terrace he would ring the bell for Turpin simply in order that the latter might open the front door to let him out. This imbecile bit of feudalism was of course heartily resented. On this particular afternoon Cedric decided to sharpen the pinprick by keeping Turpin hanging about for an additional five minutes. So he went off to the downstairs lavatory to wash his hands. Whilst he was away Turpin's attention was caught by his luggage. As usual, when he was going to or coming from his office he had a big portfolio, but today it was accompanied by a much smaller and shabbier article—an old-fashioned writing-case covered in green leather. He looked at it the more closely because he had an impression that it had been placed between the portfolio and the wall for partial concealment. Moreover it appeared vaguely familiar. After a few moments he remembered where he had seen it before; several times when he brought up tea to the *boudoir* he had noticed it lying on Mrs. Ellison's desk and once he had seen her locking it away in her safe. It may have been this last observation or pure intuition which suddenly filled him with a deep stubborn certainty that the green case was not a thing which Mrs. Ellison would ever knowingly entrust to her son. Before he could think himself into caution he had acted.

'What did you do?' I asked.

'Took my ruddy future in my 'ands,' replied Turpin.

He had picked up the case and hidden it.

'Where?'

Smirking proudly, he led me to the back of the hall where there was a radiator enclosed in a mahogany box. He undid a latch and the box opened, showing the writing-case nestling under the pipes. I took it out and looked at it curiously.

'It's going to be awkward if by any chance she did mean him to have it.'

'Ah,' said Turpin, 'but I'm a bit easier in my mind since I saw 'ow 'e wanted to keep 'is ma out of this. 'E never came by that thing straight.'

'What are you going to do with it now?'

'That's tricky. Find it again some'ow, I suppose, and 'and it in to the old lady.'

'It may involve a good deal of explaining.'

There was a pause during which the same thought evidently occurred to both of us. Finally, in his official voice, Turpin said: 'It seems, sir, that we might be better circumstanced to consider this 'ere problem, if we knew what was inside.'

My Public School morality revolted a little. But it had no deep roots, and I was just as inquisitive as Turpin.

'It might save dropping a brick,' I agreed.

The case was closed, but a small key with an elaborately pat-
terned head had been left in the lock. I turned it and instantly
the lid sprang up owing to pressure from inside. The interior
was packed with scores of letters. It would have been difficult
to imagine any more embarrassing contents, owing to the
popular disapproval of people who pry into other's correspondence. I closed the case again rapidly, but not before my eye had
taken in that the topmost layer of letters were all addressed to
Mrs. Eleanor Ellison and bore Chinese stamps of an old issue.
'Doesn't tell us much,' I said sheepishly.

Turpin felt that there was an implied slur on his judgment
and in the process of defending himself his language became
even more forcible than usual.

'Ah,' he said, 'a sod like Mr. Cedric don't nick papers to curl
'is 'air. I bet there's something in them letters that's worth a
mint of money. Help 'im to put the bite on some poor bastard,
I shouldn't wonder.'

'You mean blackmail?'

Turpin nodded. Personally, however, though I agreed that
anything which Cedric took the trouble to acquire was likely to
have a firm cash value, I did not believe that he would go in for
blatant crime. For a man in his position there were too many
opportunities of reaping equal profits by misusing rather than
contravening the law.

I was seized with a sudden impulse of *bourgeoisie oblige*.

'Look, Turpin, if you like I'll give this thing back to Mrs. Ellison.'

He was only too thankful to be rid of the task. I did not
myself much look forward to it. My hope was that I might catch
the old lady in one of her confused moments. Alas, it was not to
be. I found her sitting up in bed, clear-eyed and fresh from her
afternoon nap, and wearing her best expression of composed
benevolence.

When I produced the case she was visibly startled, but she
listened politely to my slurred explanation how I had found it
on the stairs. Clearly, however, she knew what had happened.

'Thank you, David,' she said at length. 'There has been a

misunderstanding. That case should never have left my possession.'

An instant later the complication which I most feared had come about. Nurse Fillis walked in. Seeing the object in Mrs. Ellison's hands she let out a loud involuntary gasp and the rich colour drained out of her face.

Mrs. Ellison said: 'I don't think we're ready for you yet, Nurse.' After a pause, she added: 'This is not quite your moment.'

She spoke with her normal patrician urbanity. But on the last words she allowed her glance to slide round to the bedside table on which stood a contraption of silver and velvet with an inset travelling-clock and a row of hooks for hanging up small personal objects. One of them bore a fob-watch which I had sometimes seen pinned onto Mrs. Ellison's dress and another a ring of keys. Gently Mrs. Ellison took the keys and placed them under her pillow.

I knew now to what end Cedric's nauseous persuasions had been directed.

'I—I—' said Nurse Fillis.

'That will do now,' said Mrs. Ellison. 'Come and get me up in about half an hour.'

'David,' said Mrs. Ellison, 'I'm sure that I can trust you. What do you think is in the case?'

'I don't know,' I said, and the cock crew once.

'Letters which my son, Varvara's father, sent me over a period of more than twenty years.'

'They must be very interesting.'

Her face lit up. Her next remark showed that I had accidentally given her the lead which she wanted.

'They're so interesting that many people would like to read them. And people aren't always very considerate about how they borrow. Nor do they always give things back. I should not like to lose my son's letters.

'Unfortunately,' Mrs. Ellison continued, picking her way with tired finesse, 'though I set so much store on the letters, my eyesight makes it rather a trial to re-read them. I don't know if you care for strange stories and strange places, David—'

'You mean, Doljuk? I'm absolutely sold on it.'

She smiled at this outburst of youthful enthusiasm.

'Well, if you were to look through them, you would learn a lot about the exciting side of life there—the fighting and so on.' She paused, marshalling herself for a final effort of diplomacy.

'But of course an old lady like myself tends to be more interested in domestic and family matters. For instance, I should like to read again about my dear son's wife, and anything that he may have said about his marriage. There are so many letters and after all these years I forget. . . .'

The effort of concentration was causing her voice to weaken rapidly. At the risk of a snub I tried to take some of the burden of explanation off.

'You'd like me to read them and perhaps call your attention to . . . the points you mentioned?'

Mrs. Ellison nodded. We had linked hands without ostensibly letting the right know what the left was doing. Nevertheless I do not doubt that she credited me with a full understanding of her object. After all I had been present when the meaning of 'children' under the Power of Appointment was discussed. No, she simply belonged to a period when any contortions were preferable to saying outright: 'I want to find out what evidence there is whether my granddaughter was born in wedlock.' Slowly, with shaking veined hands, she held out the case towards me. As I took it my sense of elation was damped by the reflection that I would now be responsible for the contents. Clearly Cedric thought that they might be valuable enough to make it worthwhile to suborn his mother's personal attendant. Presumably, if he had got away with them, he would have destroyed any material which was in Varvara's favour and abstracted for use in case of a legal battle the statements which told against her.

It suddenly struck me that my position would be more comfortable if there were several copies of the letters. I made the suggestion tentatively, not sure how Mrs. Ellison would take it. Rather to my surprise she did not demur at the idea of her private correspondence going through the hands of a typist. The avowed object was to enable her more easily to read the pieces which I might pick out, but I am sure that she knew the real purpose of the precaution.

A week later a large registered packet lay beside my plate at breakfast. Varvara who had taken to coming downstairs for that meal looked at it with unconcealed curiosity.

'You have not opened your big letter.'

'No.'

'It is private?'

'Most letters are.'

After some heart-searching I had decided not to tell her about my task. I had not been forbidden to do so, but I felt that if Mrs. Ellison wished her to know, she should make the disclosure herself. Besides . . . suppose I found something which was prejudicial to her? It would be more than embarrassing to have her aware of it. Varvara did not share her uncle's shameless indifference to truth, but one felt that she regarded it as subordinate to loyalty.

Nurse Fillis joined in the conversation. She had been very, very nervous of me for some days after the encounter in Mrs. Ellison's room, but of late her spirit was coming back.

'One place I was at,' she said, 'the young man of the house used to get big packets every week. He made a terrific secret of them at first. But then it turned out he was writing a novel and he kept on giving me bits of it to read. They were wicked—not spicy, I mean, but real dirt.'

'I suppose they excited your instincts,' said Varvara.

Just as heavy drinkers can usually pick out chronic alcoholics and have the greatest scorn for them, so Varvara, a highly passionate girl, detected and despised poor Nurse Fillis's complaint.

On the afternoon when I left Mrs. Ellison's room with the writing-case I had assumed that the office of nurse would change hands within the next few days. As nothing happened in forty-eight hours I thought the old lady had had some extraor-

dinary lapse of memory and I was impertinent enough to give
her a hint.

'My dear boy,' she said, 'from time to time we all lose our
heads'—she smiled faintly—'or our hearts. One must make
allowances.'

'But theft—'

Mrs. Ellison's face became quite stern. 'Not theft,' she said.
'Confusion of orders.'

She did not miss many tricks. It would have ripped to pieces
her cherished pavilion of reticence if she had had to listen to
a string of hysterical accusations against her son. She herself
gave me another modest reason for her charity.

'I'm a selfish old woman. It means a lot to have somebody
about me who's learnt to understand my helplessness and my
ailments.'

'She's very fortunate to have struck such a tolerant employer,' I said rather priggishly.

'Be kind to Nurse Fillis,' she continued. 'She has a difficult
life and she is capable of great goodness. She keeps a sister
who's slowly dying of Parkinson's disease.'

She was obviously sincere; and therefore I was the more
amazed when, having uttered these words, she suddenly began
to laugh.

'I told Barbara that,' she said, 'and do you know what her
answer was?'

'No.'

'She merely asked, "Is Parkinson's disease infectious?" ...
Oh, there's a lot of Ellison about that young woman, a terrible
lot!'

6

Altogether there were a hundred and twenty-six letters. I still
have—quite legitimately, as I shall explain—copies of all of
them. Many seem to me to be of exceptional interest; their
style, jaunty and rather self-consciously callous, says a good

deal about the character of their writer, and so indirectly of his child. This is my excuse for the limited number of quotations which I shall give.

I start with the first in the series, dated 17th November 1914, because it sets the tone and also because it may serve to correct in advance any impression that Fulk's career in Sinkiang was one long succession of *Boy's Own Paper* triumphs.

'DEAREST MOTHER,

'There are rumours here that you are having a war. Personally I think they have been put about by the Chinks to push up the price of German ammunition. But if you are, well, it is not much different here. I have had a bit of trouble, that swine Yee again, the Governor, I told you about him, I think. Last week there was a riot, the boys have been boiling up for some while, and they got a few of the garrison in a Bad House, and gave them something they didn't go in for.

'Well, it so happened that a couple of chaps who took a leading part in the disturbance were friends of mine. And furthermore it happened that I had lately sold them one or two odds and ends—for keeping off thieves and shooting quail and so on. Is it my fault if they misbehave with my goods, any more than you'd blame the ironmonger if a man bought a saucepan from him and went out into the street and bashed somebody over the head with it? But there you are. I've always been the poor fish that got the blame.

'Two or three nights after the riot I was in the outer courtyard. A couple of my caravans had come in and I was talking to the drivers and checking over the stuff. And then, damn me, if a dozen whacking great soldiers didn't barge in through the open gate. I asked what they wanted and they said they had orders to take me before the Governor. Well, the boys from the caravans who're a friendly lot were in favour of up and cut their throats. But I could see this was a special patrol because they'd been issued with the old Martini Henry rifles which go off once in two instead of once in ten like the rest of the armoury. So not wanting any bloodshed I said I'd go along. But the blasted

noise had roused up Serafina and she came out with the baby
to ask what was happening. Well, Mother, not to make a song
about it, the fact is that people who go to the Governor's palace
don't always come back, or they come back the worse for wear.
Serafina started to bawl and the baby bawled too, and then
the baby's nurse popped up, always one for a bit of grue, just
like our old nanny, and the noise would have drowned a steam
siren. There is only one way to stop Serafina lamenting and that
is to start her cursing. So I told her she was simply trying to
disguise the fact that all she cared about was my money, and
she'd be glad if I was killed, so that she could get her hands on
it. When I came back several hours later she was still making
a speech about the purity of her heart and the delicacy of her
nature. You would like S., Mother, she would give you many a
good laugh.

'Well, because of all the uproar, I'd let them take me away
without my sheepskin coat or my fur hat. The cold had just set
in, and when it's cold here believe me, Mother, it would take
the nose off a brass monkey. The colder it is, the brighter the
stars and the moon, and the mica on the slopes above the North
Gate bats back the light so that if you look long enough you
begin to imagine the whole place is winking at you. Anyway
the chill got into my bones and started me shivering. Which
would never do. Once let these Chinks think you are frightened
of them and you are finished. So when we reached the palace,
I made the soldiers let me stop in the guard-house and warm
myself over a brazier.

'You'd hardly recognize the palace by that name. Some of it
was put up about 1750 in the usual Chink style—a series of big
barns—pavilions, if you're feeling polite—with carved roofs
and long eaves. But the centre is quite different, a bit like the
castle towers in Scotland—very rough stone, slit windows and
passages, so low and narrow that you feel you're crawling along
a mole's burrow. They say it was built by either the Keraits or
the Uighurs. The Chinks don't like it, they say it is haunted, but
they don't knock it down because once or twice these four-foot
walls have turned out very useful in a siege.

'On the bottom floor there's one big room, almost circular. I don't know what it's called officially, but Yee uses it as a private audience chamber. When they took me in he was sitting at a little lacquered table, painting or doing calligraphy. Well, I ask you! What an act! It reminded me of father. You know I could never stand that trick of shuffling the papers and signing letters while people wait, just to show what a big cheese you are.

'So after a minute I waited till he was on a delicate down-stroke and I coughed as loud as I damned well could. He started all right. But he's not a man who stops on the wrong foot for long.

' "I have read", he said, "that there is a natural law which repeatedly gives symbolic warnings to the perceptive when they are in the presence of evil-doers."

'Well, I thought, my Chink is pretty good, but if the conversation is to be on that plane, I cannot run to it. So I tried to keep it simple.

' "I did not feel any warning," I said.

' "Possibly not. But just now you caused me to spoil the character which represents Peace and Harmony."

' "There can't be much use for it round here," I said, trying to put us on an easy footing.

' "You dare to tell me that!" he said. "You who have done as much as anyone to turn this city into a den of wild beasts!"

'When anything goes wrong the authorities always like to pretend that the man who sells a gun is responsible for what the buyer does with it. Of course, traffic in arms is illegal in Sinkiang and punishable by death, but everybody knows it goes on and who's in it. I scarcely thought that even Yee would be cad enough to bring that up against me.

' "I have proof against you, a hundred times over," he said.

' "There is no need to congratulate yourself on that, your Excellency," I said. "Come down to my cellar any day and I will show you my goods."

Yee is a funny-looking chap. For a Chink he has a long face and rather pronounced features. As I stood there looking at him in the lamplight he reminded me of an old mountain goat.

You stare at that long dreary mug and you don't know whether to laugh or to be sorry for the poor brute. Then if you're lucky you catch the wicked light in his eyes just before he catches you in the stomach!

' "I am willing to grant you the conventional immunity on that score, but I can no longer tolerate the fact that you have allied yourself with the enemies of the Government which has given you eight years' hospitality."

'I do not know, Mother, whether the people in England still believe that the Chinks begin every sentence by saying, "Honourable Lotus Blossom, accept my unworthy salutations". It is not so. They can talk as straight as anyone else, at least they can out here.

'So I said to him, "What are you going to do about it?"

' "I am going to put you to death," he said, "in accordance with my lawful powers."

' "There will be a frightful fuss when the news gets back to England," I said.

' "I have faced many fusses in the course of my duty," he said. "Besides, you may possibly exaggerate the concern of your Government. I shall be fully supported by mine."

'Well, I must say I was uneasy. About half the soldiers had stayed in the room, a couple guarding Yee, and three just behind my back. Even if I had been armed I shouldn't have stood a chance. Whilst I was weighing up the situation, the screen that stood across the entrance was edged aside and in strolled another brute. He was carrying one of those whacking great executioner's swords.

' "Is your Excellency not being a little hasty?" I said. "It would be a pity to do anything irreparable."

' "The whole object of this procedure is that it should be irreparable," he said.

' "Can't I at least say goodbye to my wife and child?"

' "It would only distress them," said Yee. "I shall make it my business to inform your wife that you submitted bravely to the decree of higher authority—even if the facts should not warrant that praise."

'I do not mind saying that I had begun to sweat. Do you know what I kept on thinking, Mother? I suppose it ought to have been about Serafina or you. But actually I thought "Father's still alive. I counted at least on surviving him, and now I'm going to be done out of even that satisfaction".

'Two of the soldiers suddenly put their hands on my shoulders and dragged down so that I collapsed on to my knees. That is the position from which the Chinks usually take their heads off. Its disadvantage is that the victim sometimes starts hobbling about, and the executioner has to chase round taking a slice off where he can. I have seen some of it at the city execution ground.

'There I was. I could hear the chap with the sword taking practise swings behind my back. It made a funny noise, as though the blade were somehow broad and wrinkled like a fan. Yee was looking at me with a serene benevolent expression like the old boy on the bench the time Jack Locksley and I broke the windows of that pub. Suddenly he said:

' "Do you believe that if a miracle were now to spare you, you would be able to respect your obligations to the State?"

' "Yes," I said. Who wouldn't?

' "It is a pity that we shall never know," said Yee, and he made a signal with his hand.

'The next thing I knew I heard the whistling noise for a fraction of a second, and then I stopped a sort of slap between the shoulder and the jaw. Just as if some woman had got fed up. Damn me stiff, I thought, Mother, if that's all it feels to die! Then I realized I'd gone over on my side, flat against the tiles, but looking up I could still see old Yee, and even the executioner who was laughing like a horse. His blasted sword had bent double and caved in like a Harlequin's smacker in a pantomime. And that's just about what it was. Once I looked I could see that it was made of stiff paper, painted over to imitate steel.

'Well, it wasn't the first time that trick had been worked. I'd heard of the Chinks playing it before. So much the bigger fool me. I don't know if you like your sons heroes, Mother, because, if so, you will have to make do with Cedric, which I think will be an uphill job. All I can tell you is that when I got back on my feet, I was shaking like a watch-spring.

'Old Yee said, "Today one of my subordinates appears to have made an error of judgment. We will leave it at that. But you will appreciate how rarely such a thing recurs even in the lowest civilizations."

'Mother, I do not like being made a fool of. You know that. I have it in for Yee Chen Sung. . . .'

In a broad, breezy way Fulk must have been an inconsiderate man. This comes out in the style of writing to his mother. From other evidence I believe that his language in conversation was appalling. He moderated it greatly for literary purposes, but it is improbable that a woman of Mrs. Ellison's generation much appreciated the residue of damning and blasting. More important, he never seemed to understand that the recital of danger and hairbreadth escapes was calculated to set up chronic anxiety in a loving parent. Yet the fact that his letters persisted throughout the long years of exile shows that he must have had a deep regard for his mother.

One thing about him which is unacceptable to contemporary opinion is his attitude to the Chinese. In his correspondence they are invariably referred to by the childish and derogatory nickname of Chinks. Hostility hardly excuses bad taste; but the truth was that Fulk, so much nearer to China than the average man, nevertheless saw it in a light far less likely to promote sympathy—namely, that of a colonial power, a role to which experts agree the Chinese have never been well fitted. They had made a mess of Sinkiang: they could not assimilate it, they could hardly hold it, but they would not let it go.

I have already spoken about the endless pattern of rebellion and reprisal which runs through the history of the province. Nobody who reads that history can doubt that the Chinese Government were chronically guilty of preferring reconquest to prevention, if only because it was financially cheaper. But as time went on the cost of this policy in human life rose steeply because of the infiltration of new weapons to Sinkiang.

For instance, Fulk's activities must have done a good deal to increase the rate of bloodshed.

A Russian traveller has left an account of a battle between the Tungan and Turki rebels and a Chinese army in the eighteen-nineties. It resembled a circus as much as a military operation, and more than either, a parade of weapons through the ages. Everything from Genoese crossbows to bronze cannon had drained down into that remote sump of warfare. On the rebel side there was even a detachment of men unarmed except for small pieces of paper wrapped round pebbles which they flung at the enemy; the paper was inscribed with highly damaging curses.

There was still an element of this glorious gimcrackery about the conflicts of Fulk's day. But already, above the outlandish cries and the variegated explosions, one could begin to hear the quiet padding approach of the technician with his mass-produced instruments of slaughter.

The lack of letters dating from the first nine years of Fulk's stay in Doljuk had various inconveniences. It would be interesting, for example, to know what originally decided him to settle in such an unlikely spot, how he established himself, and how the natives first reacted to his presence. But there was another disadvantage of more practical moment. No account existed of the period during which he either did or did not marry Serafina Filipovna, and their child was born. These were events which he could scarcely have avoided mentioning. But, alas, at the point where I came in all the characters were taken as introduced and familiar to his mother's mind.

I found only one passage which might bear on Varvara's legitimacy. In the summer of 1918 Doljuk was visited by a plague which must have been part of the great pandemic of Spanish 'flu. Varvara, then aged about nine, caught it and was likely to die. She was saved—or so at least Fulk thought—by her mother's doctoring. Serafina had taken up this art, mixed with a little wizardry, under the influence of one of her servants, an old Kipchak woman, who, until she broke her thigh and became unfit for a nomadic life, had been the medicine woman of her tribe. (I suppose that Varvara's similar pretensions and the stock of drugs with which she supported them were a direct inheritance.)

'. . . You know the bit about "eye of newt and toe of frog", those witches couldn't have taught Serafina anything. Thank God eighty per cent of the population are strict Sunnis who'd as soon take medicine from a woman as out of a dog's mouth; otherwise she'd kill someone, because she dearly loves a body to practise on. I stick to that, Mother, even though I now have to admit that her methods do come off at times. Well, about six on the second day the little girl was having a terrible struggle to breathe. There were black veins in her face as if the blood had gone stagnant like a pond, and with every gasp a big yellowish bubble came out of the side of her mouth. I'd seen a good many hop it in recent weeks and I knew that complexion and those bubbles showed that they were well on the road.

'I sat by the bed feeling sorry for poor little Varvara. But you know how it is, you cannot hold it, unless you are a saint or something and before long I'd slid off into feeling sorry for myself. There I am, I thought, getting on in life, no son, soon not even a daughter by the look of it. In theory I suppose I might have other children, but Serafina seems to have lost the trick of it. I am too sensitive that way, the thought of not leaving any children makes me feel Time blowing down my neck. Of course, as you know, Mother, I have had one or two little accidents, and very good you were about them in spite of all the damned fuss Father made, *but you cannot really count little accidents like your own children. . . .'*

The italics of course are mine. At the risk of labouring the point, I would draw attention to the clear distinction which he draws between the by-blows of his youthful adventures and his child by Serafina. I don't know what weight a Court would have attached to the statement. Some certainly; but it would have been far from conclusive. For it might have been that Fulk merely meant that Varvara was the only child whom he acknowledged; or even that he was lying about her status to spare his mother's feelings.

I think the story of Varvara's illness is worth completing.

'. . . Presently it seemed to get very quiet except for the child's breathing and I realized that the women had stopped their row. I'd been down and had a look at them in the cookhouse and you never saw such a sight, the daughters of the Prophet banging their heads in the muck and one queer little heathen from the Altai nursing a woollen idol in front of a charcoal fire. I do not hold with all this mourning, when we die, we die and there is no sense in making a song of it, but I will say this, they love that child as if she were their own.

'Anyhow I thought they'd given up hope, and Serafina like the rest. But suddenly she came in. She had old Daina with her and she was carrying a little earthen pot that gave off as foul a smell as I have ever smelt. They paid no attention to me, but Serafina got behind the bed and lifted the kid, and Daina from the front forced back her head and jerked the stuff down her throat. Damn me, Mother, if I have ever seen the like! After a couple of seconds that child sat up as if they'd put a thousand volts through her. You could hear her teeth rattle and her eyes opened and the eyeballs turned up till you could only see the whites looking like a couple of blood-alley marbles. That's done it, I thought, that's hastened the end. But as soon as I opened my mouth they both set on me and turned me out. . . .'

The upshot was that when he came back several hours later, Varvara was in a normal sleep and the strangling accumulation of mucus in her lungs had begun to dry up.

At the end of the letter he adds: 'So it seems I may have to go on supporting your granddaughter indefinitely. She is not a bad little thing, only a bit crazy. I bought the servants a fat sheep, but I let them know that they hadn't taken me in with their faked lamentations.'

Neither of the two letters from which I have so far quoted

contained any enclosure. But there were photographs in several of the later ones. At first it surprised me that the necessary equipment should be available in the wilds of Sinkiang. But the more I learnt about Doljuk, the more I realized how unpredictably the amenities were distributed there. Almost anything could be obtained, provided that it was specially bespoken and the buyer did not mind waiting: ultimately the goods would trickle in by railway as far as Lanchow and thereafter by bullock cart through Kansu and the desert.

Similarly, traffic in the reverse direction was slow but fairly sure. The steady continuity of Fulk's letters showed a transport system which continued to function even during rebellions. To judge from internal evidence, not more than two or three could have gone astray in the whole twelve years.

The pictures had evidently been taken with a good camera, but the development and printing were amateurish. The fading of the surface had a paradoxical effect in improving the portrait of Fulk, for it restored a dark, yellowish tinge which was near to the natural colour of his hair and his short wiry moustache. He was a big man, about six feet three inches, and he looked much as I had expected, bold, handsome, reckless, except that there was less good humour and more sensibility in his face. His appearance did not quite square up with the rollicking extrovert of the letters. He was neither a *poseur* nor yet the rumbustious ox which he sometimes pretended. I think, however, that he was well aware of his own image and when he looked in the glass he liked to see a rugged adventurer.

The photograph which I preferred showed him standing beside a pony, wearing a buttonless blouse with a high neck and a small fur hat. Behind him were some ruins stretching away into a waste of sand. His expression was watchful and slightly suspicious—the counterpart of one which I had several times seen on his daughter's face.

There were also a number of pictures of Varvara as a child and of Serafina Filipovna. Despite her beauty the latter did not photograph well, principally, I thought, because the photographer never managed to catch her with her mouth shut.

7

After several more excursions with Andrew, Varvara received her new clothes. She came down to breakfast one morning in a frock which would have looked very well at the smarter sort of Chelsea cocktail party.

The fashions of that period did not favour large well-developed girls. Skirts were longer than a few years before and breasts and bottoms had made a tentative reappearance, but the basic design of most dresses still assumed a flat, epicene figure. However carefully Varvara put on her smart garments she always looked as if she had burst her way forcibly into them and was about to attempt an equally violent exit. Nevertheless she was improved by conforming with ordinary standards. Once the impression of eccentricity was removed people could concentrate on her basic natural advantages. She belonged to that small class of women who merit the description Junoesque, which is much abused by those who forget that it was not Jove's wife but one of his mistresses who turned into a cow.

Andrew's friend, Pam Kerrison, showed herself a shrewd or at any rate a well-advised woman. When Mrs. Ellison saw the new outfit she immediately insisted on paying for every stitch of it. So far from pluming herself on her generosity she was stricken with remorse because she had not thought of re-equipping Varvara before.

The feathers also reacted on the bird inside them. It seemed to me that from the moment when Varvara first outwardly approximated to a rich upper-class girl there was a noticeable change in her speech. She made a conscious effort to acquire the fashionable catch-phrases. Sometimes they floated strangely on the surface of archaism and formality which would take another year to eliminate. Not that I personally was anxious for that day, but Andrew clearly wished to hasten it on. One afternoon he came to tea at Aynho Terrace and spent most of the time urbanely correcting her on little points of idiom. What exasperated me was the submissiveness with which she received his instructions. Rather childishly I took advantage of superior academic knowledge to refute several of his remarks about the English language. The atmosphere was cool when Varvara received a message that her grandmother wanted to see her.

Andrew and myself eyed each other in silence for several seconds. Then with the absence of malice which was one of his more admirable traits he tried to re-establish good relations.

'Extraordinary life she must have led before she came here! She's told me some things that fair curled my hair.'

It was not a very fortunate opening. However absurdly, I had come to regard Doljuk as my own property and the news that Varvara discussed it with other people made me more jealous than any sexual rebuff. My reaction was to try to show Andrew how much better I was informed about the place than he. He listened politely for a while, then broke in:

'You know, David, I can see that this really means something to you. You're one of those chaps who has a feeling for the East.'

'Perhaps,' I said, simpering slightly.

'You ought to get into some sort of practical contact with it.'

'I can't spend my vacs in Turkestan.'

'No, but there are a lot more places in that direction which have a bit of the old magic about them. . . . India, for instance.'

I thought he was suggesting that I should visit my uncle and aunt and I started to explain that it would be ruled out by expense. But he waved this aside.

'There's no need to go there, when so many of them come over here.'

'Who do?'

'Indians.'

'I know a couple at Cambridge,' I said.

My lack of enthusiasm was not due to race-prejudice, but to the fact that my acquaintances had more affinity with Bloomsbury than Doljuk.

Suddenly Andrew said: 'But do you know any Indian women?'

'No. Do you?'

'Since you ask me, yes. Actually she's only half-Indian. She's damned good value, David—ready for anything. Dentist's receptionist, but definitely a cultured girl.'

'Very nice,' I said.

'I wondered if you'd like me to introduce you?'

'Andrew,' I said, looking pointedly at Varvara's empty place, 'there wouldn't be any motive behind your offer to pimp for me?'

'Nobody but a cad would look at it in that way,' he muttered sulkily.

I believe that Andrew is now in command of his father's empire, and that he has made the historic transition from Income to Expenses with great adroitness. But in those days he still had something to learn about the art of negotiation.

Varvara and I had fallen into a routine of limited love-making.

We never indulged in any familiarity during the day, but most nights we went upstairs together at bedtime and I entered her room 'to say good night'—a process which sometimes extended to early morning. We kissed and ... But those dots mean nothing spicy, they merely indicate uncertainty about the word to use. Nobody could pet with Catherine the Great or neck Boadicea. Whatever their actual physique, their characters loom too massive in the mind. It was the same with Varvara. On the whole I think that the best term is the neutral 'embrace'—though once again I must emphasize that it does not carry its more drastic sense.

She attracted me strongly in her courage and bodily sweetness and emotional violence. The last, however, also inspired me with a salutary caution. I had enough sense to see that anybody who stirred her deeply would be caught up by a temperamental cyclone in which discretion and propriety would vanish like two straws. I had no wish to be accused of repaying Mrs. Ellison's kindness by seducing her granddaughter.

Though I was no Casanova, I had more experience than she. And it was just as well. Varvara's idea of self-control was like that of a man who drives at sixty miles an hour straight for a brick wall, relying on his brakes to stop him in the last ten feet. She had her own method of halting the runaway machine. Sometimes she would leap out of the armchair or off the bed and fling herself on her knees and pray audibly for purity. I suppose it was all frightfully bad taste, but at the time I found it romantic and exciting. I had also discovered there was nothing like amorous byplay for bringing out reminiscences of Doljuk.

I think that the same sort of familiarities probably went on with Andrew. Varvara was not essentially promiscuous, but she was an Ellison; as a family they wanted the best, and none of them would have thought it anything but common sense to explore the markets before deciding where to sell their goods.

I had tacitly assumed that contact with me and my cool British outlook would gradually wean Varvara away from her violent and melodramatic ideas. In fact the opposite began to happen. Continual exposure to a character like a superheated furnace was raising my emotional temperature to a point where fever distorted my judgment. I no longer thought it odd or unlikely that a conspiracy should be perpetually raging in the background of life; people put off their drab coverings and emerged as monsters or holy saints. I mention this because it helps to explain some of my more curious actions, and the slight fog which still hangs over my own and other people's motives.

My obsession with Doljuk and the close idle existence of almost dreamlike luxury which I enjoyed no doubt contributed to my mental state. There was every temptation to lead a second life when the real one demanded so little effort. I felt like a fish in an aquarium. For a while it seemed as if the only threat, the big pike, whose shadow had once stirred our tank to alertness, was going to fade away completely.

For over a fortnight Cedric did not come near the house, and from Turpin I learnt that he was ill.

'What's the matter with him?' I asked.

'The usual, I s'pose.'

'He has some complaint?'

'Swimming in the 'ead,' said Turpin vaguely. 'Since a boy. That's what they call it. 's my belief, though, 'e goes proper queer at times. All of a sudden 'is mind gets a straight look at 'is nature and can't stand it.'

'Do you really mean that he has fits when he's . . . not responsible?'

'Well, sir, what d'you make of this? Many's the time I've come quiet into a room when 'e thought 'e was alone. 'E'd be walking up and down talking to 'imself. And *about* 'imself, like 'e was another party. "Steady, Ellison," I'd hear 'im say. "Steady. We've got to think this out. You weren't given a first-class brain for nothing." Then 'e turn round, so to speak, and be someone else praising up Mr. Bloody Cedric. "Reliable chap, Ellison, very sound. You always get a balanced view from Ellison." '

I am sure Turpin did not invent the habit. It chimed too well with Cedric's obsessive self-absorption. Besides I did not need this evidence to believe that he was slightly mad. But whatever his precise affliction it did not last very long. Within a few days of this conversation his visits had recommenced. I returned from an afternoon walk to find Turpin in the hall, dabbing disgustedly at the hatrack with a housemaid's brush.

> 'What on earth are you up to?'
> 'Oo sweeps a floor
> As for God's Law
> Makes that and the action fine,'

said Turpin—'I don't bloody think!' Without a pause he continued. 'What do you s'pose? Mr. Bloody C. of course! Comes in 'ere and says the place is filthy and he'll see 'is ma gets value out of keeping a pack of idle, greedy lackeys. I tell 'im I'm not a ruddy skiv . . .'

It was nevertheless noticeable that Turpin had not positively refused to obey the order. Yet he was a tough and independent old warrior. The fact reminded me that, despite various set-backs, Cedric wielded many of the powers of a master at Aynho Terrace.

Changing in irony to his society voice, Turpin continued: 'Furthermore, sir, you are 'ighly privileged today. The old block 'as graciously brought 'is bloody chip along with 'im.'

'What does that mean?'

'Miss Deirdre 'as bin released from the cotton-wool in order that she may pay us a call.'

'To see her grandmother I suppose,' I said indifferently.

'She's come round to make the acquaintance of 'er little cousin,' said Turpin, mincing the words ferociously, 'which will be so naice for them both—like 'Ell! One thing, the Bud isn't 'aving any. 'E sent me up to fetch 'er from 'er room, but Ai regret to say she 'as locked 'erself in the convenience.'

I found the pair of them in the morning-room. Deirdre Ellison impressed me less unfavourably than I had expected. She was a tall girl with a face whose structure tapered down from a broad forehead to a pointed chin. She had striking eyes, between hazel and green in colour, and her mouth was conspicuously well-shaped. This was as well, for she wore it in a demure simper which could have been very unattractive. She did not approach the classic nobility of Varvara's features, but I could imagine some men thinking her more sexually desirable. She was the younger of the two by about a year and a half.

'Ah,' said Cedric, 'this is my young friend David Lindley, who occupies an indeterminate but comfortable position in the household. . . .'

No doubt he knew through Nurse Fillis that I had had something to do with the affair of the green writing-case. His remark was deliberately intended to make me feel a sponger.

A few minutes later he tried to be nasty again. I had politely given him a cigarette; after which I offered my case to the girl.

'I'm afraid David's ideas are a bit too emancipated for us,' he said. 'Where we simple, old-fashioned people come from young ladies of seventeen don't smoke. Do they, Deirdre?'

'No, Father,' she said with toneless humility.

Besides his annoyance with myself, I could see that Cedric was in a raging temper over the snub from Varvara.

'Sit up straight, Deirdre. You're lolling like an old sack.'

'Yes, Father. Is this better?'

'Have you left school?' I asked her, to make conversation.

'I never went.'

Cedric intervened: 'Deirdre has been delicate and I have had her taught at home—in my opinion the best sort of education for a young woman, at any rate from the point of view of a responsible parent.'

He gave me a glance of mingled suspicion and lubricity, contriving to suggest that I wanted to bundle his lamb into some vicious Parisian establishment.

It was a parting shot. Within a few moments he announced that he had business with Mrs. Ellison and was going to her bedroom.

As soon as his back was turned Deirdre said:

'Now give me a cigarette.'

'But I thought you didn't smoke.'

'Then you must have believed I was a pretty fair little . . .'

The timbre of her voice had changed entirely. Now it was rough and contemptuous. But what shook me was her choice of the final word. She let the obscenity drop with studied satisfaction.

'I beg your pardon,' I said.

'Don't sound so scared, I was only relieving my feelings.'

'You do it pretty drastically for a girl who's not allowed to risk the corrupting influence of school.'

'That crap!' she said. 'Father knows best—but he doesn't know what some of his selections as governesses were really like. One bitch who taught me German had been on the streets in Hamburg.' She narrowed her eyes and smiled in a way which was not wholly unattractive. 'But perhaps Father *did* know after all.'

'Steady on,' I said, really shocked by the innuendo. 'You're only doing this to get your own back for being continually bossed.'

'That's not a very brilliant discovery. . . . Father says you're frightfully conceited—always putting up mature attitudes and imagining you're impressing people. But don't worry: he says as bad or worse about everyone behind their backs.'

'It's a pity,' I said, 'he doesn't realize how generally that's known.'

She was silent for some seconds, puffing at her cigarette. From her amateur style of smoking it did not look as if her outbreaks of defiance were as many as she implied.

Then she said: 'It's my cousin who brings out the worst in him. The things I've had to listen to about her!'

'What?' I said, curious despite myself.

'Well . . . about how she's an adventuress like my Uncle Fulk who stole money . . . and how she bullies Grandma—Father says he wouldn't be surprised if she did the old girl in.'

'Nonsense!'

'Just what I think,' said Deirdre, enjoying herself. 'You see I can't help noticing that one moment poor Varvara is supposed to be an arch-fiend and the next she's a poor sucker in grave moral danger . . .'

'Who from?'

'Why, you, of course! Father says you want to compromise her so that she has to marry you and then you hope you'll get a whack at the Ellison money.'

'By God,' I said, 'what a family you are!'

Deirdre nodded without resentment. She made me feel slightly sick, but I could not dislike her. There was something pathetic and vaguely courageous about her awful malapert defiance: something for which the term resistance-movement was coined years later.

Much to my surprise Varvara stalked in.

(I heard afterwards what had happened. Cedric had made a complaint to his mother. One of the few things which Mrs. Ellison would not tolerate, at any rate in her own sex, was overt bad manners. She had sent up her personal maid to knock on the lavatory door and express the strong hope that Miss Varvara would shortly be down to meet her cousin.)

'I've been longing to meet you for ages,' said Deirdre.

'Not so,' replied Varvara cryptically.

She took the other's hand and wrung it as if it were a hen's neck.

'But you're so smart!' said Deirdre concealing her pain. 'I'd heard—'

'That I was a she-ox from the desert,' said Varvara. 'And you rejoiced.'

Deirdre, like many home-bred children, particularly females, had acquired a veneer of precocious social assurance. But Varvara bludgeoned her way through it in a couple of sentences. Deirdre suddenly looked as if she might burst into tears.

'Oh dear, have I said the wrong thing?'

Unfortunately Cedric chose that moment to reappear. The sound of his daughter's voice touched off his managerial instincts.

'What's the matter, Deirdre? What have you been saying?'

'Nothing, Father.'

'Then how could it be the wrong thing?'

'I was just rather silly.'

'Were you showing off?'

'No, Father.'

'I've had to speak to you before about that.'

This sort of slow baiting was very unacceptable to Varvara's nature.

'Your daughter spoke charitably and socially,' she said, 'to cover up a rough word of mine.'

An expression of bewilderment, followed by one which closely resembled gratitude, spread over Deirdre's face. It had obviously never occurred to her that frontal opposition was also a way of dealing with her father. I felt, alas, that the lesson might be rather dangerous as applied to anybody who had to live in financial dependence on him.

I thought we were in for a damned unpleasant scene between Varvara and her uncle. But suddenly Cedric made a retching noise in his throat and swayed visibly. He took a couple of quick steps and flopped down in the nearest chair, putting his head down between his hands.

'What's the matter, Father?' said Deirdre with a more genuine-sounding concern than I should have expected. 'Is it one of your attacks?'

There we are, I thought, if that doesn't just round off the picture! I should have realized without the need for a demonstration that when Cedric could not sufficiently assert his will by force he would fall back on an appeal to pity. 'Wicked child, do you want to kill your kind papa—who will not be with you for long anyhow?'

Despite his recent illness, this seemed a very reasonable diagnosis, and it was not my fault that it turned out to be a little too smart.

After a couple of minutes Cedric got up, still looking somewhat groggy. He muttered a brief apology and then left accompanied by Deirdre.

'On the way home,' said Varvara, 'perhaps he will die.'

'I don't think so.'

'When he lay in the chair I hoped the blood would start out of his nostrils.'

'Really,' I said, 'it's time you learnt to lay off this face-bashing attitude. It sounds perfectly ridiculous in England.'

'You have murderers here also.'

'The only person your uncle is likely to knock off is his wretched daughter. He'll send her crazy, if he doesn't look out.'

The fact that on impulse Varvara had defended her cousin did not mean that she trusted her.

'They are in league,' she said.

'You wouldn't think so if you'd heard what she was saying about him.'

'That was to put you off your guard. The cubs scratch the tiger to sharpen their claws, but they are not quarrelling.'

'Have it your own way,' I said.

I was preoccupied with a discovery which I had just made. Life is very unjust, but a high proportion of bad men manage to pay themselves out in this world: they do it simply by breeding in their own likeness.

8

I had almost forgotten my uncle's cable, and it came as a surprise when I was called to the telephone and heard his voice at the other end. He had to spend that day at the India Office, but in the evening I went round and dined with him in his Kensington hotel.

After we had chatted for a while, he asked me how I was enjoying myself at Aynho Terrace.

'Not too boring, I hope.'

'Not at all.'

'I was afraid you might be a bit short of company.'

'Mrs. Ellison has her niece staying—the one from China.'

My uncle whistled. 'That ought to liven things up.'

'How did you know?'

'Fair inference from heredity.'

My memory went back to the days in Brittany.

'Didn't you once tell me that you'd met her father?'

He nodded.

'On my great cloak-and-dagger odyssey—the one your aunt describes so excitingly. As a matter of fact I think Ellison was the only exciting thing about it.'

'Did you go to Doljuk?'

'No. He travelled down to meet me in Kashgar.'

'Why?'

'It was arranged,' said my uncle with deliberate vagueness.

'Do you mean that he was some kind of . . . British Agent?'

'Now you're getting like Edna. I can almost hear the rustling behind the arras. No. Ellison's energies were directed to the great cause of Ellison. But he was very helpful to me. And his support was worth having in those parts.'

'Perhaps you'd like to meet the daughter,' I suggested.

My uncle assented but without quite the enthusiasm which

I had expected. He was nearing the age when reminiscence is more enjoyable than fresh experience.

In the event it was just as well that he did not set any particular store on the occasion. Varvara had accepted an invitation to Sunday lunch, and earlier that morning I accompanied her to the Orthodox Church in Moscow Rd., for I had become curious about the creed to which she responded with so much fervour. I myself was impressed. I can still smell the incense and see the agonized Byzantine faces that looked down from the niches of the eikonostasis, and hear the sung litany, now plangent, now rounded and smooth like a blood-ruby. Beside me Varvara chanted in a voice which did more credit to her heart than her ear.

Afterwards the spiritual temperature fell sharply. As we stood outside on the pavement, I said:

'We might as well go straight along to the hotel.'

'What hotel?'

'Where my uncle's staying.'

Varvara gave an affected start of recollection.

'Holy Christ,' she said, 'I have forgotten the date of your damned uncle! Goodness how sad!'

'Just as well I came along to remind you.'

'You see, David,' she said, grasping me by the hand as if she were about to tear an espalier off a wall, 'unfortunately I have pledged myself to another.'

'Before or after I spoke to you?'

'Long, long before,' said Varvara with a pellucid candour which carried no conviction.

'I suppose we're being thrown over for Andrew and the Ritz?'

'I cannot spoil his party.'

'What about my wretched uncle's? It's just as bad for him.'

'Ah, no,' said Varvara with gentle reason. 'You see, you are wrong about the Ritz. This party is in Andrew's flat.'

'What the hell difference does that make?'

'Andrew's food would be wasted,' she said. 'But your uncle will suffer no loss for what is not served in a hotel.'

I don't know whether this was a flash of hard Doljuk logic

or of the spirit which had made her grandfather conserve his eyewash. At the time I was too annoyed to speculate.

'You're behaving like a slut.'

There in front of the House of the Lord, where with glistening eyes she had lately extolled the virtues of forgiveness, Varvara gave me a heavy cuff on the side of the head. It hurt and I realized again, with a tinge of humiliation, how strong she was.

I think that perhaps my uncle looked on this trip to England as a holiday from women. At any rate he waved aside my vicarious apologies.

'She only sprang it on me after we came out of church,' I said resentfully.

He began to laugh.

'Church!' he said. 'That's an odd idea to associate with one of Ellison's family.'

'She's very religious.' Spitefully I added: 'In a hysterical way.'

'I suppose it's reaction,' said my uncle. 'Frankly the only thing I didn't like about Fulk was his militant godlessness. Besides it was a bloody nuisance to me personally. The main object of my cloak-and-dagger trip was to get together the handful of our countrymen who inhabited those regions, and to pump them. Unfortunately, I was naïve enough to imagine that it would promote goodwill and confidence if I collected them all at the same time. Two of my sources were missionaries, and Ellison could hardly open his mouth to them without jeering.'

'I should have thought that white men would need to stick together out there,' I said sagely.

'It would certainly have been a help to the wretched priests. But I doubt if they could have offered any *quid pro quo*. At the time when I knew him, Ellison was one of the most famous men in Sinkiang.'

'I didn't realize that he became more than a local figure.'

'Oh yes. He'd shown himself to be something very rare: an original military thinker.'

My uncle sat back, twinkling his eyes. He always enjoyed small mystifications. But he could not have realized how much he had baffled me. The fact was I could not identify any event described in the letters with so grandiose a description.

Under his offhand Public School manner my uncle was profoundly romantic, and very English. He loved amateurism and improvisation and the triumph of underdogs. He needed little encouragement to tell a story which reeked of all three. Why Fulk himself did not relate it, seeing that he wrote at length of other events in which he played a far less glorious part, is not clear. Perhaps it was on account of the very celebrity of the operation. One of his un-Elizabethan characteristics was freedom from boasting.

As a matter of fact I later found two brief passages which must, I think, refer to the rebellion of 1917-18.

'Well, Mother, there has been another damned uproar round here. Last week we had an army of Chinks trying to break into the place, but now most of them have been persuaded to go away, and the ones who are staying will not give any more trouble....'

Between 1912 and the late twenties, Sinkiang as a whole enjoyed a spell of exceptional peace. But the term was relative, as if a doctor in plague-ridden territory were to note the absence of any pandemic outbreak. During these years the Governor-in-Chief of the provinces was a Chinese official named Yang, who, at least during the earlier years of his rule, showed unusual force and integrity. He is to be distinguished from the man whom Fulk refers to as the 'Governor' Yee. The latter was, in effect, a Resident or Deputy with local authority, who controlled Doljuk and a clutch of the northern oases. Yee was not a happy choice, perhaps because of a certain whimsicality which Confucian culture seems to impress on some of its devotees. This led him to alternate between excessive severity and excessive lenience. In any case it was not much good being cultured or whimsical with Tungans and Turkis.

A dispute about taxation set up a steady ferment which exploded in 1917. Only the cities of Yee's sub-province were involved, but within a limited area the rebels made an even cleaner sweep than usual, largely because Fulk had bought up quantities of modern arms from Russian deserters. He had also been speculating in the opposite market. Through China he imported five hundred cheap shot-guns with ammunition to match. Did he think he was going to popularize game-hunting in Doljuk? If so, he was as big an optimist as the man who tried to introduce the battle-of-flowers in Wigan. More likely he had from the first some dim notion of tactical possibilities.

At the end of spring, 1918, the expected Chinese army arrived in front of Doljuk. Two hundred miles east at Barkul, it had already inflicted a severe defeat on the rebels and had then proceeded to capture that city, executing all the notables after confiscation of their goods. Naturally there was some alarm among the upper circles in Doljuk about their future.

The Chinese sat down in front of the walls and the great wooden gates. They had no artillery except three old French guns which had been used in the Franco-Prussian war; and though these were capable of breaching the fortifications, they never continued serviceable for long enough to make an exploitable gap. Unfortunately for the defenders, however, the operations were not entirely directed by the ostensible Commander of the Chinese army, a rough-neck war-lord from Kansu. With him travelled the Governor Yee, who had skipped out at the beginning of the trouble, and spent a very pleasant year in Pekin. He was a well-educated man, and he had read the history of previous campaigns in Sinkiang. He remembered that in the rebellion of 1794 the Chinese General Huang Su had recaptured Doljuk with the loss of scarcely a man, by the simple trick of diverting its water-supply.

The wells in the city were virtually useless. Doljuk had a long history, and the sanitary habits of its population had not changed much in two thousand years. Consequently the soil and all that percolated through it were polluted to a remarkable depth. Not even the best acclimatized of the natives would venture to drink from the deep stinking holes which were to be found in the courtyards of the richer houses. Indeed it was considered reckless to wash clothes in liquid drawn from them.

In normal times all drinking water was provided by a stream which descended from a pool to the west of the oasis and flowed through the city, being conducted under the wall in two brick tunnels. In 1794 the Chinese smashed these tunnels by laying charges of gunpowder in the night. The result was doubly gratifying: not only did the men of Doljuk lose their water, but it piled up in a flood at the old point of inlet, threatening to dissolve the mud structure of the wall.

Another factor made the problem of thirst peculiarly tantalizing to the besieged. There was an alternative source of supply, which consisted of a broad pool rising in the garden of the Governor's palace. Its position had prevented it from becoming immoderately fouled; and in any case its strong mineral content was a purifier. But the latter, alas, gave it medicinal properties; it was a laxative with a harsh action. Heat exaggerated the city's plight. Towards the end of the first week of siege, the temperature stood at over 100° in the shade. People could no longer control themselves, but sucked down pints of the toxic water. The results, though not without the usual element of low farce, were ultimately horrible. Many died in great agony from the excoriation of their bowels.

The inhabitants had a long tradition of defeat which sapped their will to resist when things were going badly. There was some talk of surrender, particularly among the lower orders who might expect to escape any but a perfunctory and collective vengeance. Some of the rich tried to make their way by night through the Chinese lines.

As an infidel foreigner, Fulk Ellison had no official standing in Doljuk. Even his popularity with the Turkis which had been his chief asset was temporarily dimmed. When war turned against them, simple and faithless men found it convenient to blame the person who had provided them with the means to wage it. Nevertheless, because of his skill as an engineer, he was an informal member of the junta which had organized the defence of the city. At the meeting which, but for him, would have been the last he put forward a plan of rescue.

The key of his project was the Banner of Oirats with whom he had had previous dealings. A detachment of this tribe made an annual pilgrimage to the neighbourhood of Doljuk in order to collect salt—in which their own pastures were very poor —from the saline desert to the south of the city and they had been reported in the district several days before the beginning of the siege—of which they took not the slightest notice. Since the days of Jenghiz and Batu their nation had learnt to mind its own business.

'Still,' said my uncle, 'those who know claim that the ancient spirit has survived endemic syphilis and can still be uncorked by a good cash offer.'

That was the commission with which Fulk left. He crept alone through the Chinese lines, and rode southwards until he made contact with the Mongols. After a day of feverish negotiations, he led them to the ruined Uighur watch-tower which he used as a store for big consignments of illicit arms. There the contingent was served out with a shot-gun apiece and upwards of forty cartridges filled with duck-shot.

Fulk must at some time have asked himself the question why the nomad horsemen who had once terrorized Asia and Europe had lost their impact, and found an answer in their abandonment of rapid fire-power. Accounts of the Mongol campaigns in the thirteenth century always emphasized the dismay caused by a rain of arrows accurately directed from galloping horses. But for generations the bow had been yielding place to the gun. The snobbery of modern weapons had ruined a great military power. Bullets were indeed better than arrows —but only provided that both were delivered with approximately the same efficiency. The current arms among the Mongols were old muzzle-loaders or lengths of unrifled gas-pipe fitted with triggers by cynical and ingenious Japanese. In either case the barrels were as smooth as billiard balls, and the flight of the missile unpredictable. Consequently the irresistible charge

of Jenghiz' followers had degenerated into a mere ritual letting-
off of fire-crackers.

'Ellison told me,' said my uncle, 'that a lot of them used to
shut their eyes when they fired.'

'Why?'

'In order to pray more reverently for a hit.'

Since improvement in marksmanship would be a long job,
Fulk's idea was to reduce the margin of error.

Having equipped themselves, the party made a detour until
they were a couple of miles above the city on its north flank.
They waited until the sun was up and had begun to cast its intolerable dazzle down the mica slopes. They then charged.

'Ellison,' said my uncle, 'had that habit of deprecating his
own achievements which was so admired in my boyhood. You
remember how Rider Haggard's heroes usually insist that they
are cowards? I suppose it's really a degenerate offshoot of the
chivalric tradition. Anyhow it suited Ellison about as well as kid
gloves on a coal-heaver. . . . He pretended that he couldn't keep
up with those steppe horsemen, and that he was glad to be two
hundred yards in the rear. Personally I don't think he was too
sure that the Mongols would do their stuff and he deliberately
hung back to act as whipper-in. But whatever the reason was he
had an ideal position for seeing the whole operation.

The Mongols came down at a controlled trot for the first mile
and a half. By this time the Chinese had realized that they were
being threatened from outside their lines and had faced round
a part of their troops to meet the assault. But they had not realized how much the assailants were capable of stepping up their
speed of approach. Over the last half-mile the Mongols broke
into a furious gallop, weaving in and out of each other's paths
in a cat's cradle of movement to confuse the enemy's aim. The
Chinese were still deploying when the attackers arrived within
twenty yards of the front line. Even so their Commanders were
probably not unduly disturbed, imagining they would have to
face merely the usual random rifle-fire, followed up with a little
sword play. But at the last moment the irregular mass wheeled
broadside on, and with a fair semblance of unison both bar-

rels of every gun were discharged. Eight hundred cartridges
(excluding the minority which blew up in the faces of the firers)
amount to quite a heavy concentration of shot. Comparatively
few of the Chinese were killed, but the number of these who
lost their eyes or were shocked into helplessness by face wounds
entirely crippled the front line.

Drunk with excitement, screaming in high-pitched voices,
the small hairless men, who rode as if welded to their horses,
careered to and fro among the disordered ranks, reloading and
shooting indiscriminately in all directions. The rout was completed by a sortie from the besieged town. The whole Chinese
army broke and streamed eastwards into the desert.

During the pursuit they lost about a quarter of their strength,
and another two or three hundred were taken prisoner. Among
the latter was the Governor Yee.

Three days later when the water-supply had been restored
and the inhabitants had partially recovered from their savage
purgation, a great feast was held. Because of the numbers
attending it took place in the grounds of the Governor's palace.
All the Mongols became terribly drunk, to the scandal of the
teetotal Mohammedan natives. At the end the captive Yee was
brought out and strangled. My uncle thought that Fulk had
nothing to do with this.

These celebrations gave rise to the only other comment in
Fulk's letters on the whole chain of events.

'We had a party for some chaps who had done us a good
turn. At the end it got rather rough, and you would not have
liked it, Mother.'

Soon the Oirats rode away northward into their own land.
Before they went they begged, in addition to their covenanted
reward, a large cart and three mules. These were gladly
granted. They took bands of leather and bound them very
tautly from side to side of the cart. Then they studded them
with nails according to an ancient craftsmanship. The mules
were put between the shafts (for it was against the Mongols'

principles to harness a horse), and two men with wooden mallets mounted between the lattice of thongs. They struck them and there came out a deep humming music like the approach of a million hornets.

It was their tradition to mark great victories by the construction of a giant dulcimer on wheels. The battle at Doljuk was the first occasion for doing so in over three hundred years.

This departure from the normal pattern of events seems to have shaken the Chinese. At any rate, though the city and its confederates ultimately abandoned their resistance, they were not subjected to any penalties. The old regime returned slyly and on sufferance.

'Did you ever find out,' I asked my uncle, 'why Fulk Ellison broke so drastically with his family?'

'The story I heard in India was that old Joseph who used him as a sort of roving ambassador sent him to Mexico to negotiate a contract and gave him several thousand pounds for bribery. It so happened that he got the contract almost without paying and went off to Australia leaving the balance in his own bank account. When he returned to England he found that his father who'd grown insanely suspicious in his old age had sworn out a warrant against him for fraudulent conversion. The case was dropped of course, but it made Fulk so furious that he determined never to set foot in England again. He took on a series of jobs as mining-consultant all over the world. One of them landed him in Doljuk and there he suddenly put down fresh roots and stayed.'

'It seems a terrible waste,' I said. 'If he achieved so much in Sinkiang, think what he might have done if he'd remained among civilized surroundings!'

By this time I was somewhat excessively under the spell of Varvara's father and too ready to view him as a kind of Robin Hood. My uncle applied a mild dampener.

'I don't think that it would have made all that difference in the end. People find their own level.' He cleared his throat self-consciously as he did whenever he brought out a quotation from his considerable stock of classical knowledge: ' "*Sunt quos comitatur vastitas sua*—Some there are that carry their own wilderness with them." '

9

Turpin was looking out of his subterranean window from which the legs of a housemaid were visible halfway up the area steps.

'What are we?' he said. 'Whence do we come? Whither do we go? Dunno!'

His reflections on life had a pleasantly mixed flavour of *lacrimae rerum* and *je m'en fous*. They soothed me at a moment when I needed soothing. For I had just made a silly mistake.

The point had arrived when, having read all Fulk's letters three times, I was bound to render some account of my investigation. Accordingly I had gone to see Mrs. Ellison in her room; not much relishing the prospect of having to point out to her the only piece of evidence which I had discovered. It was the passage where Fulk distinguished between Varvara and any other children whom he might have begotten. It seemed to me that calling attention to it would rip away the veil behind which we had hitherto hidden the true aim of my search. But I had reckoned without the invincible capacity of people of Mrs. Ellison's generation to remain blind when they did not wish to see.

'Very interesting,' she said, examining the lines through her lorgnette. 'Very interesting. I think men are more sentimental than women over children. Perhaps that's because they are nearer to them. My son, for instance ... how he did love to tease by pretending all sorts of wild things about himself!'

I looked at her in astonishment, but she gave no indication of disbelieving what she said. On the whole I was delighted that the awkward corner had been rounded so easily. This gave me a false confidence; for the moment I was under the impression that I could 'manage' Mrs. Ellison. In this mood I said something which suggested fairly unequivocally that, whatever the facts about Varvara's birth, there was a moral obligation to treat her as a full member of the family.

I forget exactly what reply I received but it was one which choked me off completely. I was made to feel impertinent and vulgar. That I soon got over, but I could not so easily rid myself of the fear that I might have done Varvara some irrevocable harm. It persisted, despite the fact that for me the interview closed on a note of signal forgiveness.

When I tried to give back the originals of the letters and the copy which I had had made, Mrs. Ellison waved the latter aside.

'If you find them as interesting as you say, David, you might like to keep them. When I am dead you can do with them what you like.'

I think the sincerity of my thanks did a good deal to rehabilitate me in her eyes.

It was August Bank Holiday and stiflingly hot when Cedric brought Deirdre round for the second time. Whilst he was having one of his usual interviews with his mother she came out into the garden. Hardly wasting an instant on greetings, she launched into a long dirty story of whose point she obviously had only a dim conception. She had barely finished when her father joined us.

For once he seemed to be in a good temper.

'Tea,' he said. 'Yes, a little tea, I think, today. With cucumber sandwiches.'

He strolled back across the lawn to summon Turpin. Simply making conversation, I said to Deirdre:

'Your father doesn't usually take tea, does he?'

A truly fiendish gleam lit up her eyes.

'Because of his weight. We have to be very careful of that, otherwise he might stop being such a fine figure of a man. D'you know something . . . he wears corsets. Sometimes when he's very hurt and grieved because I've let him down, I can hear them creaking.'

Damn it, I thought, blood may be thicker than water but nothing will persuade me that that girl is in her father's camp!

Turpin brought out a couple of heavy silver trays. He was in a mutinous mood, for he had not expected to be dragged out of his cool pantry. As he passed my chair he muttered:

'Work I expect to: swink I will not.'

On a second circuit he paused behind Cedric for so long that he seemed to have fallen into a kind of catalepsy, with his eyes fixed on the upper storeys of the house.

'What's wrong, man?' said Cedric irritably. 'What are you staring at?'

'Pardon me, sir,' said Turpin in a hollow tone, 'but I 'ave just perceived a fowl effecting an entry by the museum window.'

It was one of Turpin's ways of showing his disapproval of Cedric to address him in terms of stilted and soapy euphuism; often, for greater irony, coupling them with an oriental servility. One day, with an extra drink or two inside him, I expected him to begin with the words: 'Deign to trample on this dishonourable carcase.'

The knowledge, albeit vague, that he was being guyed, showed in the sharpness of Cedric's answer.

'For God's sake, talk sense. You mean a bird's gone in. What sort?'

'Pigeon, sir.'

'Damn it. They're great big brutes. If it starts flapping about it may smash a lot of valuable stuff.'

''Ighly probable, sir,' said Turpin who realized how much any heritable property meant to Cedric. 'An 'ideous pest, the pigeon.'

'Well, don't stand there moralizing like a village idiot. Come and help me turn the damned thing out.' He swung round on the other two of us and snarled: 'Would it be too much to ask you young people to repay some fraction of the hospitality you are receiving by lending your help?'

As we crossed the hall we met Varvara, who allowed herself to be pressed into service. I did not really believe in that bird and I thought that when we reached the museum, Turpin would claim an optical illusion. But there, sure enough, strutting on top of one of the tall glass-cases was a pigeon. At first it seemed quite composed in its new surroundings, but Cedric soon altered that. He organized us into line like beaters at a shoot and gave us each a course to pursue between the cases and the *bric-à-brac*. The idea was that we should drive the intruder before us until it was forced out of the window. As a plan it neglected only one factor—that the room had a ceiling at least twelve feet high. The pigeon retreated in short hops and flutters almost to the windowsill; then it flew up on to the curtain-rail and back over our heads.

'The door!' howled Cedric. 'Shut that door, you fools!'

I made a dash and cut the bird off from the rest of the house.

'Haven't any of you any common sense?' he inquired. 'The things here are valuable, but downstairs they're priceless.'

He himself had been the last person into the room. I began to have some idea what it must be like to work in his office.

We formed up again and repeated the manoeuvre. The result was exactly the same, except that the pigeon was now becoming agitated; on its return flight it barged into a coaching-lantern which hung from the roof and left a streak of white slime on a Red Indian headdress.

'Doesn't anybody care if my mother's house is turned into a shambles?' asked Cedric, grimacing with rage.

I should never have supposed that he was one to bear up well in adversity. But this absurd loss of self-control in face of a petty crisis was something which I had not expected.

It diminished him in my eyes—an effect which was not un-welcome. I glanced significantly at Varvara to see whether she was taking in the absurdity of her bogey-man. But she appeared to be in an unusually lethargic mood. Since we met her, she had hardly spoken.

After another futile drive General Cedric decided to arm the troops. As I have mentioned, some of the museum's larger and lighter exhibits were supported on lattice racks attached to the walls. I equipped myself with the genuine prong of a swordfish; Turpin had a Dyak paddle; at the time I did not notice what the others picked up. Hooking and slashing at the air we advanced once more. Yet it was probably chance that this time the pigeon sailed out of the window, leaving a final trade-mark on the curtains.

'Well, well,' said Cedric, now mollified, 'our friend went just in time.'

'Else 'e might 'ave spoke 'arshly to the pore bastard,' said Turpin in an undertone.

Cedric continued: 'I definitely prefer humane methods. But if he'd lingered longer I should have had to dispatch Mr. Pigeon.'

'Easier said than done,' I remarked, resenting his switch from panic to complacency. 'One blast of a shotgun in here would do more harm than twenty birds.'

'Ah, but I should have used more subtle means. You see this?'

For the first time I looked at his weapon. It consisted of a thin tube made apparently from some whitish-grey wood and bound at intervals along its barrel with rings of desiccated fibre. One orifice sloped down to a mouthpiece like that of a fife, with a cut-away underpart for the lip; the other was slightly flared out in the style of a trumpet.

'Blow-pipe,' said Cedric. 'As used by the aborigines of South America.'

'You mean you'd simply have blown that pigeon out of the room?' said Deirdre (playing up, perhaps).

'I don't know what young people learn nowadays,' said Cedric, 'for all the money spent on their education. No, my dear, the blow-pipe is designed to shoot small parts dipped in poison. Look! I took the precaution of detaching these.'

He held up a narrow gourd on a string which I imagine had originally been hung round the stem of the pipe. From it he took out two or three slender shafts of wood, about six inches long, and we all gathered round to inspect them more closely. The butts were swollen with blobs of pith designed to ensure an airlock against the mouthpiece; at the other end a sharp thorn had been cemented on and its point was glazed with a film of gummy substance.

Pointing gingerly at the tip, Cedric said:

'Now I wonder how many of you have heard of curare . . .'

He elaborated on its deadly properties. It should have been interesting, for his facts were more or less correct, but the patronage of his manner made the lecture a torment. Moreover, I realized from his exceptional burst of *bonhomie* that the triumph over the pigeon counted in his eyes as a major victory.

'Excuse me,' I said, playing the young pedant, 'but surely the stuff would be pretty useless after years of keeping?'

'It is an exception in that way,' said Cedric, adding with a horrible roguishness, 'Wherein, my dear David, may we hope that it resembles your own qualities!'

I said stubbornly, 'Anyhow, I doubt whether a light dart would go through a pigeon's feathers. They'll even turn shot at a distance.'

'My dear boy,' replied Cedric with a gratifying testiness, 'you evidently know nothing about the power of these blow-guns. Now just stand aside everyone and I'll show you.'

He slipped a dart down the barrel of the tube, then indicated as his target the fold of a thick baize cloth which hung over one of the cabinets. But before he could lift the weapon to his mouth he was interrupted. Turpin, who was looking out of the window, said in a voice of sepulchral idiocy, 'Excuse me, sir, but the brute creation is again misbe'aving.'

Cedric lowered the pipe and, with the rest of us, directed his gaze down into the garden. A large ginger cat had climbed on to the tea-table and was making free with the food.

'Damn it,' said Cedric, 'those cups are best Staffordshire. Get off, get off with you!'

But the cat remained impervious to shouts and imprecations. It looked as if nothing less than our return to the garden would dislodge it; until Turpin discovered among the exhibits a rattle used in Polynesian religious ceremonies. Its din seemed to scalp the cat's nerves, for it fled as though pursued by a mastiff.

'Would you have shot the cat with the blow-gun, Daddy?' said Deirdre innocently.

'A gentleman doesn't shoot cats,' replied Cedric severely.

'Besides,' said Deirdre, 'it would be difficult to hit it at that range.'

Since her father showed no sign of resuming his demonstration, she had picked up the blow-gun and was testing its balance. Although its length was greater than that of her body she had no difficulty in handling it because of the lightness of the wood. She raised the mouthpiece idly to her lips—and then she must have given a tentative puff.

Afterwards I made experiments. I can only say that without them I should never have believed how small an effort would send the charge streaking over twenty yards. There must have been some secret in the construction which concentrated the force of the lightest breath.

The dart shot out in the direction of the door, just as Varvara, who had drifted away from the group, decided to leave the room. For a moment it seemed to have struck her squarely, high up in the nape of the neck. Then I saw that it was touch-and-go whether it had penetrated the mass of hair which she now wore curled back at the base of her skull.

The thing which made me hope for the best was the slowness of her reaction, which was not that of a person who had been hurt, even mildly. Groping, she raised a hand to the back of her head.

'Leave that thing alone,' I shouted.

I ran up to her and made her bend her head. Very carefully I plucked out the dart. Then I parted the hair so that I could see the scalp between the strong tawny hairs. I could not discover any sign of a wound, but it was difficult to be certain owing to the darkening of the skin round the roots.

'Looks as if it's all right,' I said cautiously.

To do him justice, Cedric appeared to be more shaken than anybody else. I wondered why. Then it struck me that some of the most disconcerting moments in life are when chance reveals to us our subconscious wishes.

He turned on Deirdre and started to berate her savagely for her carelessness. Somehow—perhaps from sentimental ideas of chivalry—I expected Varvara once more to intervene in her cousin's favour. I little understood how her mind was working.

She was still so silent and subdued that I thought she might be suffering from shock at her narrow escape. But suddenly she came to life. Taking advantage of a pause in Cedric's tirade, she strode up to him, her face hard with anger.

'You would have done better to take the blood on your own hands,' she said. 'It costs no more in the eye of God, and the performance would have been more certain.'

Cedric gave her a look which was either a fine bit of acting or reflected a genuine bewilderment.

'There,' he said, 'there. No wonder you're upset. We must get Nurse Fillis to have a look at your head and make sure there's really no damage.'

Varvara said: 'You tried once with your daughter, and now you want a second chance through your whore!'

Cedric still affected not to understand, but Deirdre burst into a wail like a siren.

Throughout dinner, to which I made little social contribution, I was balancing up the possibilities. I knew that I was shortly going to be involved in an argument with Varvara in which accusations of idiocy, disloyalty, and complicity in murder would be flying about like hail. It would be well to have my reasons ready. The more I considered the facts, the more firmly I was convinced of the rightness of my first assumption. The episode of the blow-gun had been a pure accident.

Mrs. Ellison, to whom nobody had mentioned the incident, sat up later than usual that evening. No sooner had she gone to bed than Varvara made for her own room, indicating clearly that she expected me to follow.

I had scarcely taken up my usual seat on the bed when the indignation which was seething inside her burst forth.

'You have deceived me,' she said.

'Me!' I said.

'You told me many times that England is not like Doljuk. "Here", you said, "they do not plot to kill. You only think these things because you are a savage."'

I sighed. It was exactly as I had feared. Varvara had the sort of fierce, medieval suspiciousness which made it impossible for our ancestors to believe that people just unaccountably died: no, there had to have been a witch at work.

'I have not changed my mind,' I said. 'What happened this afternoon wasn't planned. It was just the carelessness of a schoolgirl.'

'You fool!' said Varvara. 'That is how my uncle meant you to think. Also the judges if I had died. Did you not once tell me that here they will not execute people of less than eighteen?'

There was, I think, a faint tinge of authentic paranoia in her make-up. It came out in the awful ingenuity with which she could sweep up undoubted facts and marshal them to support some crazy theory.

Although I had not much faith in the power of reason, I carefully went through the main points which seemed to me to show that there could have been no design on Cedric's part.

First, the occasion for going to the museum had not been engineered by him. The pigeon had been responsible, and not even Varvara could suppose that the birds were in his pay.

Second, it was absolutely contrary to what we knew of the relationship between him and his daughter to suppose that he would make her his agent for murder; he scarcely trusted her to do up her own shoelaces. Nor did her private behaviour suggest that she was a devoted child, willing to pull his chestnuts out of the fire; she was far more likely to blab.

Third, I did not believe that if the dart had entered Varvara's scalp she would necessarily have died. I believe it is true that curare keeps its strength far longer than most vegetable poisons. All the same Cedric grossly exaggerated its longevity. The impregnated dart had been lying about for years, exposed to air and dust. Subsequent expert advice confirms that at most it was only likely to make a healthy girl uncomfortably ill.

On the last point, of course, it could probably well be replied that Cedric did not realize that the method he employed was chemically inefficient. In general the force of my arguments was diminished by the fact that I could not honestly pretend that I thought him to be incapable of murder. The best I could say was that on the particular facts of the case I acquitted him.

'You talk about the difference between Doljuk and England,' I wound up. 'But I don't believe that even in Doljuk people go about trying to slaughter each other by these fantastic tricks.'

Alas, I should have stuck to what I knew. Varvara was ready for me with chapter and verse from the endless chronicle of Turkestanian barbarity.

'Ishak Toghrul tied a mule's rein round his brother's neck and whipped it up so that it strangled him. Fatima Meng, the wife of the apricot-seller, pushed her husband's concubine down a well on account of the jewellery. Stefan Yefrimovitch Hamin, the refugee from Russia, took a hot iron—'

'Stop,' I said. 'Please, stop. Perhaps Doljuk is everything that you say. The point is that, whatever you believe about your uncle, you've got to keep your mouth shut. Otherwise you'll be playing into his hands.'

'How?'

'If you make a public accusation against him, he can take legal steps to restrain you. And they'll be successful. In England people just won't believe such charges against wealthy and influential citizens.'

'Would not the police?'

'They'd be more concerned to protect him than you.'

'Then,' said Varvara solemnly, 'I must make my own law and pass my own judgment.'

As I left her room the thing happened which I had long been fearing. I put out my hand for the electric switch, but before I touched it there was the sound of a door shutting and the light sprang up from the other end of the landing. Nurse Fillis came towards me from the lavatory.

As we drew abreast, she stopped and stared.

'Well, Mr. Lindley . . .' she said meaningly.

'Good night, Nurse.'

'I saw where you came from.'

'Really?'

'It was out of Miss Ellison's room. You can't fool me.'

'Even if there was anything to fool you about, I shouldn't trouble. You see, I know you wouldn't throw stones.'

Nurse Fillis's face darkened with embarrassment and anger. 'What do you mean?'

'Only that you also have your tender moments.'

'Blackmail won't get you anywhere.'

'So long as that's realized on both sides . . .'

It occurred to me that it might be better to drop the irony and end the scene on a bluffer note, showing how lightly I regarded the whole incident.

'Run along,' I said, 'if you want to get down those stairs in one piece.'

Her room was on the floor below. I merely meant that the time switch would again shortly plunge us into darkness. But when I saw the alarm on her face and the way she scurried off I realized that she had put a different interpretation on my words. At the time I was amused.

10

At the period of which I am writing, it was unusual for rich people to spend August in London, unless, like Mrs. Ellison, they were not fit to travel. Andrew was not a positive exception to this rule: he merely interpreted it to suit his own essentially urban nature. From Monday to Friday morning he was at his father's flat in Park Lane: but over the long weekend he went down to a village near Henley where he shared a bungalow with several friends.

I knew quite a lot about this resort, since it had often figured in the world-weary conversations at Cambridge with which he broke his ascent to the rooms above mine. So many of the things about which he would issue languid warnings seemed to happen there. It must have been quite a big place, for I never exhausted the list of Andrew's co-tenants—though this was no doubt partly due to the rapidity with which they changed. I had a confused impression of numerous young women guests changing partners, as in a ballet, to the accompaniment of a cricket-like noise of bickering.

Nurse Fillis and I were unexpectedly alone at lunch on the last Saturday in August.

'I'm afraid it's going to be rather a disappointing weekend for you, Mr. Lindley,' she said roguishly.

'Oh? Why?'

'Well, you won't like being alone, will you? Or perhaps you will, though I don't suppose you dare admit it!'

'I'm afraid you're being too deep for me again.'

'Miss Ellison's taken herself off.' She paused significantly. 'For the night. But I expect you knew.'

'I didn't, as it happens.'

'She has her grandmother's permission. I'm sure I hope the old lady knew what she was doing.' Another dramatic pause. 'An awfully nice-looking young fellow called for her in a great big red car. . . . It looked as if you could almost lie down in the back.'

'Never mind,' I said. 'We shall have to console each other.'

I could see her toying for a moment with the notion that I meant it. Then experience led her to conclude, quite rightly, that this was only another example of my trivial irony.

'It's a funny thing about me, but I only like men much older than myself. I don't know what it is . . .'

'Gerontophilia.'

'Pardon?'

'That's what it is. Look it up in the text-books next time you go to a dance at the Hunterian Museum.'

So another skirmish ended in open dudgeon.

Nevertheless Nurse Fillis had scored her point—or rather two points. I did not like the idea of Varvara staying at Andrew's riparian monkey-house; nor did I believe that Mrs. Ellison would have allowed her to do so, if she had had any notion what kind of things went on there. She belonged to the age of the chaperone—a role which, so far as it existed in Andrew's circle, tended to be taken over by any girl who had temporarily chased herself off the *champs d'amour* with a gin-bottle.

Varvara, I learnt, had said that she would be back in time for dinner on Sunday. But ten o'clock had struck before she reappeared—and then her lateness was the least of the things which needed explanation. She had a large black eye, and her frock had been ripped across on one side from the V of the neck to the armhole, and was held together only by safety-pins.

The car which brought her back was certainly not the luxurious sin-chariot of Nurse Fillis's description. It was a battered old Ford driven by a strange man in dungarees. In it also rode Andrew. He came up the steps with Varvara, limping heavily. As soon as the door was opened and he saw me standing in the hall, he said in a petulant voice:

'All right, David, all right. I know! But before you say your piece, do you mind if I just staunch some of this blood, and wash off the spilt brains?'

In addition to the foot injury he had a long strip of sticking plaster across his right temple.

I turned to Varvara. 'We had an accident,' she explained. 'Near Slough two lorries driven by Bolsheviks would not come apart for us.'

A few further questions elicited that they had tried to pass one big commercial vehicle whilst another was approaching from the opposite direction. The main road was in those days dangerously narrow and they had torn off the front wing of their Bugatti against the oncoming van. Then they had skidded and fetched up with a smart bang against a suburban tree.

Considering what might have happened they had got off very lightly. Both Varvara's and Andrew's injuries were superficial; although she had ripped her dress whilst being catapulted out through a broken door. Apparently the third passenger had not been damaged at all.

'By the way, who was that?'

'He is a Count,' replied Varvara. 'A friend of Andrew's.'

Andrew emerged from the cloakroom and went out to pay the garage man who had brought them home. Rejoining us in the hall, he addressed Varvara:

'You'd better go and put some raw steak on that eye if you want it to be presentable for Molly Saxby's party.'

When she was out of earshot I said:

'So the great Tino let you in for this?'

'Not entirely.'

Constantine Omolgon, styling himself Count, was an undergraduate at Cambridge, though rather older than most. He was a Phanariote Greek who claimed that his family title dated back to the days of the Byzantine Empire. Omolgon, he would explain, came from a Greek word which means 'he who confesses'; and an ancestor had been so called because, when captured by heathens, he 'confessed', or refused to deny, his religion and his emperor. For this, in Constantine's own arch phraseology, he was deprived of a great part of his happiness. Many people thought it was a pity that his misfortune occurred only after he had begotten an heir.

I could never understand why Andrew made friends with a man whose faults were a parody of his own. Omolgon cultivated an exaggerated worldliness and knowledgeability and he also had a great reputation for courtly gallantry in the Latin style—which, I'm afraid, always reminds me of a monkey with its top half dressed in satins but the basic ape peeping out below.

Outside the boudoir his favourite amusement was driving sports cars at reckless speeds. I knew for a fact that he had been involved in several accidents during the past two years. Hence my surprise at Andrew's partial disclaimer.

' "Not entirely"? Do you mean the lorry-man was to blame?'

'No,' said Andrew, 'but Tino wasn't in charge. He merely made a rather ill-judged grab for the brake at a crucial moment. Otherwise I think we should have got through.'

'Were you driving?'

'No.'

'Then ... my God! ...'

'It's all right,' said Andrew. 'I bought her a licence the other day. She's really amazingly good, if you could only make her take her foot off the accelerator. Tino thinks she'll end at Brooklands.'

'Brookwood you mean—in the cemetery! Honestly, Andrew, I realized you were pretty callous, but I'd have thought you'd hesitate before putting an exhibitionist girl with a bullock-cart-and-pony background at the wheel of a racing car. And on a main road!'

'I gave her lessons,' said Andrew sheepishly. 'She seemed to be getting on so well.'

'Couldn't you damn well see that if you drove at seventy-five miles an hour it would be a point of honour with Varvara to touch eighty?'

'Anyway,' said Andrew, 'no serious harm's done. It's just a matter between me and my insurance.'

'That won't wash. How am I to know you won't succeed in killing her next time? It so happens that I really mind about Varvara.'

'So do I, old boy.'

I noted with a wry pleasure that even in my own ears (which were apt to be hypercritical on such occasions) my protestation rang with the greater fervour. In it was the inimitable note of calf-love; whereas Andrew could not help sounding like an amiable veal-butcher.

I took him into the dining-room and gave him several large glasses of claret and soda. Unfortunately drink again raised my moral blood-pressure.

'And that damned bogus Count! Do you honestly think he's the sort of person to unleash on a girl who's come practically out of an Asiatic purdah?'

'She showed every sign of being able to cope. In fact we had a laugh about the way she capped Tino's pet build-up.'

'How do you mean?'

'Well, you know he tends to go on about the glories of the Omolgon family.'

'Do I not!'

'Just when we were all getting a bit sick of it, Varvara casually mentioned that her father had been made a prince.'

'A prince! She said that?'

'Perhaps she hadn't told you, old boy,' said Andrew, 'but

apparently the locals gave him a handle which adds up to roughly that. Of course it was only a wog title, but still . . .'

'This,' I said in a voice trembling with moral rectitude, 'has got to be stopped.'

Andrew sighed and put down his glass. For a moment I comprehended that beneath all the pretension and the 'games-manship' he was genuinely a person who had matured much younger than the average; and one who had already enjoyed certain glimpses of the obvious, from which I was still sepa-rated by a decade.

'God forbid,' he said, 'that we should start swapping home-truths. I don't feel equal to it. But you ought to watch out, David. When you find something the way you like it you want to keep it on ice, just so, for ever. That doesn't work with people. They can't help moving on. Varvara is moving on. She's come into a new world, as you're so fond of pointing out, and she's a stranger in it. But she doesn't bloody well want to stay strange. She's out to make her number, to be a roaring success. If you try to freeze her as your pet Chinese curio, just one thing will happen.'

'What?' I asked in spite of myself.

'She'll move on,' said Andrew briefly. 'Of course that may happen in any case. Good night.'

My indignation was still hot when I next saw Varvara.

'Greeting, your Royal Highness.'

'It was a joke.'

'I wonder! In any case you shouldn't play jokes until you can gauge their effect.'

'It is true,' she said, shifting her ground, 'that my father was titled by the citizens of Doljuk.'

'I know. They made him an *aksakal*, the equivalent of a town councillor. Princess, indeed! I suppose you thought you were improving your social status, but here the only people who tell that sort of lie are lunatics and broken-down night-club tarts with a White Russian background.'

I spoke even more savagely than usual in our quarrels. I was sincerely shocked not by romantic lies told for self-

aggrandizement, but by the fact that in stooping to this particular vice she seemed to have betrayed so many of the foundations
of her character—the directness, the self-sufficiency, the readi-
ness to face the world alone. She had put herself in the position of pleading for Andrew's friends to honour her with their
approval.

She must have felt some justice in my rebuke, for she did not
retaliate in her normal spirited fashion. She said nothing. The
effect was rather disconcerting: it left my outburst suspended
in mid-air. In order to re-establish contact on the normal plane
I asked her some question about the tenure of office by the
aksakals in Doljuk and their powers.

'Doljuk!' she said, not angry, but mocking. 'Doljuk! Always
Doljuk! Soon, as you go on learning and I begin to forget, it will
become your city more than mine, and I shall be questioning
you about it.'

'I've no wish to steal your legitimate thunder,' I said.

Varvara replied: 'I shall not judge against you for it, David.
You are happier when you can receive a piece of your life from
books or the mouth of another. It is so much easier to be the
master of events when they are set before you as stiff and cold
as corpses.'

She smiled at me with friendly malice. We were equal again.

I was on my way down to spend part of a wet afternoon in
Turpin's pantry when I heard him below me ushering somebody into the hall. A few moments later I was passed on the
stairs by a small, grey-haired man, wearing a monocle. He gave
me a smile but went on without speaking. When I reached the
pantry I inquired about the visitor.

'Mr. Pyne,' said Turpin gloomily. 'Lawyer. "'Ow now thou
secret black and midnight 'ag?"'

This was not a fair description. Mr. Pyne came again next day
and whilst he was waiting in the morning-room we talked for a
while. He struck me as a sensible, balanced man, and learning
that I meant to enter his profession, he threw off some *obiter
dicta* about it which remain in my mind as valuable advice.

By himself I would have relied on him to give Mrs. Ellison honest and equitable guidance. But doubts crept in when he let slip that his visit had been timed to coincide with one from Uncle Cedric. It might be too much to expect him to oppose an enormously valuable client in a matter of whose rights and wrongs he could not be sure.

Presumably he had come about Mrs. Ellison's will. In theory he might be required to make some alteration in Varvara's favour; but unhappily the opposite seemed more probable— if only because of the indications that Cedric welcomed his appearance. It looked as if the long campaign of attrition had at last succeeded.

Varvara, needless to say, had spontaneously arrived at the same conclusion. The natural prompting of her mind told her that any move was for the worse. Again I had a tremendous battle to prevent her from going to her grandmother and demanding the right to state her case. I knew from my own experience that, however justifiable such conduct, it would simply outrage Mrs. Ellison.

With the soft approach of night she became more reconciled to her injuries and even began to enjoy their pathetic flavour. As we sat on her bed drinking a bottle of white wine provided by Turpin, she said:

'Soon my grandmother will die, and I shall be left alone in this country. I shall starve.'

'Nonsense.'

'Perhaps—but only because I shall go on the streets first.' She repeated the phrase with relish, adding: 'In my good new clothes. My grandmother's ghost will come up behind me, grieving and repenting in the cold.'

'And interfering considerably with business, I should think.'

She threw one of the pillows at me. Then reluctantly she began to laugh. Her self-pity did not go very deep; it sprang from a liking for drama rather than a genuine introversion of the heart.

Whatever the reasons for Mr. Pyne's visits, I had scarcely

expected a third. Probably, however, the will was only one of many matters affecting Mrs. Ellison's vast estate which intermittently needed legal attention.

In his quiet way the solicitor had impressed me as a man who would not be put on. Cedric had been very late for the previous meeting. Accordingly I was not much surprised when at three o'clock I found him tramping up and down the morning-room, looking at his watch.

'Damn fellow!' he muttered. 'I told him quarter to.'

'I dare say he's been held up by some other business.'

'In that case,' said Cedric unpleasantly, 'perhaps I ought to consider freeing him from any trivial commissions that I can put into his hands. Do you know what my father used to say?' He quoted: ' "Never let an attorney forget that he may drive the coach, but the master's the man who sits inside." '

Old Joe's epigram seemed to have the rapier-like point of a tent-peg.

'Very crisp,' I said politely.

'I forgot, though,' said Cedric. 'You're going into that walk yourself. I trust you'll take the hint.'

He started out meaning to be nasty. But in mid-process a different idea visibly occurred to him. It was an awful demonstration of the involuntary transparency with which a just Providence had afflicted him. A smile formed on his lips and into his light-grey eyes came an expression of supernatural sincerity. He took off his tortoiseshell glasses and pointed them at me with the friendly, compelling gesture which one sees in advertisements. 'But after all,' he said, 'isn't it better that a young man should face the disadvantages of his chosen profession?'

'I don't want to go into the Law with any illusions,' I replied cautiously.

'Well then . . . frankly I should say a person of your independence and spirit, David, would find it a little trying to be always acting as . . . a, well, frankly, a professional lackey.'

I wondered whether the same applied, frankly, to doctors, actuaries, and chartered accountants.

'Because,' Cedric went on, with a glance of whimsical apology, 'I'm afraid that's how we people in a substantial way of business tend to regard our legal advisers.'

I was fascinated. I wondered very much where all this was going. That it had some preconceived goal I did not doubt. It was part of Cedric's peculiar misfortune that when he warily led up to a subject you could hear him clocking-in at each intermediate stage on the march.

'Of course,' he said, 'that attitude wouldn't apply to anybody with a legal training who happened also to be an executive of the firm. Oh, no. In my own business, for instance, I have a couple of chaps who took Law degrees, and I can't think of any of my staff for whom I have more liking and respect. I could use another of their type—to follow on behind, so to speak, because they'll both shortly be moving up to seats on the Board —where, if we're going to be vulgar, I rather suspect that their monthly cheques will look like a year's reward to a partner in some pettifogging solicitor's office.'

He intensified his stare, as if to rub in the already blatant implication. I was at a loss. I never entertained the idea that he seriously meant to give me a job in his organization; and if he had, I should not have accepted it. What I failed to understand was why he saddled himself with an offer which he would subsequently have the trouble of evading.

For reasons which will presently become clear, I still do not know the answer. I think, however, that his strangely insensitive character made him more prone than most people to employ routine gambits; it may have been his policy, when one of his enterprises was at a critical point, to conciliate any possible opposition, however unlikely it was to upset his plans. It is not inconceivable that, by some kindly reference, his mother had given him the idea that I had a little influence with her; and until he had clinched his machinations, he was not taking the smallest chance.

Foreseeing embarrassment if this conversation continued, I told him that he had given me a great deal to think about and then made an excuse to leave. I was going upstairs to my bedroom to fetch a book when I passed Varvara on the stairs. One glance showed me that her wrongs were again rampant in her mind. She was scowling all over her beautiful fierce face, and her lips were moving in a subdued mutter. Her eyes flicked over me without any lightening of expression. Unfortunately I was seized with an absurd sense of guilt. I felt that perhaps I had been disloyal in temporizing, however insincerely, with Cedric's offer. But for this I should probably have warned her that her uncle was in the morning-room. Yet I thought nothing of it when I heard her turn in at the door.

From time to time in my profession I am called on to advise or defend persons who are actually innocent of the offences with which they are charged. In these cases the main difficulty is usually to disinfect random acts of some guilty purpose. 'Why,' say the police, 'did you walk home that way, Mr. Smith? It's not your normal route and it's three hundred yards longer.' 'I don't know,' replies Mr. Smith sheepishly. 'I did it on impulse.' Despite the sceptical smiles with which this is received, it is quite possible that he is telling the truth. It ought to be widely recognized how many times a day the ordinary man exercises choices which have no basis in reason.

On fine afternoons when she did not go out Varvara generally sat on the lawn. That day the weather was excellent. Yet she chose the morning-room—and I do not think that she could ever explain why.

On reaching my room, I thought I would write a letter. I had been at this task for about twenty minutes when I heard a strange wheezing noise come up the stairs. Then my door rattled violently as someone tried to open it in the wrong direction. I got up and turned the handle from the inside.

Before me stood Turpin, or rather a disintegrated parody of him. He was too old and too fond of the bottle to run up three long flights with impunity. His breath went huck-a-huck-a-huck like a motor on a cold morning. The genial rosy varnish of his face, which was produced by a nice blending of white flesh and purple veins, had broken up starkly into its separate components. The dark worms across his cheeks looked like hæmorrhages below the skin.

'Good God!' I said. 'What's the matter?'

He could not answer at first. I dragged him into the room and put an easy chair beneath him. After a few seconds he recovered sufficiently to speak.

'It's Mr. Cedric . . . I was sitting in my pantry when suddenly there's a noise like a big bird squawking . . . and then another, like someone 'ad squashed a sack of fruit. I felt the place give a shake and, same time, it got dark. 'Ullo, I said to my budgies, thunder comin' on. . . .' As with many shrewd men, who have not had much education, Turpin's sense of relevance and logical order went to pieces under any violent shock. He tended to dwell on incidentals whilst neglecting the crux. On this occasion it took me several seconds of questioning to extract it.

Cedric Ellison had fallen off the roof-garden two storeys up, and had impaled himself on the area railings just above the pantry window. Turpin had forced himself to approach the victim closely enough to be certain that he was dead.

'I'd better ring the police,' I said. 'You see that all the maids are kept away from any window that overlooks the scene.'

As I spoke it struck me that Mrs. Ellison must be up and about for her appointment with the lawyer. Presumably she was in her boudoir, which looked on to the roadway, but if Mr. Pyne was much later she might come out to make inquiries. However she was ultimately to learn the truth, it must not be at first hand.

I had no faith in Nurse Fillis's ability to weather the news and remain competent. She was too much involved emotionally. On the other hand I saw nothing for it but to risk telling her.

As I pushed into her room I had one of the few flashes of inspiration which have ever visited me. Like most such enlightenments it was very simple. Gabbling out the essentials of the story, I deliberately slurred the title before the name so that it sounded like Miss, rather than Mr., Ellison.

To my relief wishful thinking did the rest. She did not question that it was Varvara who had been overtaken by disaster. White, but speaking quite firmly, she said:

'Certainly Mrs. Ellison must not be allowed to know anything about this at present. I'll go to her immediately.'

(Lest I now seem to be imputing callousness to a woman of whom in other respects I have found little good to say, I would point out that I had minimized the more horrible features of the case.)

Downstairs in the hall I was rapidly put through by the exchange to the nearest police station. The sergeant there was helpful, and promised that he and one of his men would be with us in a few minutes. He also said that he would arrange for a doctor and an ambulance.

'One thing, sir,' he added. 'Don't move the patient.'

'Patient?' I echoed. 'Oh, you mean the body.'

'We prefer people shouldn't draw conclusions until a doctor's been,' he said repressively.

As I finished telephoning I was facing towards the door of the drawing-room. It opened slowly and Varvara came out. I remember wondering what she had been doing in there, for she had often told me how much she hated its atmosphere of tawdry splendour.

Her face was strained and set; so that for a moment I imagined her as sharing my knowledge. Then with a sigh I realized that I must recapitulate the story once again: hoping for my nerves' sake that it would not be received in the spirit of Deborah celebrating Sisera's death.

In fact, Varvara listened with complete impassivity. She did not seem surprised or even particularly interested. But as I made for the door which gave on to the garden at ground-floor level I heard two pairs of footfalls behind me. She was following, as well as Turpin.

'Go back,' I said. 'This will be a ghastly sight.'

Varvara did not reply; nor did she slacken her step. I was not equal to arguing; if she wanted to saddle herself with a recurrent nightmare, well, let her.

As on other occasions when I tried to assert my masculin-

ity over her, the comparison of strength went humiliatingly
against me. I had underrated the revolting quality of the spec-
tacle in the garden. I shall not describe it. I will merely say that
Cedric was a large-bodied man and he had fallen from a considerable height straight across a row of iron stakes with broad
paddle heads like those of Kaffir spears.

I was forthwith sick and, through the scalding tears which
were forced into my eyes, I could hear old Turpin retching
dryly. Varvara however was not overcome—at any rate in
the physical sense. Kneeling on the grass border opposite the
impaled body, she began to pray aloud in Russian. This behaviour neither repelled me as theatrical nor touched me as an
example of spiritual valour; it seemed to me to be purely an
hieratic gesture, belonging to a world with which I had no contact.

The scene was ceasing to be the private property of No. 8.
The houses for some way along the Terrace overlooked each
other's gardens. Now we could see white caps and aprons bob-
bing at the upper windows and on the balconies, and hear a
shrill twittering, interspersed with cries of horror.

The police drove up at almost the same moment as the
doctor who came in an ambulance with two attendants. I
signalized their arrival by another lapse. As I greeted the new-
comers I was shaking with hysterical laughter. However, they
seemed to understand.

My memories of the next hour are confused. Mr. Pyne
made a belated appearance and, though badly shaken, took
charge of the domestic situation. He shepherded Varvara and
myself into the house—very properly, for the manner of Cedric's death had set the authorities a hideous mechanical task.
They had to send for more men and tackle from the hospital in
order to detach his body.

Pyne went upstairs to break the news to Mrs. Ellison, who
must by now have realized that something was amiss.

Varvara and I were left sitting in the dining-room. For half an
hour we scarcely spoke: then she leapt up quivering and slam-
ming her palms on the table.

'Why are you staring at me like that?' she said, her voice rising abruptly. 'Why?'

'I wasn't staring *at* anything.'

I went over meaning to comfort her, but she shied away from me. It seemed that old England had shown her something against which even Doljuk could not proof the nerves.

At last we heard the ambulance drive away. A few minutes later the sergeant came in with his notebook. He was extremely considerate and before he questioned us he repeatedly asked for assurances that we felt equal to the ordeal.

During his short interrogation, Varvara uttered one extraordinarily ill-judged remark. A few days before, in some chance context, I had observed that sensible people did not make important statements to the police in the absence of their lawyers.

'If that solicitor is on our side,' she said, 'perhaps we should fetch him back.'

The sergeant blenched visibly, as if he had been asked for his warrant whilst collecting for a police charity. Nevertheless his questions maintained the same level of perfunctory blandness.

My story was the one which I have already recounted in all its featureless innocence. Varvara deposed that she had entered the morning-room after passing me on the stairs. There she had exchanged a few casual words with her uncle. Then, knowing that he had a business appointment, she had excused herself and continued downstairs. As she left she had seen him walking out onto the roof-garden.

The sergeant said: 'Now, Miss Ellison, did you know of any reason why your uncle should lose his balance?'

Varvara's eyes, never inexpressive, dilated like those of the heroine in a primitive film.

'Why should I?' she countered. The man was taken aback for a second time.

'Families usually know of any little weakness in each other,' he suggested mildly.

'I knew of my uncle's wickedness, but not his weakness,' said Varvara. 'But now that he is dead I forgive him with all my heart.'

He let her go after that, rather thankfully. It was obvious that he did not know what to make of her and an expression of bewilderment verging on suspicion lingered in his eyes. As I saw him to the door I tried to apply a corrective.

'This has completely bowled everyone over,' I said. 'In a way it's harder on Miss Ellison than the rest of us because she's only been in this country a few weeks. I dare say you noticed . . .'

'Ah!' said the sergeant, interrupting. 'A foreigner, eh?'

It seemed that I had done more harm than good. Any allowance which he might make for foreigners was obviously outweighed by his conviction that, like Voltaire's Habbakuk, they were *capable de tout*.

I was retracing my steps across the hall when Turpin came up the back stairs with an immense funereal dignity which showed he had taken several bracers for his morale. He held up his hand to detain me.

' "Nothing in 'is life became 'im like the leaving of it",' he said in a sepulchral tone. 'I don't bloody think!'

When Mrs. Ellison sent for me about nine o'clock I made sure she would tell me that I must make other arrangements for the rest of my vacation. Indeed after a few stammerings of sympathy I volunteered to clear out next day.

'Please do not consider it,' she said. 'Unless you find that this house now distresses you. For myself I would welcome your staying on.'

She had borne up marvellously. Her manner was at its clearest and coolest; there was even a kind of sparkle about it. I had heard that great blows sometimes produced this effect for a short while before the shock of them was fully apprehended.

'I shall need you, David,' she said, adding with a slight catch in her voice, 'now that I no longer have another man about the house.'

'I'll be delighted to do anything I can,' I said. 'Not that it's likely to be much.'

'I shall have to manage things by myself now,' said Mrs. Ellison.

'I'm sure you'll do it excellently.'

'I shall have to manage by myself,' she repeated. 'I shan't have anyone to tell me what I must do about this and that. It's never been so for me. First there was Joseph all the time, and then poor Cedric. . . .'

Her voice tailed away in the contemplation of her future defenceless and unharried state. It was impossible to believe that she found the vision displeasing. A younger and stronger person would have been better able to conceal the fact that she had discovered a compensating aspect of the tragedy.

At the time I was a little shocked and I came to a false conclusion. I thought her attitude meant that, despite their relationship, she could not honestly mourn Cedric. I did not then understand how absurdly low is the human power of concentration and how the most sincere grief is liable to be upset by some involuntary calculation of personal advantage: nor that, so far from being blind, love is often painfully clear-sighted and permits an extraordinary degree of impartial judgment, even about such matters as the value to the world at large of the loved one's continued existence.

Mrs. Ellison gave a faint chuckle.

'Fulk never gave me orders. "Do it your own goddam way, Mother," he'd tell me.'

I had expected that Nurse Fillis would supervise my talk with Mrs. Ellison or at least that she would interrupt it as soon as she thought fit. But in fact I was left to make my own excuses when I saw that the old lady was getting tired. This indifference was so far removed from her usual professional standards that I felt vaguely disturbed. Half-knowing what I would hear, I crossed the vestibule of the invalid's self-contained suite to the room occupied by her nurse. From behind the closed door came the sound of deep laboured breathing which never quite mounted to a sob.

I was seized with pity for this unlucky young woman. She was probably suffering more acutely because she could not even demand recognition of her grief. Besides it is a bitter thing for the survivor of a one-sided passion to know that if the other party could be recalled to momentary consciousness he would not share her sense of loss.

I tapped on the door. After a few moments it was opened by Nurse Fillis. She stood there in her dressing-gown, trying to control her features.

'I'm coming,' she said. 'Just let me get her tablets and the brandy.'

'Mrs. Ellison's all right,' I replied. 'I think it's you who could do with a shot of brandy.'

She must have caught the unfamiliar kindness in my tone, for she dropped her attempt at normality. Her body sagged against the frame of the door.

'You'd better lie down again,' I said.

She went back to the bed, pushing aside the top pillow on which there was a dark patch of moisture. I found the decanter which she kept for Mrs. Ellison's emergencies and poured a tot into her tooth-glass.

'Good night,' I said. 'Try to sleep. You've had a terrible day.'

'Does everyone see it like that?' she asked bitterly.

'Yes, of course. You—you mustn't imagine things.'

I moved to the door, but she called me back.

'Stay for a moment, Mr. Lindley . . . I promise I won't be rude to you.'

'The shoe's generally on the other foot.'

She said: 'I'm not keeping you to swap compliments.' Shock and despair had tautened the loose genteelism of her speech. She went on: 'In spite of what you might think, I've always respected your cleverness and your good education. They stand out a mile.'

'That confirms my worst fears,' I said, in a feeble attempt to raise a smile.

'So I want to ask you something. . . . Do you believe in a future life?'

'I don't know,' I said. 'I'm inclined to think not. But it wouldn't surprise me.'

She accepted this equivocal answer with an ease which made

me suspect that she had already settled the basic hypothesis to her own satisfaction and had still to reach the real object of her inquiry.

'The Christian religion says that we're all miserable sinners,' she said, 'and we shall have to make up for our sins. I've never understood it properly, like my mother and my sister, who're real Church people. . . . But, Mr. Lindley, do you think a person gets credit for his death?'

'Credit?' I repeated blankly.

'You know—if he has a sad, painful sort of death, will it count towards the time he has otherwise to do in . . . purgatory or somewhere?'

I felt another stab of pity. This form of solicitude was new to me and in my eyes it had an absurd pathos like that of a doll's funeral.

'I'm sure it will,' I said. 'That's why saints like to be martyrs.'

She seemed happier and I gave her another brandy to fix her in that state. But it was an over-compensation and made her once more slightly aggressive.

'Why should he have fallen like that?'

'Swimmin' in the 'ead,' I quoted automatically.

'First I've heard.'

'He kept quiet about it,' I replied diplomatically.

'Ah,' said Nurse Fillis, 'but did he keep quiet enough?'

'I don't understand you.'

'The matron I did my training under used to say that a good many patients would still be alive unless their relatives had known what could go wrong with them. It gives people ideas.'

'You're overstrung,' I said.

Though I pooh-poohed her ambiguous yet crude suggestion, it left an uneasiness which followed me upstairs.

My landing was in darkness. As I approached its further end I heard a rustle from behind the curtains which half-covered the recessed window. Then I noticed a fold of lighter-coloured material and a stockinged foot protruding towards me. Varvara was looking out over the sweep of Aynho Terrace in which the street-lighting had just come on. She did not start when I called to her.

'What is it?' I asked softly.

'There!' she hissed, pointing at the other side of the road, directly opposite to our window.

A policeman on his beat had paused beneath one of the lamps and was idly scanning the façades around him.

'I don't see anything odd,' I said.

'Already I am being watched.'

Her whisper vibrated with dismay and dramatic satisfaction.

'What the hell! He can't see into the house.'

She dug her nails into my arm with exasperation.

'To stop me escaping, you fool.'

'Why should you want to escape?'

'You are pretending in order to keep up courage in your heart. The police believe that I have killed my uncle.'

Now that she had expressed her fear I realized that I must have made a considerable subconscious effort to avoid recognizing the grounds for it. They existed; but I could still say with a fair degree of candour:

'Nonsense. They might as well suspect me.'

'That is not unlikely,' said Varvara with conviction.

II

I had hoped that a night's rest would restore their senses of perspective, such as they were, to both Varvara and Nurse Fillis. But in the former at any rate the symptoms of persecution mania seemed to have waxed overnight. Breakfast began in an atmosphere of clotted melodrama.

'Before the police hang me,' she said, 'I shall save my breath to utter a great cry of innocence.'

I had given up trying to convince her that the English police in no way corresponded to the bodyguard of an alien Governor; consequently there did not seem much point in trying to dissociate them from the job of executioners.

'You're the only person in the world who even entertains the idea that you could be connected with your uncle's death. Anybody who accused you would probably be locked up in a looney-bin.'

'They know that he was my enemy.'

'Rot! They know absolutely nothing about the private affairs of your family. Nor want to.'

It was unfortunate that Nurse Fillis should have entered a few minutes later and announced that she had just been answering the telephone; the police had rung up to say that they would be coming round again that afternoon.

'I hope they're not going to ask you a lot of awkward questions,' she said.

I think she had forgotten the transient suspicions which cropped up when her mind was excited by brandy. Her remark did not strike me as carrying any innuendo. But of course her back was scarcely turned before Varvara had fitted her neatly into the Websterian plot.

'She is their agent. She has given information against us.'

'Can't you forget your feuds for a couple of minutes?'

'Why are they coming? Answer me that!'

'Because there's been a fatal accident. In this country inquiries into a death don't mean suspicion of murder. The police are simply out to help the coroner and his jury.'

Varvara changed her tack.

'On the roof edge, even if a man slipped, there is a little wall to stop him. How did it not stop my uncle?'

'Varvara,' I said after a long pause, 'if you go on in this way, you'll soon have me and a lot of other people asking just that question.'

'There you are,' she said, with the splendid obtuseness of a lioness worrying at the jaws of a lion-trap.

'Varvara . . . you don't know any more about Cedric's death than you've told me?'

'I am innocent,' she proclaimed.

'That wasn't exactly what I asked you. But never mind.'

'You are innocent also. But who will believe us?'

'I wish you'd leave me out of your damned fantasies,' I said crossly.

The persistent linking of our fates had begun to jar me. Varvara had a compulsive power which seemed to wax rather than wane with the absurdity of the idea which she was trying to impose.

Possibly I have given the impression that she was in a panic. Far from it. She believed in her peril but she was facing it with a good deal of the joy of battle in her heart.

The police were as good as their word. At three o'clock a party of them arrived: an inspector, a sergeant, and two constables. They asked to be shown on to the roof-garden. Varvara insisted on watching them from the morning-room and I was sticking to her like a shadow for fear that she would drop some disastrous brick.

Thus it happened that I witnessed an experiment which further shook my complacency. The sergeant—not the one who had come on the day of the accident—was a big-boned man, about six feet in height, not fat, but well-covered. First he bound a couple of thick strips of sorbo-rubber round the middle part of his thighs. Then he put on a sort of rough waistcoat of very strong canvas; threaded through it, so as to run round his chest, was a rope, whose ends trailed behind him until the two constables picked them up.

The harnessed man went to the parapet at the edge of the roof-garden, and stood sideways against it. I noticed that the piece of rubber on his thigh just about coincided with the coping.

'O.K.,' said the Inspector. 'Watch out!'

The last words were addressed to the constables and one soon saw why. The big sergeant began leaning gradually out over the drop. The ropes were still slack and it was remarkable what an angle his body could attain without needing their support. But suddenly he gave a shout and the two policemen jerked him back before he could fall.

This procedure was repeated several times from different

positions—with the face to the parapet, backing on to it, and half-turned. Then the experiment entered on a new and more exciting phase. The sergeant retreated a few yards and deliberately put himself into a stagger, so that he struck the parapet whilst still in motion. He was obviously simulating the action of a man who—for one reason or another—had lost his balance.

I wondered whether it was tact and the awareness of our watching eyes that prevented the Inspector from starting his guinea-pig off with a good push.

I must say I developed a respect for that sergeant. Even with his protective leggings it must have been a painful business to hurl oneself repeatedly against a sharp stone edge. Moreover, though the ropes were there to save him, his position would not have been pleasant if the constables had taken up the slack too late and allowed him to fall and dangle with only the dubious support of his canvas belt. But he stuck to his task and was rewarded by success in demonstrating several things to the most casual observer. The first was that a human body stationary by the parapet would not go over unless something happened completely to unsettle its centre of gravity. Secondly, though a man in motion would take the hurdle more easily, he would have to be pretty well out of control to get up sufficient impetus.

There were two obvious ways in which this last condition could be satisfied: a suicidal rush or unexpected violence.

I began to feel more than ever uneasy, and I was only slightly reassured by the bright candid friendliness with which the police took their departure. Surely they could not suspect Varvara when they called her Miss so deferentially and thanked her, as Mrs. Ellison's representative, for putting the roof at their disposal? And yet—and yet—

When we were alone, Varvara did not make any comment on the proceedings, and I thought that perhaps their significance had escaped her. After a while she disappeared. I sat on, however, gloomily pondering the situation and shying away at intervals from my own conclusions.

Presently I heard soft footsteps passing the door on their way downstairs. One of the maids, I thought idly. But after they had reached the landing below there was an irresolute pause. Then they started to come up again with a firmer, louder beat. Now they unmistakably belonged to Varvara. The door opened and she walked in carrying a small suitcase and wearing outdoor clothes.

'I could not do it,' she announced.

'What?'

'Leave you here to be captured.'

'What is this nonsense? And what are you doing with that bag?'

'It holds my clothes and some poison in case I am caught.'

The truth suddenly dawned on me.

'My God, you little imbecile, you're not running away!'

'I am going into hiding,' said Varvara with dignity.

'How long d'you think that would last?'

'Months, perhaps.'

'More like hours! The police would be on your tracks immediately.'

'Once a thief or murderer is outside the city and away in the country nobody troubles about him,' she said stubbornly. 'It is well known.'

It was hard to keep in mind the shortness of her acquaintance with Britain and the gaps in her knowledge of it. Apart from the road to Henley and its environs she knew nothing of the countryside which she seemingly regarded as interfused with great stretches of desolation where outlaws could roam indefinitely. Her geography and her history were both about seven hundred years out of date.

'Listen,' I said. 'You're pushing your head straight into the noose. If there's one thing that could persuade the police to charge you, it's bolting. They're bound to interpret it as an admission of guilt—particularly when you've been warned that you'll be wanted at the inquest.'

The Inspector had given us both this notification before he left.

'They have already made up their minds,' said Varvara. 'The fat one was proving that you cannot fall off our roof without ... help.'

'But you can, Varvara. You must be able to. Because Uncle Cedric did it ... didn't he?'

'Yes,' said Varvara glumly.

In the aggregate I recognized the psychological forces to which she responded. But I was like a layman in an engine-room, confronted by a tangle of anonymous pipes and taps. To-gether they made the machinery go but I had no idea which did precisely what. To me the signs were equally consistent with her having played some part in her uncle's death (I could not believe that she had deliberately killed him); or with a morbid pleasure in the idea of being wrongly accused of a capital crime.

'For God's sake,' I implored her, 'let yourself be guided by somebody who knows the ways of this country!'

'Who?'

I had forgotten that she did not recognize the modest Eng-lish idiom whereby people recommend themselves imperson-ally. Since she did not accept me as filling the bill I was virtually bound to produce an outside arbiter. Apart from other difficul-ties, there were not many persons to whom I would have cared to explain the situation.

'Andrew, for instance,' I said reluctantly.

'Andrew would take me to a safe refuge in his car,' she said.

'Let's see, then.'

'Except that his car is still broken.'

'Never mind. If he agrees with your tactics he can hire a horse.'

The merits of Andrew as a referee grew with reflection. He was a calculator, a man who kept his own head and discouraged other people from losing theirs. He had no use for hysteria or melodramatics.

Alas, Varvara seemed subconsciously to realize this. She would not agree to call him in. Several times she picked up her bag and made for the door. But a wedge of doubt had entered her mind. She was no longer anxious to take the plunge of departure. As she had apparently no goal except some imaginary wilderness, her hesitation was not surprising.

Eventually, rather by the use of prayers than argument, I persuaded her to postpone her flight till next day.

'But what if the police come and seize me tonight?'

'They won't.'

'Why not?'

'Well ... after dark they're too busy catching burglars and assassins.'

'Where?' said Varvara.

In misfortune she had developed an embarrassing vein of scepticism.

'Oh, Limehouse. The Chinese quarter, you know.'

She nodded with satisfied comprehension and I knew that I had gained a respite.

Later that evening it struck me that her refusal did not invalidate my plan of consulting Andrew. I could go by myself. The dangers of the situation were multiplying like yeast in my mind and I longed for support from any quarter.

Andrew's father's flat was furnished in a way which seems to have died out in the nineteen-thirties. And small cause for lamentation. The prominent objects were in an off-centre Second Empire style and all quite useless—cabinets without shelves, console tables with pin-point tops and tabourets too low for a human and too high for a dog. Amongst this blaze of ornamentation the effective articles, those actually intended for use, skulked in corners as if aware of their own inadequacy.

With difficulty I perched myself on a small black satin settee. Andrew stood in front of me, holding a drink, whilst I gave him a résumé of events. It was simplified by the fact that he had seen a paragraph about Cedric's death in one of the papers.

'I wonder you didn't ring up,' I said unthinkingly.

'Why?' he replied with unnecessary vehemence. 'I didn't see that I could do any good. People usually have too many 'phone calls at these times.'

Very true, very just, very considerate. All the same it gave me a chilly feeling that, in time of trouble, Andrew might show remarkable powers of absence.

When I had finished he asked one or two sensible questions. 'What was Ellison's build?'

'Just over six feet and pretty solid. I'd put his weight at about fourteen stone.'

'Could Varvara have thrown a man that size?'

'She's as strong as an ox,' I said gloomily. 'Besides, if you catch anyone unawares . . .'

'Well, my God, David, I'm bound to agree with you. If the daft girl doesn't show up at the inquest—the police *will* get ideas.'

'To my mind it's inconceivable she should imagine that decamping would solve any problems. What does she think she's going to do with the rest of her life? Flit about Sherwood Forest like Maid Marian?'

The slightly smug expression which both Andrew and I were inclined to wear when exhibiting our trophies of confidence came over his face.

'It's ridiculous, I grant you. But not entirely unintelligible— at any rate if one knows the background.'

'What background?'

'When she was five or six, before her father became such a big pot in their God-forsaken town, he and his servants had a dispute with some characters who were either Customs officials whom they mistook for bandits or bandits whom they mistook for Customs officials—I'm not sure which. Anyway, they killed half a dozen of them and it caused a certain amount of sickness on the part of the authorities. So, to escape arrest, the whole household migrated about fifty miles into the desert and camped at some monastery. They stayed there for six months; then they came back, and by that time nobody was interested in a few stale old murders. She thinks it would work out the same in England.'

As usual I was not very pleased when I found somebody else knowing things about Doljuk which I did not. Shifting the subject, I said:

'Well, anyway, you agree that it will be fatal if she runs away?'

'Yes,' said Andrew, but he paused with his head on one side as if he were listening to the echo of his own answer. After an interval he corrected himself: 'I'm not sure that I do.'

'What!' I said, thunderstruck. 'You must be as crazy as she is. She'll—'

'Wait a moment,' he interrupted, 'and give me credit for what I actually said. It's not the running away which will cause the trouble, it's being absent when wanted by the authorities.'

'That sounds to me like a quibble.'

'It isn't, though,' said Andrew, smiling whimsically. 'I'm just pointing out that there's no reason why she shouldn't have the satisfaction of flight provided that we can get her back before she's missed.'

'That's damned likely! Once she takes the bit between her teeth, it'll need a public hue and cry to fetch her home.'

Andrew did not take offence. Indeed he scarcely seemed to hear me, so deeply was he plunged in thought. At intervals he gave me little bulletins on his progress.

'I'm getting it. . . . No, that won't do. . . . What we want is something like ju-jutsu! You let the other party make his own move: then you give a subtle tweak which lands him exactly where you want.'

'Very nice. But what does it mean?'

'A bit of self-sacrifice, old boy, I'm afraid.'

There came into his eyes a warm, human look which augured well for his public relations as a future captain of finance. To me it was faintly alarming.

'Suppose,' he continued, 'you were to say, "All right, clear out, if you're set on it. But you'll need someone to look after you. I'm coming too"?'

'This is me saying it?'

'I can't think who else would,' said Andrew with a regretful shake of his head. 'Besides, didn't you tell me she insisted that the police were after you as well?'

'Damned nonsense!'

'Still, if she does bring them down on her, I shouldn't be surprised if they began to wonder about her associates. Bad luck of course, but it does give you a sort of special stake in the business.'

'O.K.,' I said. 'We both run away. And then?'

'You choose the day before the inquest and some place not too far from London, so that you might be on an ordinary short trip. There you commit an offence—quite a small one, but enough to get you both locked up for the night. Drunk and disorderly would do. Next morning you explain that it's vital you should be back in London for an important inquest. Either you're brought before the magistrate and given a brisk fine or you're let out on bail. Either way you're shipped back to London and Varvara has to give her evidence before the coroner. What do you think of that?'

'I've heard of nothing like it since Harry Tate's mousetrap,' I said. 'It seems just an elaborate way of piling one mess on top of another.'

'That's because you haven't had time to take in the beauty of the scheme,' said Andrew kindly. 'For instance, you may say, "As soon as the girl is out of her cell, she'll be off like a scalded cat". But that's not psychology. When she's really been nabbed once, it won't seem worth while running away. Damn it, it'll probably give her confidence, like playing round a golf course before a competition.'

I felt that in a crazy way he was right—though not quite for the reasons he gave. After the harrowing programme which he had sketched out, it seemed unlikely that anyone would feel equal to trying to escape even from summary execution. My objections began to come down from the general to the particular.

'You suggest we should get drunk or pretend to. Varvara wouldn't play on that.'

'Oh,' said Andrew, 'it'll be enough if you start something. Have you ever known that girl fail to join in any row that's going?'

Again I had to concede him at least half a point.

'Well then ... what about bail? They might not accept our

own recognizances. You don't suggest we should call on poor old Mrs. Ellison?'

'We're all in this,' said Andrew warmly. 'I wouldn't mind coming down and springing the pair of you.'

How far would it be effective? How great would be the cost? These questions kept me awake for most of the night.

About the first, closer thought only strengthened my conviction that Andrew was right. It seemed to be an instance in human affairs when the homœopathic principle of countering one evil with another might pay off. Nothing except shock-treatment would cure Varvara of her stubborn folly.

I accepted these conclusions reluctantly. I foresaw their corollary all too clearly. They required that somebody should not only make an objectionable ass of himself, but also run the risk of being pilloried as a corrupter of innocent girls. Drunk and disorderly, said Andrew light-heartedly. But what if the Press got hold of the case? It would be a trivial one but they had a *penchant* for taking the mike out of college boys. If the authorities at Cambridge learnt that I had been up before the Courts it would do me no good.

Unfortunately, however, I could not pretend that it would be harmful enough to let me cancel the plan with a clear conscience. The damage bulked very small beside an indictment for murder.

My taste for disinterested action was probably rather smaller then than it is now. I suppose I must have been over the borderline of love. But it was not a clear-cut dominant passion and by itself I doubt if it would have swayed me to risk my reputation. More potent than affection for Varvara was an absurd, esoteric sense of loyalty to her dead father. With all his opportunism and amorality Fulk had obviously been a man who would stand by his friends and, if necessary, die with them.

Next day got off to a bad start. Turpin came in at breakfast and announced that there had been yet another call from the police. It was only to say that the inquest had now been defi-

nitely fixed for three o'clock on the morrow. For Varvara it was
a reminder of her obsession. For me it meant that if I intended
to act I must do so immediately.

I cornered her afterwards, when we were alone.

'I hope you've given up the idea of leaving everybody in the
lurch.'

'If I am caught, I shall poison myself before they can torture
me. But I shall leave a letter between my breasts swearing by
God that you are innocent.'

It was as impossible to ignore her repeated threats as those
of a deranged person. Yet Varvara was averagely sane. In her,
false premises gave the same effect as advanced paranoia.
How I cursed myself for the laziness and complacency which
had blinded me until too late to the fact that a few weeks in
Britain had hardly touched her ignorance of Western thought
and customs. It all seemed ludicrous until one made the imagi-
native effort of reversing the positions. If I had been dumped
unprepared in Doljuk, should I have made an appreciably better
estimate of the dangers and impunities?

I took the crucial step.

'Very well, Varvara. I believe you're wrong. But I believe
even more strongly that it would be a mistake for us two to take
different lines. If you go, I go too.'

'Christ reward you, my dear friend!' said Varvara, making
me feel a monster of duplicity. 'Let us start quickly. Where shall
we go?'

The order of her last two remarks was significant. But her
failure to descend to details suited me. It would have been awkward if she had possessed a business-like mind which fixed on
the destination as firmly as the resolve to travel.

I had given some consideration to the choice of altars for
my self-sacrifice. As Andrew had pointed out, we needed a
place from which, when the *débâcle* was complete, it would be
possible to return quickly to London. To this I added the re-
quirement that it should be somewhere where a bit of minor
roistering would not be uncommon or exciting enough to
induce the local paper to dwell on it. I wanted to get away with

a small paragraph at the bottom of a page. This ruled out a number of little towns in Sussex and Hampshire and Surrey. Besides it was essential to the plan that we should be able, if necessary, to point to some reason for being in the locality.

In the upshot I had not been able to think of anywhere more suitable than my old home. Before their death my parents lived at Horrage between Dartford and Gravesend, where my father was a doctor. It was the kind of indeterminate area which we needed. During my childhood it had been a small independent Kentish town. But since then, its two great neighbours had been stretching their tentacles over it and merging it with them in a single urban block. Like most riverside districts it contained a pretty tough element and it had learnt to take the smaller delinquencies in its stride.

'Where shall we go?' repeated Varvara with a trace of impatience.

'What about the Thames Marshes?' I said, trying to make my tone conjure up an illimitable maze of sedge and water.

'Is it wild?' said Varvara.

'Oh, pretty wild, if that's what you're looking for.'

I inwardly excused myself with the plea that there were indeed some stretches of half-flooded meadow and mud-banks just outside the town.

'Perhaps we shall find a hut to live in,' said Varvara more happily.

'Yes. There are quite a lot of huts too. Boarding-huts.' Seeing a look of disappointment and suspicion growing on her face, I hastily added: 'You know, in a small country, when you're running away from the police it's often better to choose somewhere crowded. Here it's easier to lose yourself against the people than the scenery.'

Varvara meditated this for some seconds.

'The English have a nobler character,' she said at length. 'In Doljuk when a wrongdoer hid in the bazaar his fellows would wait till he was asleep and then they would stab him and bring out his body for the reward.'

'What happened if there was no reward?'

'Then the man went on living,' said Varvara, surprised by so obvious a question.

Despite Varvara's impatience, I refused to budge until after lunch, partly because I had no desire to loiter for hours round Horrage until the licensing laws allowed us to set about the task of disgracing ourselves; and partly because the preparations which I thought necessary were not yet complete.

Humanity demanded that some safeguard should be devised for Mrs. Ellison. I had no intention of letting the police know that we had any connection with her. But if she merely discovered that we were both inexplicably absent for the night it would prey on her nerves. Already the delayed action of shock had caught up with her and the doctor was calling twice a day.

I enlisted my old ally, but I dared not tell the truth even to him. Turpin's face was blank as he listened to my explanation that I was taking Varvara to see some friends outside London in order to distract her mind.

'There's something going on in it,' agreed Turpin, 'but I wouldn't have said it was grief for 'er uncle.'

'That's as may be. The point is that the trains back from this place are very irregular. If we were to miss our connection we might decide to stay the night. No one is to worry.'

'Wheels within wheels,' said Turpin.

'I wish I could be sure which way most of them are going round.'

I am afraid that, for once, he was slightly shocked by a suspicion that I was using the disorganization of the household to indulge in a frolic with the Bud. But I knew that I could rely on him.

Later I went out to my bank and drew an uncomfortably large sum. I was toying with the idea that if we could pay an immediate fine in cash we might get away under the old guise of John Smith and Jane Brown.

I had never before realized the appalling number of minor snags which crop up along any trail of deception. For instance, I should not need luggage nor would Varvara; but I could not

tell that to a girl who believed that she might be away for weeks.
Even on the basis of the story which I had told to Turpin, our
two small suitcases added an embarrassing hazard to our joint
exit. And of course, as we stole downstairs, we walked straight
into Nurse Fillis. She gave an audible gasp: then with a convul-
sive effort she screwed her features into a sad, forgiving smile.
It revealed an unexpected degree of charity, but not, I feared,
enough to act as a permanent silencer.

We went by taxi to Charing Cross where we found that
there was half an hour to wait for the next train. The station
bar was still open, so I took Varvara in and we had a couple of
drinks. Although I had no intention of enacting my role literally—indeed it would have been fatal to lose control of my wits
—I doubted whether I should have the nerve to carry out the
programme in cold blood.

Since it was a rather sordid stretch of line, with rolling-stock
to match, I had taken first-class tickets. Even so an interesting
black dust came out of the cushions as we sat down. We shared
the carriage with another couple who appeared strangely out
of their element: an amiable-looking youngish man who might
have been an ex-Guards stockbroker, and a very smartly dressed
girl who turned out to be his wife. It was impossible not to learn
the relationship between them and a number of additional
facts, because they addressed each other with that penetrating
clarity which belongs either to the lowest or the highest circles.
He was, I gathered, a prospective Parliamentary candidate for
one of the riverside constituencies, and he was going down to
speak at some function.

The woman began to stare at Varvara with the same frankness which marked her speech. Nevertheless, of their type,
neither of them struck me as objectionable people. But I was
surprised when they took the opportunity provided by a struggle with a jammed window to get into conversation. Perhaps
they thought that nobody would travel on that line unless he
had local ties which made him a potential voter.

'Goodness, how foul!' said the woman, warding off a large
smut. 'By train, this journey really is the end.'

'It's as bad by car,' said her husband.

'Oh no, darling. That way you get the sights, but not the dirt.' She turned to Varvara with a smile. 'Don't you agree?'

Varvara looked out of the window at a sordid procession of backyards.

'It is as poor as a dunghill,' she said.

The girl blenched slightly, but both of them were more broad-minded or made of sterner stuff than their appearance suggested. The man seemed to think that there might be some political implication in Varvara's remark and tried to improve the occasion.

'I don't say there isn't a lot round here and elsewhere that needs putting right. But it's a great mistake to suppose that the Government is doing nothing. They have their eye on the situation.'

Varvara nodded understandingly.

'No doubt their troops are ready.'

This sabre-slashing approach to economic problems was too much for even the keenest Right Winger.

'Really, I don't think there's any risk of that being necessary.'

His wife, however, either did not believe in criticizing allies for too much zeal or else she realized that they had chosen the wrong subject for a canvass, for she went back to her previous theme about the horrors of rail-travel. 'I dare say you're in the same boat as us—car laid up.'

'Yes,' said Varvara, 'one of our cars is smashed at Maidenhead.'

'Really?' said the man with a slightly satirical smile. 'And the other?'

Varvara thought for a moment.

'We have lent it to a poor trader to carry his merchandise,' she replied magnificently.

The exchanges continued, but less briskly because they were clogged by mystification. Varvara in her present state was probably more baffling to strangers than when she had first arrived in England. Her choice of words and idioms was still touched with eccentricity: but her former gruff, rather alien accent had

been fined down to vanishing-point. This combination, when
superimposed on her unexpected outlook, sometimes made
people wonder whether they were being guyed.

At Horrage we duly got out and left our bags in the cloak-
room. When we had given up our tickets and were walking
across the familiar cobbled forecourt of the station, I said:

'Why the devil did you want to tell them those lies?'

'It was her feet,' said Varvara.

'Her what?'

'They were so small,' said Varvara, looking down at her
own, which were shapely but bore the same relation to the
feet of the girl in the carriage as the fetlock of a Percheron to
that of a first-class hunter. 'Also, she spoke with a very ladylike
voice.'

'One day,' I said unpleasantly, 'you'll know enough not to be
jealous of a pseudo-Mayfair whine.'

These asperities were partly calculated in order to take
Varvara's mind off the fact that, so far as the present vista of
Horrage extended, we might never have left London. There
stretched before us the same sort of dingy street as we had left
sleeping in the sunshine behind the main thoroughfares of Pad-
dington and Bayswater. If Varvara jibbed and began to demand
forests and deserts it might wreck my plan. It was not easy to
find a piece of unoccupied country in that area, nor, having
done so, to create an effective disturbance in it. However, I need
not have worried, for she accepted her surroundings without
demur. The fact was that so many things had recently happened to her within an alien framework that she no longer had
any orientations.

We wandered up the main street which had always been a
dismal succession of suburban chain stores. I automatically
think of it in connection with the sale of innumerable packets
of cheap tea. But behind it, on the north side, were two or three
older streets running one behind the other in parallel with the
Thames. These still retained something of the jaunty, dingy,
junk-shop air which Dickens fastened on another and more
famous riverside town. You could smell the mud on the flats:

its scent, neither seductive nor actively unpleasant, was like that of a trout which has been landed a few hours. The lowest of these roads, the one which actually contained the riparian embankment, was well-known to me: years before it had been one of my favourite walks, partly because it had the reputation of being dangerous to children.

It had a violent camber. On one side some odd little houses were sunk by three or four steps below the level of the road-way. On the other a low wall, broken by little embrasures in which seats were placed, surmounted a bluff or small cliff about twenty feet in height. It is one of the few spots along the flat lower reaches of the Thames where the shore rises at all sharply above the water-level. At some point during the late-Victorian engineering operations which regulated the banks of the Thames a couple of small jetties had been built below the highest point of the bluff. There was a bench immediately overlooking them and giving a further view across the wide dirty expanse of water to some so-called marshes, which were really only a few flooded meadows, bordered with the hulks of derelict barges.

Varvara and I seated ourselves on the bench. It was hot; after the journey and a couple of miles' walk we were a little tired. I thought again of my duty which now coincided happily with my inclinations. Before I left Aynho Terrace I had asked Turpin to put me up a flask of something drinkable. Now I produced it and unscrewed the stopper. With his usual acute instinct Turpin must have realized that I needed the maximum of stimulant in the minimum of space. For his own taste he dealt in wines; gin he once told me—perhaps quoting his old master, the port-loving professor—was a drink only fit for ostlers. But on this occasion he had stifled his aesthetic sense, and mixed the coarse spirit very cunningly with lemon juice and dashes of Mrs. Ellison's expensive liqueurs. After a couple of mouth-fuls the sunlight began to fall with a softer glow over the great drain and the hoot of a passing tug evoked the image of foreign ports.

'Have some?' I said to Varvara.

'No.'

'I thought it might be a good idea if we had a few drinks this evening. It would relax us.'

Varvara did not see it: she was both young enough and temperamentally robust enough to prefer staying tense.

After an interval she said in an unexpectedly sentimental tone:

'This is very sad for you, David.'

'What is?'

'That you should be ruined in your life.'

'How's that?' I asked, carelessly allowing my role to slip.

'Now that you have run away with me there will be a great scandal on account not only of murder but also morals.' There was a pause whilst I took in the subtle distinction; then she continued: 'Do not think that I shall be ungrateful.'

'Oh, no,' I said reassuringly. 'I wouldn't think that.'

Varvara appeared slightly huffed, as if I had taken too much for granted.

'Tonight,' she said, 'I shall grant you my supreme favours.'

I yelped with involuntary agony.

'Good God, where do you pick up language like that?'

'In a book. One that came from my grandmother's library.'

'Well, it contains all the essentials of bad taste—archness, genteelism, and imprecision.'

'Tonight,' said Varvara, 'you shall have a cut off the joint.'

'Now we've moved down from My Ladye's Bower to the *palais de danse*. May I ask where that bit of your repertoire came from?'

'A friend of Andrew's says it.'

'Suppose we stop talking this nonsense and go for another walk.'

I thought she might start worrying about a room for the night. But she did not seem to care if the joints and favours were granted under the sky. We strolled about half a mile towards the outskirts of the town where my former home was situated. The building looked even less distinguished than in the eye of memory, but the garden had not suffered the customary shrink-

age. It was still big and untidy and surrounded by wild shrub-
beries.

Varvara said: 'We can hide there from the policemen.'

I sighed. 'My dear, what on earth is going to happen to you?
In the end, I mean?'

Varvara replied: 'I shall become important.'

'What makes you think that?'

'In this country,' said Varvara, 'I do not know my fanny from
my finger-tips—as you are always telling me.' (I must disclaim
the phraseology which presumably came from the same source
as her previous remark.) 'But wherever I am I shall always know
better than you how to advance myself in the world.'

I sighed again. It would be a bad day when the granddaughter of Joseph Ellison, the go-getter, finally drove out my Noble
Savage.

We wandered back by the way we had come, except that this
time our course took us into the topmost of the three small
roads which separated the main street from the river. Though
it was chiefly residential it had a pleasant humble brown-faced
little pub in it. Since it was after half-past five, and Turpin's cocktail had gone, with all but a memory of its 'lift', I turned in and
soon we were drinking mugs of Kentish cider. It was last year's
and pretty near the end of the barrel which is said to make it
more intoxicating.

Varvara was not very interested in drink. She had lived in a
rabid Sunnite community where, for Moslems, the Prophet's
ban on alcohol was rigidly enforced. Nevertheless, I gather
that there was plenty of liquor about for those who wanted it:
certainly her father, when in the mood, did not go short. The
trouble was—and this tends to be true of any product which is
manufactured in defiance of popular opinion—that the quality
was execrable, more fitted for the bottom of a petrol-can than a
young girl's stomach.

Still, she had no prejudices. And she possessed the kind of
'good head' which is often associated with a generous capacity elsewhere. She was thirsty and down it went by halves to
my full pints. I was keeping control of the situation until pub-

freemasonry set in and we became involved with the regular customers. They consisted chiefly of men who earned their living in the warehouses by the waterside, with a sprinkling of mechanics and small shopkeepers. I woke up from a long session of dirty stories to see her far away on the other side of the bar surrounded by a different group. She was sitting on the counter with her hat on the back of her head, singing in the Turki language.

A man next to me nodded knowingly.

'Belge, I'd say. 'Ot—I seen 'em in Ostend.'

My action in running her out of the place was not popular. Many doubts were expressed about my parentage and virility. But eventually we broke free. All the way up the street Varvara reproached me in ringing tones for my infirmity of purpose.

'You have taken me from among the servants of God,' she cried. 'I knew them and they were as pure as apricots!'

I gritted my teeth but did not answer. I had begun to realize how much more I had bitten off than I could chew. Now that it loomed over me the climax of my plan seemed quite impossible. Not just dangerous, but so utterly foreign to my nature that I could never execute it. I should almost certainly have thrown in my hand, if chance had not thrust the means of law-breaking across my path.

We had turned back towards the river and were traversing the street below the one which contained the pub. Here a part of the roadway was up for repairs. Just beyond the fenced-off cavity, a few bicycles with crates in front were leaning against the kerb outside a shop: I suppose they belonged to delivery-boys. But the significant factor was the presence of a policeman marching slowly up the opposite pavement. I was overcome by this hint from the auspices.

As we passed the first bicycle I casually pushed it over: the constable did not turn. But at the fall of the second he looked round briefly. With his eye still on me, I kicked the third under the handlebars so that it fell with a crash. The officer turned round and began slowly to retrace his steps in our direction.

I felt that I was committed, yet, at the same time, I had not done enough to ensure my object. There was a mild weariness about the policeman's approach which suggested that in Horrage vulgar horseplay with bicycles was too common to earn more than a rebuke. I cast about for something more actively reprehensible. Whilst he was still twenty yards off I took a penny out of my pocket and shied it at the glass of a street-lamp. Rather humiliatingly it missed, but at any rate it showed that I was a serious criminal who would not stop at damaging municipal property.

I was reminded of Varvara by a loud, challenging cry. She had ducked under the roadmakers' barrier and was standing beside a dump of tarred blocks piled up for laying. She had one of them in her hand. Uttering another happy yell of defiance she flung it smartly through the window of a tobacconist.

What did she think she was doing? I don't suppose she had the least idea. For the moment she was a creature not of reason but pure heredity. She was her father happily plunging into the thick of one of his 'damned uproars'.

The constable quickened his pace to a trot. But the next instant he was forced to double up to avoid a couple more of the blocks which Varvara had dispatched straight at his head.

This was getting too serious for me. I had not bargained for assaults on the police. Calling Varvara to follow—I suppose a real gentleman would have made her lead the way—I fled up the street. I had abandoned my plan and I no longer intended to be caught after a mere token flight. I made for the riverside because I remembered that lower down where the embankment ceased there was a series of wharves which had always used to be dotted with timber stacks and dumps of scrap metal. If we could reach that area we might be able to play hide-and-seek until dark came on.

An ominous sound struck my ears. The constable had drawn his whistle out and was blowing it as he ran. The strain of listening for an answering blast made me careless. I was crossing the road towards the seat in the embrasure where we had sat earlier that evening, and I stepped off the kerb before I was ready. Immediately a sharp pain shot through my ankle, turning my run into a series of rapid hops. I glanced round and saw that my pursuer was closer than I had imagined. Indeed whilst I looked he overhauled Varvara on the opposite side of the road but continued after me on the honourable but incorrect assumption that the man must be the chief desperado.

I realized that I could not get away and resistance would only make my case worse. Panting I sank down on the bench overlooking the river. Next moment the policeman's hand was on my shoulder, not roughly, but with a grip that showed he was ready for trouble. He was a big ginger-haired man and his face was covered with the largest and most individually defined beads of sweat which I have ever seen on a human being: they were like marbles.

'I'll come quietly,' I gasped. But these words, spoken honestly for myself, soon took on a treacherous air. Varvara had other ideas. When she approached panting heavily my captor probably thought that she was sportingly putting herself in the bag in order to take her share of the blame. I would not swear but that a faint smile of complacency crossed his face. If so, it was soon wiped off. Slowing to a walk, she came right up to him. Then, without the slightest warning, she advanced her forearm, held like a horizontal bar, under his chin. At the same time she put her leg behind his and pushed. It was simply a variant of a common wrestling throw, but the element of surprise was increased by the fact that one did not associate such aggressive tactics with a woman.

The man let go his hold on me. He went back so quickly that one had the illusion that he had been lifted off the ground. In fact he must have taken a couple of rapid unbalanced steps before he came up against the wall of the embankment. He struck it about the level of his buttocks, his feet flew up, and he toppled over. There was a moment of agonizing silence and then from below there rose an awful squelching noise. To my brain, fevered by one frightful accident, this sound could only indicate the breaking up of the human body. I did not stop to reflect that such consequences were a little too dramatic for a fall of a mere twenty feet.

Varvara and I looked at each other—I appalled, she still flushed with berserk joy. Gingerly I approached the edge and peered over. What I saw gave me a sense of relief so exquisite it almost made the previous anguish worth while.

Between the two small jetties built from hard stone a short stretch of the river-bank had been left in its primeval state. There were perhaps five yards of good Thames-side mud, having a consistency somewhere between those of treacle and suet. By good fortune the constable had landed on this substance. Otherwise he would probably have broken his back or staved in his skull. As it was, he had obviously been winded by the fall. But whilst I watched he began to stir. Slowly he disengaged himself from the clinging slime leaving behind an almost perfect impression of his rear view.

Varvara joined me for a moment. But she wasted no time in gratitude to Providence.

'Run,' she said. 'Or he will catch us again and next time he will know to beware of me.'

That last was a very unfortunate phrase. We both knew it. When we set off again, I had the impression that we were running away from certain parallels and inferences rather than the police.

If there had been any pursuit, my ankle, though not so bad as I had feared, would have undone us. But the constable must have been severely shaken up, and perhaps he had lost his whistle. Our greatest luck was that the road happened to have been empty throughout the incident, otherwise some public-spirited person might have raised a hue and cry.

Even so I realized that if there was any search it would certainly include Horrage station. I pushed Varvara on to the first bus we saw in the High Street. It happened to go to Dartford, from where we got a train almost immediately. I don't think we spoke at all during the journey.

From one point of view my crusade had been an outstanding success. I had set out to confuse the issues and to bamboozle Varvara by folly out of worse folly. Yet I would have foregone this achievement. I would have let her involve herself with the

Law if I could have won back my old certainty that she had nothing to fear except the shadows in her own mind. But that parapet, that policeman, that throw . . . and that uncle. . . .

It was after ten when we arrived back at Aynho Terrace and everybody in the house seemed to have gone to bed. Still avoiding each other's eyes we did likewise.

I lay awake for a long time, examining the rusty underpinning and defective supports of my moral sense. I was not even quite sure that the thing was there at all. Did I recognize wickedness? Well . . . yes, in selected forms, principally mean dealing and gross cruelty. But I did not seem able to accept any crime as heinous, merely because authority had so labelled it, or because of the gravity of its consequences. Murder was a terrible offence. It took away something which could never be replaced. But when it came down to particular cases, who wanted Cedric back?

In the last resort, however, training and the reasoned opinion of humanity had their effect. Without actively blaming Varvara I felt that she had somehow burdened herself . . . not exactly with a load of guilt but with a sort of persistent disability or taint.

At one point I forced myself to envisage the scene on the roof-garden in the hope that I could reduce the charge to manslaughter or pure accident. But it was hard to believe that a push or trip was administered in a high unfenced place with any object but that of throwing the victim off. The only plea which could be readily sustained was a misguided self-defence. There had never been any doubt about the genuineness of her belief that her uncle had tried to kill her.

Eventually I fell into an uneasy sleep; from which I roused up at the first squeak of my door. By the light of the moon which was now shining brightly I saw Varvara enter, statuesque in her dressing-gown. Though we made pretty free with one another's rooms, we never paid visits after we had finally said good night. Something must have happened to make her deviate from this custom. I was suddenly afraid lest I should have to listen to a confession.

'David? Are you awake?'

'What's the matter?'

'There is a ghost trying to get into the house,' said Varvara.

'Whose?'

'That of my uncle, naturally.'

'You're dreaming. Where did you see this thing?'

'I heard it,' she corrected.

'You mean a voice seemed to speak to you?'

'I know what you are thinking, David,' she said sadly. 'But my conscience is silent because it is pure. Besides the ghost has not spoken yet. It is outside sawing through the railings.'

'Why in God's name should it do that?'

'To escape the impalement.'

I suppose my face showed what I thought of this beautiful notion, for she continued: 'If you go to the window you will hear it.'

I did so and became aware that she was not talking nonsense. A faint but insistent noise of a kind not readily identified was rising from below, and as far as I could judge its point of origin was in the garden directly below the flat roof from which Cedric had fallen. It was an odd rasping sound which seemed to change quality from moment to moment without changing volume; now it did indeed resemble somebody working on metal with a file, but then again it would soften to a sort of harsh snoring. Aynho Terrace was quiet at night but it was still uncanny that the noise could reach us so clearly without any cause being visible. Though I was well situated for scanning every yard of the small moonlit garden, I could see nothing to account for it.

'Come on,' I said. 'There's only one way of setting your mind at rest.'

Yawning, I pulled on my trousers. But when I made for the door Varvara hung back. I fear that I was delighted for once to be able to appear as the bold and resourceful male. It was clear that she believed in ghosts: I did not. When I was little I was afraid of large dogs and rude boys with knobbly fists and most of the other things that a real little man should face valiantly. On the other hand I did not mind dark cupboards or empty houses or stories told on winter nights. This, as the annoyed mother of a schoolfellow once pointed out, was due to my innate lack of reverence and sense of the mystery of life.

'I'll tell you what it was when I come back,' I said.

Varvara gritted her teeth and followed. We went down to the back-door which led into the garden at ground level. It had glass panels and whilst I was easing back the bolts I could look through on to the moonlit gravel and grass. Except for a few small patches of shadow the visibility was excellent. And still out of nowhere came the noise, louder now and faintly apoplectic. Despite my vaunted insensitiveness I felt the hair crisp a little on the back of my head. It really did sound as if an animal was trying with pain and labour to extricate itself from some horrible trap.

We skirted the back of the house. The rasping was so near now that it seemed to rise from the ground beneath our feet. And yet I was almost convinced that there must be some auditory illusion and it was being carried over from the next-door garden; when suddenly from behind me Varvara gave a cry. I whipped round and saw her pointing at a spot immediately beneath the railings. The stone foundation into which they were sunk cast a few inches of deep shadow. Still I could see nothing at all, until I stood behind her and followed the exact line of her finger. On the ground was a rough ball, less than a foot in diameter. It seemed to be disturbed by an internal agitation which caused slight changes of shape but not of place.

I went up and poked it with my foot—as good a way of testing apparitions as has yet been devised. But the next instant I drew back sharply, for something had pricked me through the cloth of my bedroom slippers. Slowly, still uttering their extraordinary mating noise, two hedgehogs separated themselves from an embrace.

'What is it?' said Varvara, breathing almost as heavily.

I explained. I had heard of this phenomenon before though I had never personally witnessed it, and without experience it is hard to believe how much row these animals will kick up in their erotic transports. Since I also knew that they were often deliberately introduced into London gardens to keep down pests, the affair had lost all its mystery for me. But Varvara was not entirely satisfied. She bent over the hedgehogs, inspecting them closely.

'They look like wicked, long-nosed old men,' she said. 'Why should they come to trouble us on this of all nights?'

'We have had ghosts,' I said firmly, 'and we are not going to have transmigration as well. Doesn't your Church forbid these superstitions?'

Varvara went into a heavy sulk compounded of shame and annoyance at having her orthodoxy impugned.

I led the way back upstairs, hoping that we had not disturbed the household. Between us we already had enough to laugh off.

She did not speak again until we were outside her room. Then she tried to recoup herself with a little of the smart jargon which she was picking up from Andrew and his friends.

'Sorry to have been such a nitwit. Too boring!'

'It was enough to scare anybody. I didn't understand it.'

'Nor yet do you!' she said with a sudden vehement change of manner. 'If you had lived in Doljuk, of which you are so fond, you would be wiser and less brave.'

By this time, despite my weariness, my blood was up in defence of rationalism.

'Can you honestly pretend that you've ever seen an evil spirit or a ghost?' I countered.

'I have heard them hooting and chattering in the desert to lead the caravans astray.'

'I said—have you *seen* such things?'

'That also,' she replied, though more reluctantly.

My eyes were fixed on her with satirical challenge and she knew that she had got to justify her claim.

'It was nearly a year after my mother's death,' she began, 'and I was sleeping alone in my room, when suddenly I heard a noise of something moving outside. I took a lamp and a knife and I ran into the passage. There I saw a figure dressed in coat and trousers like a Tungan woman, but unveiled. It stood beside the sockets for the water-jugs outside the room of my father.

For a moment I thought that it was a thief or an assassin sent by the new Governor, but it threw up its arms with a thin cry, and vanished down the stairs which ran into the courtyard. Some of the servants were sleeping there, but when I questioned them, they swore that they had seen nothing.'

'Had your father?'

'No,' said Varvara. 'Nor did he ever, though the thing came again several times and it was always lurking near his bed. I believe that it was sent by the sorcery of an enemy to harm him, but his nature was too strong for it.'

I looked at Varvara hard but she returned my gaze with unembarrassed candour, and I knew that I could not touch her ghost. It was a situation in which even the most determined iconoclast must be powerless. So oddly, when she spoke as a daughter, did inhibition and frankness mingle in her mind.

Next day the inquest duly took place. It was held in a depressing building of red brick with tall chimneys and a domed skylight over the well of the Court which gave it an odd resemblance to a mosque. Turpin, who with Varvara and myself made up the witnesses from Aynho Terrace, remarked on the likeness in characteristic fashion:

'Up the Prophet!' he said as we went in. ''And me my 'ouri.'

The coroner seemed a nice man. He had a pleasant but discreetly depreciatory touch. By the time he had done with it no incident was very large or very surprising. You felt that he could have held an inquest on somebody torn to death by wolves in Oxford Street without raising more than a paragraph in the Press.

The first two witnesses were the police sergeant and the surgeon who had examined Cedric's body. Then Turpin, I, and Varvara gave evidence in that order. None of us were in the box more than five minutes and there was hardly any questioning beyond a general invitation to tell our respective stories. I had been apprehensive about how Varvara would behave and in particular lest she should show that she regarded herself as under suspicion. But the fact that she had almost committed an indubitable murder by killing a police officer in the course of resisting arrest seemed to have had an admirably steadying influence on her. She told the tale of her brief neutral exchanges with Cedric unemotionally, almost woodenly, in a fashion which drew the minimum of attention to her eccentricities of speech. When she stood down the coroner made some sympathetic remarks about the trying nature of the experience for a young girl.

'Up the Bud!' said Turpin under his breath. 'Box on.'

I thought we were heading for an open verdict which would leave the cause of Cedric's fall unexplained. Because it had originally been presented in a frivolous manner, I had unjustifiably discounted what I knew of his medical history. But there was still one more witness, an elderly man in a morning coat. He gave his name as Mortimer Giles and his profession as physician. He was a Harley Street specialist, who had attended the dead man on a number of occasions.

'Will you tell us why he consulted you?' said the coroner.

'Owing to a condition known as Menière's symptom-complex.'

'What does that involve?'

'Intermittent noises in the head; dizziness combined with a desire to vomit; in bad attacks actual loss of balance and inability to rise after a fall. Its causes are not altogether understood but it is associated with disturbance in the inner tube of the ear.'

'I see. Was Mr. Ellison suffering from this complaint at the time of his death?'

The doctor shrugged slightly.

'The general condition was there. It is not one that can be cured. But of course I'm in no position to say whether he was actually attacked at the—'

The coroner interrupted:

'Quite, Dr. Giles, quite. We understand your position. All the jury will want to know is whether, in your opinion, the deceased might have been suddenly overcome so that he staggered off the roof.'

Dr. Giles shrugged again. He was not a man who found it

easy to accept approximations, a trait for which his patients may often have been grateful.

'Yes . . . it might have so happened. But usually the sufferer retains enough temporary control to avoid danger.'

'Yes, yes,' said the coroner, seeing his neatly packaged solution being untied at the corners. 'But we are trying to find a reasonably possible explanation of an unwitnessed accident. And if I understand you rightly, the disease in question supplies that.'

'Yes,' said Dr. Giles. 'But with a wall there, I should have expected—'

'Thank you, Doctor.'

After that, of course, Accidental Death was the only starter. Although their experiments showed that they must at one time have entertained other possibilities, the police representatives did not appear either surprised or dissatisfied.

I suppose I cannot sit on the fence indefinitely, nor pretend that over all these years I have retained an open mind about Cedric's death. I believe—though I have no proof—that what really happened was something like this.

Varvara unexpectedly ran across him in the morning-room. Either because of her general indignation at his legal man-œuvres or because he specifically provoked her, the smouldering hatred between them blazed into an open row. Arguing and slanging each other they went out on to the roof. And then? . . . Well, perhaps Cedric in his greasy way thought he would try for a reconciliation and laid an avuncular hand on her. If so it would certainly have come off double-quick. And what more natural than that the rejection should have been accompanied by a little push. Varvara's little pushes were pretty drastic, and supposing that this one coincided with an upset in Cedric's ear he might easily have gone into a long stagger which would carry him over a considerable obstacle.

It may be that I have invented this theory only because the alternatives are either too improbable or too painful. But it has the merit of explaining Varvara's curious attitude, which seemed to be based not on guilt itself but on a conviction that it would be imputed to her. Once the Law had had its negative say, she gave no sign that anything was preying on her mind. If she could look back on whatever happened with equanimity, why should not I?

Mrs. Ellison was too ill to attend the funeral. But by her wish the cortège started from the door of 8 Aynho Terrace. As I went out to take my place in one of the black Daimlers, Turpin was in the hall looking out at the hearse.

' "Beautiful Dreamer, Goodbye," ' he said; and then, still faithful to his ancient enmity: 'I don't bloody think!'

12

Before I went down from Cambridge I had tentatively arranged to join a reading-party in Cornwall for the last three weeks of the vacation. Mrs. Ellison again asked me to stay on, but she was by then so ill with delayed shock that I could not decently accept her invitation.

Oddly enough, I can remember very little about my farewell to Varvara. It was not like her to miss such an opportunity for memorable drama. I do, however, know that we swore to write to each other regularly—a promise which I kept, partly from inclination, and partly because, God help me, I thought that she would be lost without my guiding hand. Her replies began on a one-for-one basis but soon tailed off; until by the middle of November she had ceased to write at all. Correctly or not, I associated this defection with the news contained in her final letter.

'... The lawyer has come again, but on a worthier errand. My grandmother purposes to convey money to me to give me face with the bankers. She is acting very rightly in this and consequently her mind is serene. I pray for her, and that she may continue to do well. Perhaps you do not understand what a responsibility there is in money. ...'

*

From time to time there went through my mind a variant of
Keyserling's celebrated remark about America: I hoped Varvara
would never lay herself open to the verdict that she had passed
from savagery to rich bitchiness without even an intervening
period of civilization.

At Cambridge I had one continuing source of first-hand
news. Andrew still lived on my staircase, and though we did not
maintain the close contact of earlier weeks, he continued to
pay me occasional nocturnal visits. (I suspected that one day I
should overhear him tell somebody that he dropped in 'to cheer
me up.') He went to town a good deal and from various remarks
which he let fall I knew that he saw something of Varvara. Her
description and status varied interestingly with the item which
he had to recount:

'. . . Our protégée has taken up golf and tennis. I gather she
already strikes a pretty formidable ball.'

'. . . My partner was Varvara. That girl's beginning to get
around. I mean, really circulating in the right places.'

'. . . Your girl-friend will have to watch her step. The other
day at Sadie Prince's she had a row with some woman and
threw a vase of flowers over her. Somebody ought to warn her
that people won't stand for that kind of thing.'

Alas, in mid-term even this irregular flow of information
was cut off. Andrew had an accident—which arose, rather im-
probably, from putting too much faith in human nature. One
of his girls fell asleep in his rooms and so remained until long
after the hour when women were supposed to be out of college. Andrew not unreasonably decided to keep her for the
night. Next morning he made no particular effort to conceal
her presence from his bedmaker: whom, to his credit, he always
treated with great liberality. But the crafty brain of a Cambridge woman easily struck a balance between the tips of one
transient undergraduate and a lifelong wage from the college.
She went straight to the authorities and reported him. Regretfully they sent him down.

I could of course have taken a day off and gone to London
and called at Aynho Terrace. There was no quarrel between

us or other reason why she should refuse to see me. Common
sense argued that her failure to answer letters was probably
due to nothing more than laziness and an expanding social programme. But on the other side was ranged the self-immolating
pride common in young men. If keeping in touch with me was
not a matter of overriding importance to her we had better stay
apart. At least that was what I pretended to think.

A week before the end of term, in the middle of a wet afternoon, a knock sounded unexpectedly on my door. Outside
were two women, neither of whom appeared in the least familiar. I imagined that they had come to the wrong set of rooms:
until the younger said hesitantly:

'It is Mr. Lindley, isn't it? . . . Don't pretend you remember
me because there's absolutely no reason why you should.'

But her voice had done the trick.

'Miss Ellison . . . Deirdre!'

' "Miss Ellison—or may I call you Deirdre?" ' said the other
woman in a light ironic voice. 'Sorry, but that's how it sounded!'

She was considerably the older of the pair—about thirty, I
judged. She was outstandingly well-dressed in a style which I
have learnt to associate particularly with women who combine
elegant bodies and ugly faces.

Deirdre said: 'You are a swine, Tilda. Now you've made me
feel so silly that I can't possibly ask him.'

'All right, then I will. . . . Mr. Lindley, Deirdre is sharing a flat
with me now, and we're giving a small party on 22nd December. Would you care to come?'

'Yes, of course. And now you must let me give you some tea.'

But they refused, saying that they were visiting Cambridge
with friends whom they were due to rejoin in a few minutes. I
don't imagine that when they arrived Deirdre had any intention of calling on me. Probably my name on the board at the
bottom of the staircase caught her eye and she came up on
impulse.

'I hope you won't be bored,' she said with the diffidence
which had been her public front before the days of her orphan-
hood.

'Of course not.'

'Two or three quite clever people have promised to come. Perhaps they will. Tilda's friends, of course. And Varvara will be there.'

I could not resist asking: 'Do you see much of her?'

'Speaking for myself,' said Tilda, in her cool, light voice, 'too much.'

'You mustn't say that,' said Deirdre, giggling. 'Not to David.'

They went, leaving me with an address in South Kensington. I wondered about their set-up, but came to no conclusion except that somebody had taken a wise step in deciding that Mrs. Ellison's other granddaughter should not join the house-hold in Aynho Terrace. Varvara, Deirdre, Nurse Fillis—it would have been like three Red Indians with raised tomahawks perpetually stalking each other round a camp-fire. To keep the peace, Turpin would have had to mix them knock-out drops every night.

My aunt had returned to England and I was spending that vacation with her in a hotel at Wimbledon. It was she who, so far from raising any objection to being left alone, prevented me from cutting Deirdre's party. For the last few days of term I had felt vaguely unwell and since then idleness seemed to have intensified my lassitude and the aching in my limbs. I thought I had suppressed 'flu. On the morning of 22nd December noth-ing appeared less attractive than three hours of making conver-sation with strangers.

But Aunt Edna said:

'Nonsense. Of course you must go.'

'It hardly seems worth it.'

'The Ellisons are very well worth anybody's while—yours, certainly.'

Suddenly I greatly wanted to annoy my aunt.

'You think, don't you, that everybody ought to be flat out to improve his or her social position?'

'You're old enough,' said my aunt, 'to understand the advan-tages of looking after yourself in that way.' (Her crisp, aggressively sensible tone made it sound as if she were talking about some embarrassing aspect of health.) 'There's nothing to be ashamed of in making suitable friends, even if you have to go out of your way to do it.'

'But don't you see,' I persisted, 'that if everybody follows your policy it's bound to be self-defeating? Smith is trying to put salt on Brown's tail, but just as he's getting there Brown jerks himself another couple of rungs up the ladder in pursuit of Jones. And suppose that one day they all arrived together at the top of the ladder, and there was nowhere left to climb! What would it be like—Nirvana or the Black Hole of Calcutta?'

'I hope,' said my aunt, 'that you will save a little of this clever talk for tonight. It may impress some nice young girl.'

Nevertheless when I came downstairs that evening in my best suit, my appearance evidently caused Aunt Edna some misgiving.

'David,' she said as we stood in the hall, 'at South Kensington Underground Station there is a refreshment room. I know because Diana Maddox-Faure was once taken faint there after her operation. When you arrive, you can go in there and order yourself a double brandy. Only one mind. I don't want you either drooping or whooping at this party.'

She insisted on giving me one-and-eightpence which was the current price of the drink she had prescribed.

I spent the money as she had directed. But by the time I reached South Kensington I no longer badly needed any stimulus. As on other occasions a rising temperature in the blood had a curiously liberating effect on my mind: which in this instance was not counteracted by headache.

Frensham Gardens lay back at one remove from the Old Brompton Road. 'Mrs. M. Norroy—Miss D. Ellison' I read on the card below the first-floor bell of No. 76. Up I went humming merrily to myself, until the escaping noise of the party drowned my voice in my own ears. Allowing for the fact that I was late and the first guests must have been there for nearly an hour, it did not sound like the staid assembly which I had expected.

I soon found out why. This was not so much a rackety party as one organized regardless of expense. The only drink seemed to be plain champagne or champagne cocktails, both of which go straight to the lungs. On my entry I was greeted, rather vaguely, by the woman Tilda and introduced to a number of people who were already absorbed in their own conversations. Of neither Deirdre nor Varvara did I see any sign at first. This was not altogether surprising, for the flat was a big one and the party had diffused itself over three rooms. Finally, however, whilst circulating alone, I ran across Deirdre in a passage.

After the usual greetings she said: 'I'll let you know as soon as *she* comes.'

The arch note of conspiracy jarred on me.

'Thank you, but that's not necessary.'

'No, probably not. She'll let everybody know for herself.'

She looked at me with that confiding gleam of malice which, when first we met, had done much to remove my prejudice against her heredity.

'Come on,' she said. 'I'll find you someone nice to talk to in the meanwhile.'

She was as good as her word. I spent the next half-hour very pleasantly with the help of several glasses of champagne and a small pretty woman of about Tilda's age. Seeing that she was far more at home than I in these surroundings, I took the opportunity to ask about the occupants of the flat.

'They're related,' she said. 'Pretty distantly, but still related—Tilda was a cousin of Deirdre's mother. You may say what you like, but I happen to know for a fact that years ago she was kind to Deirdre and stood up for her against that dreadful father.'

'He *was* dreadful, wasn't he?'

'My dear, the absolute sub-basement! So whatever anybody says—'

'By the way, what exactly is it that people would say?'

She looked significantly at the luxurious room and the maid coming round with another tray of shallow golden glasses.

'I adore Tilda. She's brave and gay and she has a sort of heavenly poise. Besides being terribly well-connected. But those aren't things that necessarily bring you a bank balance. When her antique-shop failed, I think she was in rather a tight spot . . . until she had the chance to make this generous offer about having Deirdre to live with her.'

'In fact Deirdre pays.'

'Oh, I'm sure it's utterly above board. Anyhow she's still a minor, with trustees and whatnot. But half a million is half a million and I believe there's a prospect of more to come.'

My little acquaintance was a nice person and I think she was genuinely well-disposed to Tilda. But she had that distinctively feminine way of coming to the defence of another woman, which is like a rescue from drowning performed by a shark. She seemed herself to feel that some of the rough edges needed smoothing.

'I should be the last to suggest that Deirdre gets nothing out of the arrangement. In fact I think it's absolutely vital at this stage in her life that she should be under the eye of somebody with a really cool head. Tilda won't let her make mistakes . . .'

'Is she likely to, then?'

'Well'—my informant sank her voice—'it all comes back to that father. He so badgered the poor girl and suppressed her personality that she thinks anyone is doing a favour by noticing her. Well, you can see that's dangerous, can't you?'

'Not for the moment.'

She giggled. 'I haven't drunk quite enough yet to get into my frank mood. But if you've no belief in the value of your society in itself you're liable to start throwing in other attractions.'

She may have thought that I disapproved of her hints, for during the next couple of minutes I cannot have appeared to be paying her much attention. The fact was that I had heard Varvara's voice somewhere in the throng behind me, and I was engaged in stealing quick glances over my shoulder.

At last my eye lit on her. She had come in with Andrew whom she must have brought on her own initiative. But even as I looked he moved away in a manner which suggested petulance, and she was left with an older man in a dinner-jacket. Varvara herself was wearing a frock bordered with golden discs like spade-guineas. Her clothes-sense had obviously come on since the previous September: but there was still something to learn. Her dress, though intrinsically pretty, would have been more suited to vivifying and colouring up a type of looks which ran the risk of insipidity; for her to wear it was like gilding a peony.

'Of course,' said my companion, who must have followed my gaze, 'the other Ellison girl might get it all.'

'I beg your pardon?'

'The extra money we were talking about. But I'd rather it went to Deirdre.'

'You don't like her cousin?'

'Not much. I can't stand people who're larger than life—particularly outsize *prima donnas*.'

'I'm sorry she's getting that name.'

'I didn't realize you knew her. Perhaps I'm prejudiced. And anyhow I admit you've got to hand it to her for her work among those natives.'

'I hadn't heard about that.'

'You know she was brought up in darkest Asia? I mean real Asiatic Asia, not India or somewhere like that. Well, naturally the inhabitants were continually ravaged by every sort of disease. I'm told that this girl used to go about nursing them quite regardless.'

I began to laugh. 'Which will you have?' I said. 'Cholera or the ministering angel?'

My companion looked at me indignantly for a moment, then she too broke into a titter. We drank another glass of champagne apiece and then parted on that basis of mutual esteem which is often so unfairly engendered by malicious conversation about third parties. I made my way across the room and took up a strategic position behind Varvara's back. She was still talking to the man in the dinner-jacket, and he was listening, his face inclined towards her with an expression of almost super-human urbanity.

'. . . My father would scarcely ever leave his estates in Turkestan, so consequently my mother and I never got a glimpse of

the Season. Poor daddy, it was only his terrific sense of responsibility towards the tenants that made him—'

I stepped round to the front.

'Hallo, Varvara!'

'David! Where have you come from?'

'My ancestral duck-shoot in the Carpathians.'

Varvara was not pleased, more especially as a grin of surprising intelligence flashed over the face of the other man. She
retaliated on me by means of an introduction.

'This is Sir James Lexing. And this, Jim, is David Lindley, a
boy whom my grandmother took in for his holidays.'

It was sad to see what results were produced by incomplete
transition between two worlds. The old Varvara would have
denounced me with ringing violence, ending with a box on the
ear; but this new edition, attempting a sleek insolence, sounded
merely vulgar. I was not annoyed; I merely prayed that she
would not get stuck in this intermediate stage.

My offence in her eyes was not yet complete. After a few
banal remarks Lexing took skilful advantage of the break in the
flow of fiction to which she had been treating him and moved
away. She stared after him with undisguised disappointment.

'What does he do?' I asked.

'He is at the Court.' She mentioned quite an important office
in the Royal Household.

'My, my, you are coming up!'

'I am taking my proper place in the world.'

'What's happened to Andrew? I saw him slink off looking
vaguely disgruntled.'

Varvara said: 'Most of the time now he is rather stupid. He
presumes. Old acquaintances are not necessarily the ones best
suited to each other. And because you knew a person when
she was a child or sick, that does not give you the right to hang
round criticizing and managing when she can look after herself.'

'Ah,' I said, 'I see.'

'I hope you do,' she said pointedly.

'I see that you're losing any little sense of proportion which you once had. I hardly thought I should be defending Andrew, but your talk about presumption makes me sick. Who on earth do you think you are? ... No, I'm going to tell you. You're a rich girl of the English commercial middle classes and basically very well-attuned to your station. You just happen to have had a freak upbringing. But that doesn't give you any title to play the aristocrat. What right have you got to ask for more than your own equivalent in a man? That's Andrew. In fact he's rather the better bet of the two because his father made the money and according to the "clogs-to-clogs" rule it'll last another generation.'

Varvara began to curse in several languages. The noise round us must have been pretty considerable, for nobody took much notice; then she seized a champagne cocktail and dashed it down her throat as if she were putting out a fire. Meanwhile I had switched from acerbity to righteous sorrow.

'Nothing's good enough for you now. It's a pity, because you have so much if you'd only be content with it. Why should anybody who knew Doljuk as it really was want to tinker about with a lot of melodramatic pretences? Trying to pass yourself off as a mixture of Florence Nightingale and Lady Bountiful! What would your father have said, if he could have heard you?'

This last remark was unfair as I knew before it was out of my mouth. I was so ashamed of it that I had not the heart to evade the just consequence. I saw Varvara's arm going up and a loose gold bangle slipping back against a line of short blonde hairs. I remember thinking, I hope she throws that glass; if she hits me it'll break off and form an edge.

Of course I may have exaggerated a mere gesture of disgust. In any case the attack was never delivered. Innocent, wide-eyed, and rather red-faced, Deirdre slipped in between us.

'Finding lots to talk about?'

Varvara glared at us both for a moment. Then she said something brief and unrepeatable and stalked away.

Deirdre put her hand on my arm.

'Never mind. She'll forgive you in the morning.'

She began to laugh.

'I don't see what's so funny,' I said.

'Oh, I wasn't laughing at you. I was just thinking . . . how one person gives something up and another takes it on.'

'What does that mean?'

'Well . . . bad language for instance. You heard what she said. Not that I'm in a position to throw stones—in front of you at any rate, because I once told you an absolutely filthy story in the garden at Aynho Terrace.'

'I remember.'

'I only hope it didn't embarrass you too much.'

'Tell me another if you like,' I said rather warily.

At one moment I thought she was a little bit tight, but the next I caught a whiff of heredity, a reminiscence of that deadly methodical carelessness with which her father had tramped from one objective to another. And then again my suspicion seemed to be buried under a gush of spontaneous self-revelation.

'I realized that talking like that was not only vulgar, but it gave one away.'

'Gave people wrong ideas, you mean?'

'Not so much that,' said Deirdre with a warm smile. 'But it labelled one as a repressed innocent. Every time I tried to be daring people could see my whole life with father. What's the point of breaking out when you aren't in prison any longer?'

Her language had a flavour of quotation. I thought that Tilda must be quite a clever woman.

'Let's drink to purity,' I said, facetious because I was not sure of my ground.

'Let's drink to not advertising,' said Deirdre. She gave me another glance which suggested that she had merely substituted the door-to-door canvass.

I should have been warned. It was not intoxication but the liberating sense of feeling really well for the first time in weeks which made me reckless. In this mood I sympathized intensely with any other escaped prisoner. We began to talk about her new life, and it appeared that she was taking lessons at an art school.

'I'm very keen, but I'm not sure that I have any talent.'

'I bet you have.'

'You can't possibly tell without seeing.' She paused as if expecting me to say something. 'Would you like to see?'

'Well...'

'Oh, come on. Nobody will notice if we go to my room for a moment.'

I was caught off-balance. My hesitation had been due to the belief that she was inviting me to come round one day and inspect her exhibits at the school, and I was not sure that I wanted to carry my patronage so far. Unprepared with excuses, I followed her out of the room, in which the number of guests was rapidly dwindling.

'It's straight down the corridor,' she said. 'Second door on the left.'

As she spoke she fell a little behind me and a moment later I heard a swish and a soft flopping noise on the parquet. Looking round, I saw that she had brushed a woman's fur coat off a heavily laden row of pegs.

'There are too many parked here,' she said. 'They'll get trampled on. I'll drop this one on my bed.'

She slipped ahead again and threw open the door. Perhaps it was Tilda's system for decompressing the personality; at any rate Deirdre had been allowed to launch out into a scheme of decoration which was feminine to the point of tartiness. A full-length mirror had been let into the wall; and behind it stood the bed quilted in white satin with an ornate doll on the pillow and a white sofa at its foot. The only object which struck a sterner note was the writing-desk. This she opened and took out a portfolio of drawings.

As far as I remember, they weren't bad. But even at the time it was hard to form an impression because, as we bent over them, she kept on sweeping her loose-cut coiffure across my face. It was like doing an art gallery with a yak, only nicer.

I was aware of the absolute constancy of my feelings about Deirdre. When I had first met her I thought she was an awful little girl, but I took a liking to her, which was only intermittently tainted by the memory of whose flesh and blood she was. Those were still my sentiments.

Presently I had my arm round her shoulders and then we were kissing and then we were on the sofa. Deirdre was not so passionate as Varvara but much more lascivious. You felt an ulterior motive, closely connected with self-esteem, behind her love-making.

Presently she said: 'I do feel mean about this.'

'Why?'

'Poaching, sort of.'

'My dear, I'm not anybody's exclusive possession.'

'You mayn't think so,' she said. 'But Varvara has a very strong sense of property. I wouldn't like to come between her and her rights. . . . Why did you shiver?'

'I've a bit of a chill.'

'I thought you might be disgusted with me for talking like that about my cousin. Really I admire her.'

'Is that true?'

One of Deirdre's more engaging characteristics was her willingness to give serious thought to any reasonable question.

'Yes,' she said after a pause. 'But it doesn't prevent me from thinking that she's rather frightening and at the same time rather ridiculous.' She sighed. 'Of course she and I have one great thing in common.'

'What's that?'

'We both hated my father.'

Words failing me, I resumed the embrace. At that age I found girls like Deirdre, though they were often called rude names, rather restful for a necking-party. With them there was no problem of not going too far, they saw to that. Nevertheless she put me sufficiently under her spell to kill my sense of time. When we went out the party had obviously been in its later stages, and if I had been allowed to think, nothing would have induced me to risk making myself grossly conspicuous. I dare say that subconsciously I was relying on Deirdre, whose position was still more vulnerable, to gauge how long we could safely linger.

From time to time there were still noises of people leaving and before they did so they often came along the corridor to fetch their outdoor clothes. But they all entered a room lower down on the other side, and their movements had long ceased to disturb me. I thought nothing of it when two voices seemed to come closer than usual. In my false security I had no time to disengage myself before the door was thrown open. On the threshold Tilda was saying:

'But I don't think any of them were put in here.'

She saw us and a look of well-bred nausea flitted across her face. 'Deirdre! Do you realize that people have been looking for you everywhere to say goodbye?'

Tilda was a lady; it showed in the way that, despite her annoyance and disgust, she instinctively moved across in order to block out the view of the person who was with her. It was a manœuvre which would have worked very well if that person had not been Varvara who could easily see over her head.

Deirdre separated herself from me without obvious discomposure.

'Are you looking for a coat?' she said. 'I found that one on the floor so I brought it in here.'

Varvara's eyes were sparkling with rage.

'Now it will smell of bitches,' she said.

'Smell more of bitches, perhaps,' said Deirdre with surprising quickness.

'Stop it, both of you!' said Tilda. 'You're behaving like sluts.'

'I was only showing David my pictures,' said Deirdre.

As the joke about etchings had not then been invented, this remark did not convey quite the same impression of calculated impudence as it would today. But it was blatant enough to add fuel to Varvara's anger. Under the strain of conflict her new flossy manner and her conventional vocabulary temporarily disappeared.

'You tempted his lust,' she said, and I saw Tilda wince. 'I know his weak and sexful nature.'

'None better,' said Deirdre, 'I'm sure. But the point is, my dear, you're acting like a dog-in-the-manger. You have a row with David—oh yes, anyone who wasn't blind could see that—and you throw him over for people who you think will be more useful in helping you to forget your unfortunate background. Then you're furious because somebody else out of the kindness of her heart tries to make it up to the poor boy.'

I was too fascinated by the argument to care about the undignified role which had been thrust upon me.

Varvara drew a deep breath and pointed at the coverlet.

'If you and I were laid side by side on that bed and David came in to us ... I know whose side he would bloody well choose!'

'You'd be welcome,' said Deirdre in the fashionable mock-Cockney. 'You can have all your property.'

She dropped her glance to the coat as if to indicate that it and I had shared the same status of pawns in a campaign for Varvara's discomfiture. (I believe she really had planned the whole episode.) But the next instant she gave me a look of mingled defiance and apology: I had to do it, her face said, if I was to keep my end up.

Tilda turned on me: 'Can't you do anything to stop them?'

'I can do one thing,' I said brusquely, and pushed her out of the way.

I was not practising rudeness and violence for their own sakes. Indeed my object was to prevent the latter. Although it was December and wet, the weather had continued unusually mild. All the time that Deirdre and I had been in the room the white net curtains had been billowing gently in front of a half-open window. But they would not have made much of a barrier against a falling body. As Varvara moved towards her cousin I dived hastily across and slammed down the sash.

Varvara did not seem to notice any significance in my action. There was an extraordinary and baffling expression on her face: I knew that it represented the extreme of some emotion but which I could not tell. When she reached Deirdre, who was trembling visibly, she folded her in a brisk embrace and placed a kiss on her forehead. Then she stood back, beaming seraphically.

'You have done well,' she said. 'You are the servant of God.'

Whereat she kissed her again.

'What's that for?' said Deirdre in a tremulous voice. Despite her brave pert show, she knew she was outweighted and the row had told on her.

'For love,' said Varvara. 'And for compassion.'

'I still don't see it.'

'You have rebuked my sin,' said Varvara, 'with your own. Therefore I have compassion and humility towards you. The Chinese say: "What meat for the man who goes to bed in dirty boots? His wife will certainly put a toad in the pot."'

I took it on myself to interpret further.

'*Reductio ad absurdum*,' I said blithely. 'There's no way of bringing home people's bad conduct like behaving worse.'

'I wish,' said Tilda, 'that you wouldn't be so smug about your part in these barnyard gambols.'

Varvara took Tilda's hand and looked into her chilly green eyes with two enormous rings of glowing blue fire.

'You also,' she said, 'are a good woman. All you wish is to save two poor girls for a little longer from their folly and their appetite. . . .'

'Please!' said Tilda wriggling.

But Varvara's charity was inexorable.

'Some day I shall come to you and implore you to advise me how to become happy by keeping my place in the world and making no trouble there. . . . But I think I shall wait for the summer because you would speak best under a shady tree in a sun-hat.'

I suppose this was equivalent to telling Tilda that she would carry more weight if her face were hidden; but the result was the reverse of what I expected. Tilda was visibly melting, from frozen hauteur, through bewilderment, to a sort of resigned benevolence. I looked round and saw a corresponding change in Deirdre: she was simpering amiably.

And damn me, as Fulk might have said, if I didn't catch it! I suddenly felt what a beautiful thing it was to have enemies and to forgive them; to do wrong and to confess it; to make an ass of oneself and not to mind. The air was saturated with an impulse towards such feelings, diffused from one abnormally power-ful personality. I have had a similar experience once or twice since, but on the darker side, involving the radiation of hatred or embarrassment. Nor have I ever seen three such dissimilar types as Tilda and Deirdre and myself rendered sensitive to a single influence.

Tilda said: 'Well, we are a bunch of fools'—and I noticed how generously she included herself—'Next time we have a party it's going to be gin and lime and perhaps you'll work it off quietly by weeping in corners. Come on, if that frightful old bore Colonel Hammond has taken himself off, I'll cook us all some eggs in the pantry.'

'Darling,' said Deirdre, 'I do hope I haven't embarrassed you too much with the guests—particularly the older contingent.'

'The ones who noticed,' said Tilda, 'are the ones who've done that kind of thing themselves.'

'Very good,' said Varvara, like a teacher approving the per-formance of a class. She looked at me with smiling expectancy as if I were a favourite pupil who had failed to answer up.

'I'm afraid I'm really to blame,' I said. 'I expect you'll be glad to see the back of me. I think I'll go home now.'

I had not the slightest fear of being taken at my word. It was all part of the curious game of playing at saints which had somehow been imposed on us.

We went into the kitchen where Tilda made us an omelette whilst the maid was clearing up the débris of the party. The spirit of brotherly love continued strong throughout the brief meal. The others were probably aware that some unusual force had been let loose, for Deirdre said with a giggle:

'I hope this evening we haven't used up our ration of good-will for the season. It'll be too sad if we spend Christmas biting the nose off anybody who comes near us!'

It was the first remark for a good many minutes which showed any degree of self-consciousness. I don't know whether Varvara obscurely recognized it as a sign that her period as ring-mistress was expiring. At any rate, almost immediately afterwards she rose and said smilingly that she must go home.

'I ought to be on my way too,' I said.

Undoubtedly the magic was fading, for there was a moment of embarrassed silence in which one could almost hear the rasping of ulterior thoughts. Then buoyed up on the last remnants of the spell, Deirdre said:

'You should share a taxi to Aynho Terrace. David can pick up the Underground just beyond.'

I hope I have not suggested that we went through some kind of joint mystical experience. What happened—unless it was due to chance or my imagination—approximated more closely to light hypnosis. Yet it was not without its genuine spiritual content. At its best the power which Varvara generated could transcend her own interests. She would risk looking silly or undignified, she would even eat a kind of humble-pie, in order to make other people collaborate in producing effects which she felt to be beautiful and dramatically true. She was like a medieval painter who was willing to put his own face on Judas if he thought it would help the picture.

She had, too, the inflating vision of the artist. Usually it was directed towards the magnification of feuds—which are the easiest material for histrionics. All her rows were like the harrowing of Hell. Sometimes, however, her spirit would veer sharply. Perhaps it was due to her Slavonic blood that she would suddenly become obsessed with the splendours of Christian charity. When this happened, it did so, not as a mere shading off of mood, but like the recoil of an explosion or a powerful engine thrown suddenly into reverse. The shock was transmitted to outsiders, so that for a short while they were coerced into taking their responses from her, and the atmosphere became almost Franciscan.

Alas, her potentialities for spiritual leadership were limited by the general tenor of her nature. Sooner or later she would always turn an agapemone into a brawl. But at least inconsistency was likely to prevent her from putting her considerable psychic gifts to any serious misuse.

She let me in at Aynho Terrace with her own latch-key. The hall was in darkness. As we entered, one of the lusher clocks which had broken loose from the unison of the choir began prematurely to strike eleven. Its isolated warbling sounded weird and faintly idiotic and yet significant, as if it had struck a sick note which harmonized with something in the constitution of that great plutocratic mansion.

Varvara led the way to the dining-room. She was not trying to conceal my presence in the house; still less, at that stage, can she have seen any reason for sparing me a climb to the upper floors. All the same I was glad to avoid it. Since I left Deirdre's flat and the stimulus of the party was withdrawn the sensations of weakness had become stronger and more generally diffused throughout my body. Every molehill was a mountain now; and yet my illness was not positive enough to make any difference to the balance or clarity of my mind.

There were several decanters and wine-bottles on the side-board.

'One for the road,' said Varvara in her social accents. Then suddenly, changing to tones of tragic disillusionment: 'God knows it's likely to be a long road!' She locked her arms behind her head so that the loose sleeves of her frock fell back almost to her shoulders. This exhibition was immediately followed by a peal of laughter. 'Do you know, David, I actually said that to a young man the other day!'

'How did he react?'

'He told me it was easy to see I had suffered and he tried to console me by putting his hand on my leg.'

'Shocking!'

We were both laughing almost hysterically whilst Varvara postured round the room in attitudes of exaggerated despair, hauteur, and outraged chastity. I did not know before that she had any capacity for relaxation, let alone self-parody. Finally, however, she became serious again and pulling up two chairs, close together, in front of the electric fire she pushed me into one of them and sat beside me clutching my arm.

'We will make an agreement,' she said. 'You will give me

a free licence to show off as much as I like. But the condition will be that I shall repeat all my vanities and stupidities just as they happened, except that you alone shall be the audience. You shall keep me in order with your sneering.'

I said: 'Don't try too hard to escape from your own faults. You know the proverb about the baby and the bathwater?' When I had explained it she nodded.

'Already I have thrown away a great deal of my old self, the one of Doljuk, so as to be a figure and not a guy at nice English parties.'

'I suppose in the end it will make for your happiness,' I said sighing. 'But thank God you've still got to flatten a few idiosyncrasies the size of Everest before you become just another Kensington rose.'

'That is right,' said Varvara, not without complacency. 'I shall never entirely learn. One reason is that I shall not stay here long enough.'

'Stay where?'

'England.'

'Do you mean that seriously?'

'Of course.'

'But where will you go?'

'I have no idea,' she said. 'This is not a matter of plans nor even of intention. It is something which I know about the form of my life and it will happen with or without my will.'

After a pause I asked:

'Do you think you'll ever go back to Doljuk?'

'Never. Never. Never. . . . Except in my sleep.'

'You dream about it then?'

'Often.' She blenched perceptibly.

I could not bring myself to believe that a few more months of Europe had so softened her that her previous brisk acceptance of the facts of Central Asian life had been replaced by shuddering horror. There must be some cause intrinsic to the dreams themselves rather than their setting. She admitted this.

'Mostly,' she said. 'I see how it was when they brought back my father, dead.'

'You never told me about that.'

'He had bought some goods and he was anxious to collect them away from the town because of the dishonesty of the Customs—'

As I have said, Varvara's fits of delicacy were unpredictable, but she always referred to her father's trade with great circumspection. The fact was that he supplied persons who knew no better with the means of murdering each other, and I think she realized that as an occupation it was open to criticism.

'—So he went out with his carters that lived in our courtyard and four little carts drawn by oxen. It was summer and very hot, and the whole sky was like a ripe plum about to burst. When he came to the meeting-place, his friends were there before him and everything was in good order. But as soon as he began to count the goods and they the money, out from behind a tall dune charged a great mob of bestials. They were of a kind which they have in America and an American has told me they are called high-knackers—'

'Hi-jackers,' I corrected. 'It means people who steal contraband from other—' I had been going to use the word crooks, but when I realized where the sentence was leading me, I left it unfinished.

'My father and his servants lay down behind the carts and began to shoot. But presently the thieves were on them and the fighting was at hand-to-hand. Owing to God our side were about to conquer when the captain of the robbers took out an old pistol stuffed with stones and hard paper and pressed it against my father's throat whilst he wrestled with another man. Christ save me, but it fired and the blood came out of my father's gorge where the flesh and veins had been swept away, as if a woman had emptied a tub full of blood. Soon his body was as white as veal and he was stark dead.'

'At least it must have been pretty quick,' I said, fumbling. Perhaps fortunately Varvara did not seem to hear.

'My father was economic,' she said, 'and he had taught his carters that whatever happened it was their first duty to lose no cargo. In the uproar that followed his wounding the thieves had escaped with one of the carts full of goods. So when he was clearly dead the chief carter took all the men except the two weakest and pursued after them. But the pair, of whom one was dumb and the other coughed blood, put my father's body on the smallest cart with bullets below and old rifles on either side and began to push him back to Doljuk. On the way the blood-spitter was overcome by a great gush from his lungs and he lay down on a bank of stones, so that the dumb man had to go on alone.'

A slow procession of tears was running down her face, orderly and controlled, the product of a sorrow which has lost the capacity to present any new aspect. The firmness of her voice was unaffected.

'It happened,' she said, 'that I had gone down to the East Gate to meet my father on his return. I had been uneasy all day, per-haps because of the heat or perhaps for another reason which you would call boasting and mystery. At any rate I sat there beside the sentry's stairway and looked out into the desert. It was about sunset and getting dark except for one patch where the light fell in a square box with a streamer beneath it as if somebody were flying a great kite and it had caught fire. Then I saw the dumb man coming along the track heaving and strain-ing at the cart. So I went down to meet him, knowing what I should find. My father was covered with sacking up to the chin and as I have told you he was pale white. The dumb man wept and danced about but he could not make me understand what had happened, until he seized one of the arms from the cart and held it to his own throat. It happened to be loaded and it went off in his hand and the bullet went through the corner of his mouth and out of the cheek.'

'My God,' I said. 'Doljuk never gave you a straight run at your tragedies. The farce would keep butting in. Did the poor chap die?'

'No,' said Varvara casually. 'He recovered in a few weeks. And after that it was found that he could speak, though not much. . . . We put my father in a brass cauldron and sealed the mouth with clay and buried it in an orchard of apricots which he owned. All the people came to the burial though they regarded him as an infidel. Even the Governor sent his chief secretary.'

Seeing that she was in the mood to talk, I meant to ask her about the weeks when she lived solitary and unprotected whilst she prepared for her journey home. But before I could do so we were interrupted by a light irregular tattoo on the closed door. Uneasily I rose and opened it.

Turpin was standing outside. Above his head and a little behind it he held a candle set in a reflector-shade. (I suppose he did not care to race Joseph Ellison's economy device up the stairs.) The angle of the light and its surprisingly intense concentration made his face look like semi-transparent butter in which somebody had traced innumerable lines. He was very, very drunk and intoxication had ironed out his shrewd old face to a benevolence which was almost idiotic and yet significant. Further in the hinterland, dully illuminated by the backglow of the candle, stood an ornate multi-branched Victorian hat-and-coat stand. In the gloom it resembled a bit of primeval forest. As if I were recollecting something viewed in a dream, I seemed to be walking through a magic wood: I looked up and there peering down between two dusky branches was the yellow, mellow, internally radiant moon-face of ... not a fairy ... no ... but a very amiable, very old elemental of the forest. . . .

'My dear Turpin,' I said. 'How nice to see you again!'

But elementals do not talk English. His lips moved silently several times with the delicate precision of fish-mouths behind glass walls. No sound came at first. Then:

'Poop, poop, poop,' said Turpin very gently.

'What was that?'

'Poop,' said Turpin.

He raised two fingers towards us in an improper gesture to which he lent the force of a pagan benediction. Then slowly he turned away.

'Would you like me to give you a hand up the stairs?' I said anxiously.

Turpin did not deign to answer. Already he was ascending

into the darkness, with the candle throwing a saucer of fire on the wall above his head. On the first landing there was a pause and I feared lest his legs might after all have deserted him. Then soft but clear, in a perfectly produced stage whisper, came down the message of reassurance: 'Poop!'

He was a drunken old sot who had temporarily reduced himself to incoherence: but for me his shameful state and the absolute tranquillity which accompanied it rekindled an afterglow of the universal benevolence which we had experienced earlier. I think that Varvara felt the same, for she received impressions as easily as she broadcast them. Presently we had an exchange which may have been an illustration of this truth.

I was talking about the future and in particular how we must not again run the risk of losing touch with each other.

'Should I come round again tomorrow?'

'Tomorrow I go away for the day to meet a friend.'

I forbore to ask any impertinent questions.

'Well, then, you'll be back on Christmas Eve. What about that?'

'Yes.'

'Or would you rather we met somewhere outside? We could go and do some agonized last-minute shopping.'

'Yes.'

'I say—you do want to see some more of me? If not, it would be as well to say so now.'

Varvara sighed and leant towards me.

'Sometimes I cannot make plans.'

'Why's that?'

'Not because I don't wish to, but because I know that they will be interrupted.'

'Nothing can interrupt us if you don't want it to.'

She leant further over, not provocatively, but searching my face intently in the dim light. Under that scrutiny I suddenly realized what she might mean, either in reference to herself or me. Frankly I was a little annoyed at what seemed a reversion to an inferior mood and an attempt to conjure up tragedy in order to spice the possibilities of friendship.

'Now, now,' I said. 'We don't need the Gipsy Queen among your impersonations.'

Varvara took my sarcasm without resentment: her forbearance with its implications of pity caused me a momentary dismay which the dark hints themselves had failed to produce. But it was soon forgotten. For the brief additional time I remained with her she was at her best. I had the warm, humble feeling that we both knew the worst about each other and it would never be enough to deter either of us.

13

Probably there is no need to attribute Varvara's fear of an 'interruption' in our relations to anything more esoteric than intelligent reading of physical signs. I dare say that I looked pretty ill by half-past one on the morning after Deirdre's party. Certainly my state was not improved by having to walk two miles through a drizzle before I could find a taxi.

Next morning I could scarcely get up owing to a violent pain in my back and a throbbing headache. The only thing that drove me to my feet was the certainty that remaining in bed would be put down to hangover. Even at this lapse of time I can remember the agonies of that day, in which I dragged myself round like a half-crushed worm. Only one ray comes back to me from amidst the gloom. After lunch, feeling a little less moribund, I thought I would try the effect of fresh air. As I tottered down a side street I saw a small shop displaying Christmas cards, mostly rather vulgar. One showed a scene in which three drunken lumberjacks had been sitting in a row; now only the two at the ends remained; the place of the third one had been taken by an enormous bear to which one of the men had just handed a bottle in the belief that it was his companion.

I went in and bought this monstrosity. Before I posted it to Turpin I inscribed on it the lines, several times quoted in Tchekov's *Three Sisters*:

> *He had not time to say Alack*
> *Before the bear was on his back.*

I don't know why, but I thought they would make a nice addition to his repertoire.

If I had not a bear on my back, I had something almost as formidable wrapped round my vitals. Next day there was no question of leaving my bed. A doctor came and went and came back with a radiographer. When the film was developed it showed that I was suffering from fairly acute T.B. For good measure I also had pneumonia. The latter nearly killed me within a week; and by the time that I had thrown it off the T.B. germs had further strengthened their hold on the ravaged area.

I went from a London hospital to a sanatorium which specialized in my disease. There, for months, I was allowed no visitors except my aunt and no correspondence at all. The effect of this, combined with illness, was strange: the external world sank like a coin dropped in clear water: you can still see it shimmering and distorted on the bottom, so that it does not entirely cease to be an object of interest and regret to you, but you no longer count it in any way amongst your possessions.

I heard nothing from Varvara during this period. Possibly she tried to send messages but they were stopped in my own supposed interests. Anyhow it never occurred to me to feel resentment at her silence. She was so many light-years away that silence seemed the only natural condition.

When I improved somewhat and they sent me to Arosa in Switzerland, it began to be different. They tell you that consumptives are optimistic and amorous; but these amiable qualities are the products of an abnormal emotional quickness, which also gives rise to easy suspicions and grudges. I spent a long time lying in my bed looking out over the shining snow-fields and holding imaginary scenes with Varvara, somewhat on the Dr. Johnson–Lord Chesterfield lines. That is to say, at some undefined point in the future she would again seek my company; but I would turn away with a few, or not so few, apt words about the value of fair-weather friendship.

Of course the proof or remedy was in my own hands. I could have written, and wherever she was, my letter would no doubt have reached her in the end. But that would have invited the blow hardest to bear in my morbid condition: a sensible cool explanation of her silence—unlikely as such a thing seems from Varvara. Nevertheless my conduct was so perverse that I cannot put it down entirely to self-pity and despair. In it there may well have been a subconscious recognition that, faced with death or chronic invalidism, I was morally bound to avoid involvement.

I touched the nadir of uncharity during my third year at Arosa. Aunt Edna came out to see me and I put to her a question which had been bothering me for some time. Who was paying for my long stay in an expensive sanatorium? My uncle was now retired and I knew that he had very little beyond his pension. I hoped that he and my aunt were not making desperate sacrifices on my behalf—even though, if they were, they both looked pretty well on it.

When I asked Aunt Edna she dabbed her lips delicately and put on the saintly expression which many of her generation wore when speaking about money.

'We didn't like to tell you before . . . in case your pride made you interfere with the arrangements.'

'I'd be just as quick to refuse charity as a lion would a lump of meat.'

'Now you're being cynical. And anyway there's no such thing as charity between friends. . . . You made a very good friend, David. I don't know how you did it, considering the difference of your ages and so on.'

'Let's come to the point,' I said. 'Who did what?'

'Mrs. Ellison, whom you stayed with that summer, heard that you were very ill and had got to live out of England. She sent me a cheque for £5,000 to be used on your behalf. She said that anyway she was going to leave it to you in her will.'

Suddenly there rose up before me an enormously magnified simulacrum of that will: ravaged and cracked and torn like a battlefield by the march and counter-march of rival armies:

bearing in its corner what might seem to be a great rough seal until one perceived that it was composed not of wax but clotted blood. At the same time I felt a gratitude so intense that the tears came into my eyes. Old, sick, mentally weakened Mrs. Ellison had still been able to take thought for the misery of a chance acquaintance. Thank God, I thought, I really liked her when I had no cause, beyond a little hospitality, for doing so: otherwise it would be unbearable now.

'You've put me in a very false position,' I said to my aunt with unnecessary harshness. 'All this time I've been enjoying her money with never a word of thanks. I must write immediately.'

'I'm afraid you can't. You see, Mrs. Ellison died about a year after you were taken ill.'

'Oh!'

'You may be sure,' said my aunt, 'that she knows what's in your heart at this minute far better than you could put it in any letter.'

Aunt Edna was a clergyman's daughter, and, I think, a concealed agnostic of the deepest dye. The concealment covered herself but not anybody who had had opportunities of noting the absolute spiritual indifference behind her distribution of religious clichés. It contrasted oddly with the sincere piety in her every reference to social matters.

After a pause I said:

'What became of the granddaughter who lived with her?'

'I saw her at the funeral. A striking girl, but too *outrée* for my taste. She married somebody a few months later.'

'Can you remember his name?'

My aunt thought for a moment, then shook her head.

'It was someone rather queer. Not exactly unsuitable, but queer. Like a foreigner or an artist or a person who'd been in the papers.'

Even if I had pressed her I don't think she could have told me more.

The injustice to which I referred earlier grew gradually out of this conversation. I chose to believe that Varvara was angry with me because of her grandmother's generosity, and

I reminded myself of the fanatical proprietary sense which she had shown towards her family inheritance. A girl who thought it quite natural that she should be suspected of murder in defence of her rights would not take kindly to an interloper who walked off with even the smallest sums. So I told myself. But really it was too nonsensical even for my inflamed mind. Varvara was no more mean than those medieval barons who fought to the death for a few fields: most of them were not interested in rental values but they all regarded property as an adjunct of their personalities, and if it was diminished against their will, so were the latter. But no such disparagement applied to free gifts and they would hand over to charity the thing for which they had slaughtered their neighbours.

From this time a reaction began in my feelings about Varvara. It coincided with an improvement in my health. The rest of my personal story, so far as it is relevant, can be told in a few words.

I left Arosa cured after five years, and I have never had any recurrence of the disease. Whilst I was in the sanatorium one of my fellow-patients and a close friend happened to be a boy of my own age whose father was an English solicitor settled in Paris where he carried on a profitable practice among the English community. The son died, and his father offered me the place which he would have taken in the firm, partly out of sentiment and partly because it was essential in his business to have someone who not only possessed legal knowledge but could also speak first-class German and French. When I had served my articles and passed my exams I became a partner, and with the interruption of the war I have held that position ever since.

For present purposes the point is that the break in my life which occurred at Christmas 1928 was prolonged by the nature of my career. I lived entirely in Paris, seldom visiting England more than three or four times in one year. All the cracks of separation widened, first into ravines and then canyons. Twice on my brief trips I went back and looked at Aynho Terrace. The first time the front badly wanted painting but there was a Rolls Royce outside. The next, the façade had been done up but there was a board attached to it advertising flats to let. All down the road the great monsters of the late Victorian age were being chopped up into more usable forms: and the once quiet air was full of dust and loud with the whistling of labourers as they slammed matchboard partitions into the enormous rooms.

I don't know what practical object these visits served. Certainly if I wanted to learn about Varvara they were completely useless, and I ought to have made inquiries by means which by that time I knew only too well. A competent firm of private detectives would soon have tracked her down. The more remarkable her history, the simpler the task. But I never even toyed with the idea because in my heart I felt that a contact deliberately and artificially renewed would be somehow vitiated.

This may have been a way of disguising from myself the warnings of common sense: there was at least a chance that Varvara would have grown into an unpleasant woman, and a fair certainty that her gift for disorganizing people's lives would have matured along with her other traits.

But inaction is not resignation. One may take no physical steps and yet the mind may be full of the patter of their inner equivalents. I often thought about Varvara—not in the earlier jaundiced way but with affectionate speculation: indeed I still do so. Under this treatment the ghost of her personality began to develop as its real presence might have, choosing certain definite lines of progression out of all those which had been possible at the time when we parted.

This seemed to happen without any assistance from my mind. Not that I entirely excluded my own conscious conclusions. For instance I saw in retrospect that, during her early days in England, I had much overestimated her confidence in herself. She was in reality very lost, and at times probably frightened. But the ferocious tradition in which she had been bred caused her to react to threats like a wild animal, with bared teeth and tense muscles: whereas a creature with a more civilized background would have tried to slide through her troubles.

Apart from this, it was easy to exaggerate the influence of her pre-English environment. Doljuk accentuated and adorned the oddities of her character, but it did not create them. If she had been brought up in Brighton she would still have been a somewhat ferocious young woman: nor would regular attendance at Sunday School have killed her capacity for self-dramatization against a religious background. But take away one or the other of her parents, and the result would certainly have been different, whatever part of the world she had inhabited. She was born at a point of confluence where strong currents of valour, brutality, and practical intelligence poured into a steamy lake surrounded by rather theatrical scenery.

Curiously enough, the material circumstance which now seems to attach to her most firmly is not one to which, in the days of our acquaintance, she had any real title. Then—whatever the future might hold in store—she was certainly not rich. Nor do I know what happened afterwards. If I assume that, with Cedric removed, Mrs. Ellison divided her fortune between her two granddaughters, it is not so much because that would have been the natural thing to do, as because I totally fail to envisage Varvara as anything but a very wealthy woman. Her personality needed a large income for its expansion, and by one or another means, inheritance or marriage or both, I am convinced that she obtained it. She was not a person who would submit to any cramping of her destiny.

It seems perhaps a little fatuous to lay down conditions of life for somebody whose actual history remains unknown. Here I must plead guilty to playing a sort of private game. Ignorance of facts can be an advantage in that it gives one a freer hand. Years ago I realized that, so long as I did not burden myself with the narrow truth, I could give Varvara any career I liked, or indeed the choice of several. If I had had stronger creative powers, I should probably have simply made up a series of fantasies about her. But being, as it were, tied by one foot to earth I fell back on ready-made material, merely using my imagination to establish identity. In concrete terms, I have for many years been picking out items from the newspapers and other sources about women who might be the present Varvara. It is a little like the Eton Wall Game in which goals are scored only at long intervals, for, if it is to be played fairly, not only does the story have to ring psychologically true, but the details, such as names, initials, ages, etc., have to avoid contradicting any known facts. Hence it is that, though I have come across a good many cases where identification at first seems possible, there are only three to which I would accord a diploma of spiritual truth.

The first, dated 1936, comes from the columns of a French weekly paper which has now been extinguished for the part which it played before and during the German Occupation. In its day it was a most disreputable rag, far exceeding in scurrility anything which would be tolerated from the British Press. Still, on occasions when only its routine malice, not its political passions, were aroused it could produce some amusing snippets. That, however, is perhaps the wrong word, for the editor devoted considerable space to any story which pleased him.

I translate fairly literally:

'A boat tossing alone on the Gulf of Guinea has written another chapter in the tumultuous history of Mme Barbara Peigneret, English-born widow of soap-millionaire Marcel Peigneret, whose mysterious death of four years ago so much embroiled the discreet police of Lyons. Undeterred by her narrow escape from charges following her husband's fall from a third-floor window, Mme Barbara became a noted solicitress of the French Law. At one time scarcely a month passed without the Courts being cheered and electrified by a stage in her innumerable processes against the relatives of her late husband. At length however the triumphs of the witness-box began to pall and the beautiful protagonist made a poignant declaration to the Press. "Modern life is corrupt. I have determined to quit it, alone with a few other sympathetic spirits." On further inquiry it appeared that, employing a fortune already sufficiently large before she began to assert her rights, she had leased from the Portuguese Government the uninhabited island of Sao Onofrio in the Bissagos Group just off the Guinea coast. "I plan to settle there", she said, "and found the perfect democratic society. I

SEA OF GLASS 215

shall be Queen and my subjects will have completely free access to me."

'The last at any rate seems to have been true, for the new paradise had not been instituted for more than six months before representations were made by the Catholic Church in Lisbon to abolish it on the grounds that a public desecration of morals was taking place on Portuguese territory. Evidently this lady had her own interpretation of democracy. If it permitted a Queen, how could a Court be forbidden? When the chartered vessel, *Secours de Sainte Anne*, set out from Marseilles in November 1934 it carried not only five families of ordinary colonists, about whom one could say that they sought nothing more than to change very moderate gifts of fortune, but also the direct entourage and inner council of Mme Peigneret. The latter, who happened to be all males, consisted of: M. Jean-Raymond Manitou who acted in several films until his conviction for harbouring narcotics; M. Edmond Sameuil, twice-divorced international Rugby-footballer; M. Robert Conte, business man, who in 1934 adroitly dissociated himself from the scandal of Blum-Stavisky; and finally a mysterious character, Stefan Tourdieff, ex-Polish miner and mystagogue who was reputed to instruct his paymistress in the arts of Yoga.

'A fair landing was made on the chosen island. Thereafter no more was heard from Sao Onofrio until M. André Ledoux, a French journalist who had occasion to visit Bolama, decided to extend his journey so as to obtain a glimpse of the new settlement. His visit was not altogether welcome, but before ejection he managed to obtain certain details of Mme Peigneret's social experiment. Tragedy, alas, had already struck the little community. Whilst the worthy plebeians set about producing quarters from the jungle which prevailed over most of the island, Mme Peigneret and her friends were already pursuing an active social life. It appears that, at first, M. Manitou was most favoured with the intimate confidences of the leading lady; but that after a while his position began to be sapped by the spiritual machinations of M. Tourdieff, who expressed doubts not only whether M. Manitou's etheric vibrations were suited to his position but also whether he had satisfactorily recovered from a certain disability which he had contracted round the film studios.

'Sequel—both men went off on a bathing-trip to talk over the situation. Neither returned, but four days later the body of M. Manitou was washed ashore covered with the stabs of a small knife. Query—M. Tourdieff, had he suffered a mutual fate, or had he perhaps dematerialized himself in order to avoid hurtful gossip?

'M. Conte succeeded to the status of consort, but his tenure was a short one, for he was swept away in convulsions by a mysterious fever. Remained only the athletic M. Sameuil who endured for more than a year. Unhappily his experience among the scrums and mêlées had given him a taste for variety and quick movement and he began simultaneously to pay addresses to the most attractive wife among the commoners. No harm would perhaps have ensued if he had not tripped and accidentally split his skull on an axe with which the husband happened to be following him.

'Too late Sao Onofrio came to regret the high marital standards of the avenger. In agricultural terms one says that the balance of nature has been upset when the removal of one pest leads to new ravages by creatures on which it formerly preyed. Queen Barbara, being now entirely deprived of high-class satisfactions, began to look towards lower sources. The quiet sunbaked air of the island was continually rent with hideous rows and altercations [rixes et bagarres] and the perpetual booming of the surf was almost drowned by the cries of outraged womanhood. Finally the men themselves, reduced to a simple taste for peace, conspired with their wives to rid the island of its turbulent ruler. Mme Peigneret was seized whilst she slept and thrown into a small row-boat which had been equipped with a few provisions and a keg of water. In true pirate fashion she was cast adrift and the current rapidly bore her out of sight of her relieved subjects.

'This one must admit, Mme Peigneret has never lacked resolution or courage. For eleven days, long after her food was exhausted, she floated over a little-known expanse of the

Atlantic. Her water too had just given out when she was saved from certain death by a chance sighting of the Greek vessel, *Louloudhi.*

'Tanned to the colour of old bronze she stood once more on the quay at Marseilles being interviewed by our representative. "Life is a pilgrimage," she said, "and Sao Onofrio was not the most curious place to which it has taken me. I spent much of my early life in the Far East where I was adored by the natives and learnt resignation." Asked where next she proposed to direct her pilgrim footsteps Mme Peigneret drew up her magnificent frame to its full six feet and said: "Towards the fulfilment of my essential destiny. I find that I am pregnant." '

What is the betting on this identification? Varvara might easily have anglicized her name, and also married a Frenchman. If she did the second, I should be willing to stake a great deal against the success of the union. Amidst a French family circle she would have been like a lioness in a formal garden. The physique and the claim to Eastern experience are suggestive but hardly more. I say nothing about the husband's briefly hinted fate.

Personally I hope Varvara never became Mme Peigneret nor ruled over her self-devouring flock on Sao Onofrio. Even allowing for a high percentage of malicious exaggeration in the presentment of the story, one has to admit that it is not only comic but also brutal and sordid. To my mind the features which point most strongly to Varvara are not the atmosphere of nymphomania and homicide—for neither of which have I any substantial grounds to indict her—but the way in which the heroine, even when seen through the eye of a debunking journalist, contrived to invest her adventures with a kind of grotesque dignity.

The second of these oblique and doubtful glimpses I owe to my own experience. In the summer of 1943 I was returning from a leave spent in the West of England. The train was ambling gently along a branch line not far from Weymouth. It happened to be unusually empty, and I and another Army officer had a first-class carriage to ourselves. He was a small, brisk man who opened a conversation in a fashion difficult to repel —by producing half a bottle of Scotch and two paper cups.

For a while we talked casually. Somehow we came on to the subject of the large houses which could be seen at intervals along the track, standing out preternaturally white against the scarves of woodland. I ventured on the usual speculation about what would happen to them after the war.

'Don't know,' said my companion. 'Some'll go for schools and hotels, I suppose. They may knock others down for the materials.' He began to laugh to himself. 'If you'll wait another five minutes I'll show you one that's bloody lucky to be still standing.'

'You know the neighbourhood?'

'I was stationed here for a bit in 1940.'

'Was this some place where you were billeted?'

I suppose the suggestion connected unfortunately with his earlier remark. At any rate he looked at me rather coldly before replying:

'Not in the house itself. In the grounds.'

Evidently, I thought, the story of some stray bomb. But the memory seemed to give him a surprising pleasure, for he had glued himself against the window, scanning the landscape and uttering short chuckles.

'There,' he said suddenly, 'there, between those two copses, with the hill behind.'

It looked a very decent Georgian mansion with a double bay front and a flat roof, large and handsome but not remarkable for sheer size or beauty.

'Yes?' I said, knowing that, even if I wished to, I could not stop so cherished an anecdote.

'That's where I saw my only active service so far in this war! Serbright Manor. I shan't forget that night in a hurry. We'd been in camp at the village just over the hill. Then, about the end of June 1940, after France had packed up, there was a flood of refugee soldiery and two of our companies were told to move out to tents in the Manor grounds. Some of our officers were a bit fed up and thought the authorities ought to have taken over the house for them. But there wasn't really anything to complain about, particularly as the weather that summer was so good. At least it was until the day of the move. But that morning the hell of a thunderstorm blew up, and by the time it was over the temperature had dropped nearly fifteen degrees.'

He paused, poured another drink, glancing at me anxiously to see if he was doing his story justice.

'There's a point there, old boy. I'm not just nattering. If it hadn't turned quite cold, Clara would never have put on her leopard-skin coat. Clara was my C.O.'s wife—not bad but rather a bitch, really. Frankly I never thought she was quite worthy of old Colin. He was a magnificent chap. I suppose she caught him.

'Anyway Clara had some keen ideas about etiquette and doing things properly. So she'd made up her mind to call on the lady of Serbright Manor. We'd heard one or two things about her and frankly she sounded pretty peculiar. The villagers never mentioned her without sniggering in a scared sort of way. But none of us knew anything positive about her except that she was a widow and as rich as hell.

'I don't think Clara was really paying the call in a very friendly spirit. She was the leader of the school of thought which held that the Manor ought to have been requisitioned for the battalion. But she had every chance to get into a charitable state of mind because, outside the gates of the lodge, she met a couple of nuns from the convent at Ossington who were going up to the house to visit a sick R.C. servant. Clara was a R.C. herself and she knew these two good women, so naturally she got off her bicycle and they all proceeded together.

'Well, they'd just rounded a bend in the drive when something went whee-ee over their heads. You can't expect nuns to know much about bullets, and the first time Clara probably thought it was some kind of flying beetle. But beetles don't bust bicycles—and that's what happened. Whilst she was still wheeling it the hub-cap was knocked out of the front wheel. That made them look at the house and what they saw so staggered them that they could hardly run away. There on the roof, dancing about and waving a rifle, was a ruddy great woman. She was shouting and making signs at them, but they were too far off to make out what she was saying. They'd ducked into the woods at the side of the drive and were lying low when an awful suspicion came over Clara; she was practically sure that the words had been German.

'I don't need to tell you, old boy, what a state everybody was in at that time: or how many stories of Jerry tricks were going round—including the one about using Hitler Youth Maidens as parachutists in Holland and Belgium. So naturally Clara who was never backward in jumping to conclusions thought that she'd discovered at least a raid and probably the first wave of invasion. She and the nuns bashed their way out through the undergrowth, then she leapt on to her bicycle and shot straight down to our lines. Colin was out when she arrived, and I happened to be in charge, God help me! Clara was soon in a towering rage. She went straight through the roof when I suggested that before doing anything drastic we should ring up the Manor and see whether they could explain the incident. I stuck to my point, but unfortunately when I tried to 'phone I couldn't get through. The exchange said the wires must have been damaged in the storm, but of course for Clara that simply meant they'd been cut.

'It was beginning to look as if I should have to do something on my own when, thank God, Colin turned up. He ticked Clara off for being in the camp, but he couldn't shake her story or put it down to imagination. He tried to get through to Brigade H.Q. to see if they had any information about raids or subversive activity by fifth columnists; but that bloody line was down too. So he told me to take Sergeant Dewes with half a platoon and carry out an armed reconnaissance. Then, at the last moment, he decided that as the situation was so peculiar, he'd come along as well. He could never bear to be left out of any uproar.'

'What did you say?'

'—any uproar. Well, we set off and when I got to the Manor grounds I fanned the men out in battle order—still feeling a bit of a fool. But, sure enough, we hadn't been in sight of the house for more than a minute before we heard "ping", "ping", "ping". It was fire all right from some kind of light rifle and it came out of an upper window. I thought, hell, the balloon really has gone up! By this time we were all flat on our faces. Colin crawled up to me and said that he was going to take half the men round to the back and try to break in that way. My orders were to stay put with the other half and keep up a slow rate of answering fire. "Don't try to hit anyone," he said. "If this lot are what they seem, they're worth more in the bag than dead."

'It was just as well he said that and I got the word round; because, when he'd been gone a few minutes, we saw the woman strolling about on the roof. She was a dead target, particularly when she stood still fixing something to one of the chimney-pots. I nearly collapsed when I saw what it was—a bloody Union Jack! It seemed a bit optimistic to think they were going to fox us that way after trying to blow our heads off. But you can't tell with Jerries.

'We must have remained under cover for about half an hour. Then there was another outbreak of shooting, but this time no bullets came our way. The reports sounded as if they were actually inside the house. I was just wondering whether to give the order to rush the place from the front, when the front door burst open and Colin came staggering out. Even at that distance I could see that he had blood on his forehead, and he was walking bent forward with one hand pressed to his middle. I said to Sergeant Dewes, "My God, he's hit in the stomach." Old Dewes didn't answer for a moment, then he muttered, "Ask me, sir, I should say the Captain was laughing." I could have bashed him at that moment: but when I looked again, Colin was near enough for me to see the expression on his face. He was practically doubled up with mirth. In another few yards he began to make signs and shout to us—"O.K., you can all come out now. There's been a slight misunderstanding." Then he went off into another fit of laughing.

'I ran across the lawn feeling sure that it was all a dream. Nothing Colin said at first made me change my mind. He kept on repeating the words, "leopard skin", and "nuns" and "bicycle" and then going off into another paroxysm. I had to tell him quite sharply to pull himself together in front of the men.

'Finally I got the story out of him. He and his detachment had worked round to the back of the house where everything was quiet. They forced up a window and climbed into the pantry where they found an old butler-chap soundly stewed and sleeping in front of an empty bottle of port. To cut a long story short, they went up through the various floors without meeting a soul until they came out by a trapdoor onto the roof. There behind one of the chimney-stacks was an outsize bit of crumpet, in the act of drawing another bead on me and my wretched chaps. Colin crept up behind her, but just when he was a couple of paces away she heard him and whipped round and bashed him over the face with the butt of her gun. There was a terrific battle and it took practically every man to immobilize her. In the process Colin gathered something rather peculiar. He naturally thought she was a German, but it took him back when he found that the idea was mutual. You see, she told him that he would be captured and shot for wearing British uniform.

'At last they got it straight. This girl had been reading the usual newspaper stories about Jerry ruses. I don't know if you remember but some of the Dutch towns were supposed to have been attacked by parachutists who were dressed as women either in leopard-skin coats or nuns' habits. They carried folding bicycles too. Quite a coincidence, eh? Anyhow, when the girl saw Clara and the two holy women proceeding up the drive she drew her own deductions. After that, of course, everybody who came along must be in disguise. Rather gallant of her to engage the enemy single-handed! She was bloody tough and as brave as a lion.'

'Did you actually meet her?' I asked.

'Most certainly. She gave us a terrific party. The old butler chap was woken up and swayed round with lashings of drink. The men were hitting it up in the kitchen. It was just as well a real invasion scare didn't blow up that evening. Still it was very enjoyable. She was a damned odd woman and frightfully disconcerting at times, but I liked her. She was bloody pretty, too, if you could take the size.'

For the first time in his narrative my friend showed a certain hesitation; but finally he went on:

'I don't know whether I ought to tell you this . . . but what I found embarrassing was the way she went for Colin; though I must say he came halfway to meet her. They suited each other, both being big and full of the same kind of energy. She spoke quite normally, but I think she must have been a bit foreign. I mean, you wouldn't find a real English girl telling you how hard it was for her to be a widow because of her instincts and how she prayed to overcome them.'

He tipped the remains of the whisky briskly into our cups. 'Somehow, I don't think her prayers were answered that night. I could see they wanted to be alone, so I decanted the men and poured them back into camp. I'm not sure whether Colin came back at all that night. Certainly he was up at the Manor at all hours for the next two weeks. Nosey Clara soon got wind of it and was she furious! Does these managing women a lot of good to be wronged occasionally.'

'What happened in the end?'

'Oh, nothing dramatic. We were shunted up to Warwick-shire. I never saw the place again till this evening.'

The train began to slow as we pulled into the junction at which our local line joined the main one. My companion got up and gathered his cane and respirator from the rack.

I interrupted his goodbyes, rather rudely, I am afraid:

'Can you remember her name?'

'That's funny! Now you mention it, I can't.'

'Not either sur—or Christian?'

He tried for a moment.

'Sorry, but they've both clean gone.' He looked at me, amused. 'Were you thinking of trying your luck in that quarter? If so, I'm afraid you're too late. Fellow I met in a pub who knew the district told me some different people had the Manor now.'

I like that one better. In fact, it is my favourite of the three, perhaps because it seems to point up a factor which was always strong in my affection for Varvara; I mean the admiration which I bore towards her father. If she it was upon the rooftop, he was certainly there beside her, blazing away in spirit at the supposed Nazis, grumbling about the damned uproar but secretly glorying in it.

The sequel with Colin, however morally deplorable, gives me a cosy sense of still moving within the family. I am sure that he was rather like Fulk. But perhaps this is a line better left unpursued. At any rate I am not jealous.

And then that ancient and boozy butler. . . . Turpin would not have been much more than seventy in 1940. How nice to think that he had survived, defying the moralists, to follow his Blasting Bud through her efflorescence! Box on, Bud!

I return to the Press for my third and most transient glimpse, seen as from an express train through an arrow-slit. This time the material comes from a well-known American magazine.

'Tangling again this week with Californian State Police was blonde, six-foot high priestess of T.I.N.D. sect, Mrs. Varvara Calderon. T.I.N.D.'s, claiming membership of two hundred thousand, take title from initials of the succinct phrase embodying their basic belief—There Is No Death—a proposition they support by appeal to authorities ranging from Isaiah to time-theorist J. W. Dunne. Of the two, Dunne is more important as supplying, allegedly, the mechanics of the creed. Idea is that every living "observer" is geared to an infinite number of view-points. Death is merely a shift from one to the next and is never felt or observed by the sufferer. For him life appears to go on without a break, though so-called decease of other people is noted. Reading her views described in Catholic Los Angeles *Harvester* as a "collection of poisonous drivel, propagated by cowards who cannot face our mortal destiny", eloquent, uninhibited Mrs. Calderon reacted strongly. Form of reaction was to hire Aspiration Stadium for mass-meeting of T.I.N.D.'s critics and sympathizers. At end of meeting Mrs. Calderon undertook to refute accusations of cowardice and give practical testimony to faith in T.I.N.D. doctrine by shooting herself through the head.

'Intervention of Floyd C. Deil, Los Angeles' chunky, lantern-jawed top cop, scotched her disinterested project. Cracked he: "If there ain't no death, she's wasting time. If there is, she's violating the law against suicide . . .'

When I knew her Varvara was a most fervent devotee of the Orthodox Church, a religion which does not lack colour. In it she would no doubt find her ultimate spiritual refuge. All the same, I would bet that there was some period in her life when she craved for still brighter hues. Given fertile environment, she was capable of plunging into the extremes of mystic crankery, and probably of inventing her own material.

T.I.N.D.-ism is not an impossible faith to have gained her allegiance. She spoke much and familiarly of death, which she must often have seen at close quarters. Yet, despite her Christianity, I never had the impression that she could reconcile herself to it, either then or in later years. All her references to mortality were impliedly identified in her mind with some loss of power or failure of vigilance; in fact with the triumph of an enemy who had been allowed to prove himself the stronger. Against him, in middle age, I can imagine her hardening her heart; and when he proved intractable, not trying to placate him or beg him off, but deciding to abolish his existence. She was not a woman who would ever willingly lie down without her faculties.

There is no reason to accept any of these conjectures. My belief in them is purely collective and undistributed; it rests on a conviction that a person of Varvara's force could not disappear, even in a world as big as that of today, without leaving some ripples by which an alert mind could trace her. That does not mean that I expect to see her again. I do not; when the interval is too long the wheels of chance grow stiff and rusty. A belated reunion might bring only disappointment. Her oddity might have become a mere commonplace pretentiousness. If so, she would destroy more than a personal image; a whole panorama would be wiped out, and with it part of the permanent furniture of my mind. Railed off in a corner, where it has survived many years of conscientious pettifogging, is a small zone in which Doljuk blends with Aynho Terrace. The Swiss clocks are chiming over enormous empty spaces, wicked Cedric marshals his forces and storms and bullies and plots, and the nomad horsemen come charging down with cups of tea.